ALEC

A Reed Security Romance

GIULIA LAGOMARSINO

Cover Design courtesy of T.E. Black Designs

www.teblackdesigns.com

❀ Created with Vellum

Thank you to all my fans and new readers. I couldn't keep doing this without your support.

CAST OF CHARACTERS

Sebastian "Cap" Reed- owner
  Maggie "Freckles" Reed
  Caitlin Reed
  Clara Reed
  Gunner Reed

Team 1:

Derek "Irish" Cortell- team leader and part owner
  Claire Cortell

Hunter "Pappy" Papacosta
  Lucy Papacosta
  Rylee Papacosta

Rocco Turner
  Evelyn Rose Turner

Team 2:

Sam "Cazzo" Galmacci- team leader and part owner
    Vanessa Galmacci
    Sofia Galmacci
    Leo Galmacci

Mark "Sinner" Sinn
    Cara Sinn
    Violet Sinn
    Asher Sinn

Blake "Burg" Reasenburg
    Emma Reasenburg
    Ryker Reasenburg
    Beatrix (Bea)

Team 3:

John "Ice" Peters- team leader and part owner
    Lindsey Peters
    Zoe Peters
    Cade Peters
    Willow Peters

Julian "Jules" Siegrist
    Ivy Siegrist
    John Christopher Hudson Siegrist

Chris "Jack" McKay
    Alison (Ali) McKay
    Axel McKay
    Elizabeth (Lizzie) McKay

Team 4:

Chance "Sniper" Hendrix
    Morgan James (Shyla)

Payton James

Jackson Lewis
    Raegan Cartwright
    Parents: Susan and Robert Cartwright

Gabe Moore
    Isabella (Isa) Moore
    Vittoria
    Lorenzo (Enzo)
    Grayson Moore

Team 5:

Alec Wesley

Florrie Younge

Craig Devereux

Training:

Hudson Knight- formerly known as Garrick Knight
    Kate Knight
    Raven Knight
    Griffin Knight

Lola "Brave" Pruitt
    Ryan Jackson
    James Jackson (Cassandra Jackson- mother)
    Piper Jackson
    Ryder Jackson

Team 6:

Storm Hart

Daniel "Coop" Cooper
    Kayla Cooper (daughter)

Tony "Tacos" Russo

IT Department:

Becky Harding

Robert "Rob" Markum

Chapter One

FLORRIE

Present Day...

He was staring at me again. Those intense eyes were boring into me from across the table. When he was around the guys, he was just another one of the guys, hanging out and joking around. With me, he was possessive and overbearing. The stupid, sexy man was the epitome of tall, dark, and dangerous. He had black hair and a dark complexion. His eyes though were a bright, vibrant blue. If not for that particular feature, he would remind me of Knight. They both had the same dark and scary personality. Alec didn't like that reminder though, and he actually had a sense of humor which helped keep his dark tendencies at bay. I could hardly breathe around him. All he had to do was look at me and all the air was sucked from my lungs. It was too much being in the same room with him, but I somehow managed. It was getting more and more difficult every day to work with him.

My only saving grace was that I was very focused on the job. Alec was too, but for the last three years, those eyes were always trained on me. Meaning that at times, he was more concerned for me than the client. Not that he wasn't doing his job, but he took on my personal safety like it was the only thing that mattered in life. And I understood it. The few times that Alec had been injured, I thought I would go out of my mind with worry. But those injuries seemed to be more self-inflicted than anything lately. By self-inflicted, I mean that he purposely put himself in harm's way so that I wouldn't get injured. He didn't even give me a chance to defend myself anymore because he worried so goddamn much.

"Are you two even paying attention?" Cap snapped. I broke my stare down with Alec and glanced over at Cap.

"Sorry."

"Is it always like this?" Cap asked Craig.

"Pretty much."

"How did you not see this before?" he asked Craig. "They're practically fucking each other on the table."

I flushed in embarrassment and glared at Alec. As far as I was concerned, this was all his fault. We had broken up. If he would just stop staring me down everywhere we went, I could have moved on.

"Trust me," Alec muttered, still staring me down. "If I was fucking her on the table, you'd know it."

"I don't really need to see that. I see enough of you guys as it is around here. It amazes me that the women are more conservative than any of you guys. Hell, you guys wax each other."

"I've never waxed anyone," Alec said. "And if I did, it would be my woman."

"Oh, God," I groaned. "Here we go again."

"I thought you two were broken up?" Cap asked. "So why are you two burning holes into each other from across the table?"

"We are broken up," Alec responded.

"Good, then that should make things easier-"

"I'm still fucking her."

"Here we go again," I said irritatedly.

"What? Are you not aware that he's fucking you?"

"I was referring to the fact that Alec's going all caveman on me again," I said, barely restraining my anger. "See, I like to keep things professional, whereas Alec seems to think he's in charge of all things that involve me at all times, including in front of my boss."

"I don't think that at all," Alec said calmly.

"Really?"

"I know that I'm in charge," he retorted. "You're my woman and it's my job-"

"One, I am not your woman. You *just said* that we aren't together, so it should be really easy for you to ignore me when we're working." I interrupted, hoping to stop this little lover's spat. "We're at work, so please try to remember that we both have jobs to do."

He grinned that sexy half smirk at me as his thumb ran along his lip. God, I wanted to get him alone and beat his ass so I could fuck him. "And it just so happens that at work I'm also your boss."

After a heated moment of him staring at my mouth, like he wanted to shove his cock inside, Cap cleared his throat.

"Right, so anyway, as I was saying, I have a job for you. I know you just got back from a job, but with our teams all beaten up at the moment, we need to start bringing in the income. And you're the only team that's whole."

"I'm good with that," I said immediately. If I hung around here with Alec, he'd just maul me all the time. At least if we were out on a job, he had to direct his attention to the client. Well, that's what I kept telling myself.

"Good. This job is pretty simple. Jamie Hanson is a philanthropist attending a charity auction in New York City this weekend. He's stopping by Philadelphia on the way to visit family and would like an escort into the city and then protection during and after the event. We're looking at about a week on the road. Florrie, you'll serve as his close protection-"

"Whoa, just a fucking minute," Alec interrupted. "She's not doing close protection on a male."

"I'm sorry," Cap said, a frown marring his face. "I didn't realize that I was supposed to ask *you* who was going to be doing what jobs."

"I'm the team leader."

"You're also too fucking possessive."

"So, your solution is to put my woman on guarding another man?" he asked incredulously.

"Let's just call it retribution for you hiding your relationship for so long. You're going to have to learn to share and I think now's a good time to start."

"I'm not fucking sharing."

"Oh, sorry, I meant learning to accept reality and let your team do their fucking jobs."

That shut Alec up right away. One thing Alec never wanted to be accused of was not doing his job. And part of his job was making sure we were all performing the way we should.

"Now, Florrie will go as his date to the auction. This is all pretty standard. There are no current threats on his life that we have to worry about-"

"So, why does he want the protection?" Craig asked.

"He's had a bit of a windfall and his net worth has just reached $550 million. He's more worried that he's going to be kidnapped and held for ransom. He hasn't been able to finish getting a security team together, so if he needs additional security after this event, you'll be following him back to Seattle."

"Who currently holds control on his money in the even that he's kidnapped?" Alec asked.

"That would be his wife, whom he's currently in the process of divorcing. It's very messy at the moment and he's quite sure that she'll do anything to get his money. Everything he's sent on her makes her appear to be a gold-digging whore."

"So, we need to be on the lookout for anything," I surmised.

"Exactly. Nothing's off limits as far as I'm concerned. I may send a few extra guys along just to ensure that everything's secure. The last thing we want are any problems when we hold the contract for a very lucrative deal."

"Then we should have me on close protection the whole time," I said. "If I pose as his girlfriend and stay by his side wherever he goes, we may be able to ward off any potential threats. A second person makes kidnapping a little trickier."

"Or it could put a target on your back," Alec argued. "As his girl-friend, you'd be a target that needs to be taken out. You'd be disposable because you're a threat to his wealth. If someone wants to kidnap him, what's to prevent them from shooting you and snatching him?"

"Me," I said testily. "You keep forgetting that I'm former military and can take care of myself. Not only that, but you and Craig will be there to protect him also."

"She's right," Cap sighed. "We minimize the threat if there's another person right beside him. She can take care of herself, and you need to trust that she'll be looking out for both him and herself."

Alec looked like he was about to explode, but held back. That could have been because Craig was gripping his arm like Alec might jump up from the chair and beat someone.

"When do we leave?" I asked.

"Let me talk with Cazzo first. I need to work out logistics with him and Sinner, see if they can take this trip with you. We'll meet up again once I have another team in place."

We all nodded and I stood, ready to head back to the training center for a little extra time in the ring with Knight. I was frustrated and needed to work out the tension.

"Oh, and Florrie, nice dresses for this trip."

"Sure, Cap."

"No combat boots."

I turned and glared at him, but he just shrugged. "Combat boots don't go with ball gowns."

"They do in my world," I muttered as I walked out of the room.

Chapter Two

ALEC

Present Day...

I stalked up behind her. There was no way she was getting in the ring with Knight right now. If she needed to blow off some steam, it was gonna be with me.

"What the fuck was that back there?" I asked as I closed the distance between us.

"Don't know what you're talking about." She didn't even bother to turn around and look at me. She just kept walking like I was any other asshole in the place.

"Hey, I'm fucking talking to you."

"And I'm going to train. If you want to talk, we can do that when I'm done."

I grabbed her arm and swung her around, pushing her up against the wall. "We're going to talk now."

She broke my hold, ducking under my arm and twisting my arm up behind my back, shoving me face first into the wall. Damn, she made me hard when she got rough.

"We have nothing to talk about right now. We have a job to prepare for, and if you don't want me to break your neck, you're going to let me work off my anger."

She eased back slightly and I slipped my foot between her legs, kicking out and tripping her up. Her leg gave way and her grip slackened. Before she could react, I had her swung over my shoulder and I was carrying her to the ring. If she was taking her aggression out on anyone, it would be me.

"Put me down, Alec. We're not doing this."

"Yes, we are."

"Fuck you!"

"Oh, I plan to fuck you hard when we're through, but we have a few things to set straight first."

"Yeah? Like how much of a controlling asshole you're being?"

"Among other things."

I tossed her down outside the ring and she whipped her shirt and pants off. All she had on was a sports bra and some boy shorts. It was so fucking sexy. She pulled her blonde hair up off her neck and tied it up in a high ponytail, then wrapped it in a bun. She was smart, not leaving anything for me to fight dirty with.

I stripped down to my own boxers, leaving my body open for her personal enjoyment. If I was going to have trouble concentrating, so was she. I hopped in the ring and held the ropes open for her, but being the little minx that she is, she pushed the ropes down and climbed over on her own.

"So, tell me what your issues are," I said as we bounced around the ring.

"I can't work with you. You're too possessive."

She came at me, using my leg as a bouncing board, then wrapped her leg around my neck and swung us down to the ground. I rolled into it, hooking my legs around her body so we were pinned together. "You like me possessive."

"Sure, in the bedroom. Not when we're working."

She wrenched my arm back and rolled away from me, springing to her feet.

"You agreed to be that man's girlfriend for a whole fucking week."

I charged her, driving my shoulder into her slender waist, but being careful not to hurt her. I pinned her in the corner with my body, hooking her legs on either sides of the ropes.

"It's part of the job."

"It's you driving me fucking crazy. You'll be touching him."

"That's part of the job."

"Yeah?" I slid my hand up her thigh, right to her core where she was wet and waiting for me. "What if he touches you inappropriately? If you're playing his girlfriend, how are you gonna get out of that?" My fingers dipped into her soaking panties and slid between her folds. "Are you going to let him touch you like this?"

"Definitely not in public," she retorted, trying not to let me see her panting.

"Not at all. You're mine."

"That's debatable."

"Nothing is debatable about us." I slid two fingers inside her and slowly pumped them in and out. She squirmed to close her legs, but I held them open. Not that I really could keep her like this. If she didn't want this, she could easily break my hold.

"You can't keep doing this, Alec. We're good together and I like fucking you, but we agreed that we wouldn't go down this road again."

I stopped and stared at her. What did I want? I sure as hell didn't want what we had before, but Florrie had been very clear that we were just fucking. Not that it mattered anyway. I was still fucking pissed at her for what went down. I wasn't even sure that I could handle trying to have more with her. But it still bugged the fuck out of me.

"Why?"

"Why what?"

"Why can't you just admit that you're mine? Hell, I know that we're just fucking, but you can't even bring yourself to admit what we're really doing here."

"We're fucking. That doesn't need further explanation."

"But you're only fucking me, which makes you mine. Why not just say it?"

"Because you demand it," she huffed, shoving her pussy forward toward my hand.

"So, I'm good enough to fuck, but that's it?"

"That's not what I said."

"You don't have to. I know you. You'll do anything to have an out."

"What is it you really want? Because when we started fucking the other day, it was about lust. Now you're in a meeting, calling me yours in front of Cap and Craig. We've already been through all this bullshit. We've done that whole relationship bit where you pretend that we're in one. It didn't work. Why the fuck would you even hint at it again?"

"Because I still fucking love you," I shouted before I could stop myself. I hung my head and took a step back. It was the truth. No matter how much I tried to deny it, I had stayed away for six months, but she was never really out of my thoughts. Just one taste of her was all it took to reel me back in. I should have never fallen for it. I should have listened to Craig when he told me to back off, but I didn't. And now I was back in the position I was in for three fucking years. I was in love with a woman that would never love me back.

"We're toxic to each other," she said quietly. "You expect too much and I don't give enough. I can see that now. We'll never work and you know it. It doesn't matter how much you love me or how good the sex is. We're just not going to work."

"Why do you always say that? That I love you. Can you honestly say that you don't feel anything for me?"

"I know I feel something, but I don't know what love feels like. I imagine that it's something like an overwhelming feeling that suffocates you. I don't feel that. So, I know I feel something, but it's not enough."

"After three fucking years, you've never wanted anyone else, but you still can't admit what I see plain as day."

"Alec, you have to stop. I should have known this wasn't going to work. I knew that you would get like this, and I knew that I would push you away. I think...I think we need to end this for good."

"There's nothing to end. The only thing we do is fuck, remember?"

"It's all got to stop. We can't keep doing this to each other."

"You mean, you can't keep screwing me over."

She sighed and hopped down from the ring. "When we're done with this job, I'm going to ask to be reassigned to another team."

"What?"

"It's for the best, Alec. We have to stop this now. We're only going to continue hurting each other. And I just can't do that to you anymore."

She got dressed and walked away, leaving me standing there with my heart in my hands, bleeding out all over the fucking floor.

Chapter Three

FLORRIE

Three years ago...

Fuck, he was so sexy. I watched Alec run the training course against some of the other guys. He wasn't wearing a shirt, having just finished training with Knight. His biceps flexed as he climbed the wall and flung himself over the other side. His thick, muscular thighs gripped the rope as he grappled down to the floor. I blew out a long, slow breath as I continued to watch him move.

I had never had any particular interest in Alec or Craig. They were my teammates and that was it, but lately, something was different. I noticed Alec more for some reason. Maybe it was a touch or a look. Maybe it was working with him day in and day out for so many years. It was hard to say, but even harder to watch him working out like this and not be able to touch him like I wanted.

Not that I really could. We were teammates. Besides, I didn't do relationships. I had never found a man that I actually wanted to be with. I had seen it happen over the years when I was in the military. Guys would fall in love with some woman back home and they would get married. Then, after coming home from a long deployment, the woman would give some excuse of how things were too hard to deal with. And it was. Life in the military sucked for a relationship.

I went out to dinner with friends once when I was home on leave. It was uncomfortable. The husband asked if she was done going off playing G.I. Joe. He didn't understand what point she was trying to prove. They were divorced by later that year.

So, I never really saw the point. I wasn't looking for anything serious anyway. When I was deployed, I basically needed someone to get my rocks off with. There was always a willing male that needed it just as much as I did. There were never any hurt feelings when we walked away because there had never been any expectations. For some reason, when I came home, I stuck with that mindset. I had just been looking to get my life back on track, and I wasn't ready for anything more. Besides, it wasn't like there had been any prospects that were so great that I just couldn't walk away. I always walked away.

But then there was Alec. The man that had somehow slipped in under the radar and made my body thrum with excitement just by being close to me. As I watched him, I wondered *why not?* Neither of us had any serious relationships, so maybe he would be okay with just having a fling. The only issue was work. We would have to make sure that the lines between us didn't get blurred. This was just sex.

"Sexy, huh?" Lola joined me in watching the men. She was already married and deeply in love. I knew that she didn't get any kicks out of watching the other guys work out. She was onto me.

"Well, they're sexy men running around shirtless and I haven't gotten laid in months, so, yeah, sexy."

"Mmhmm." She didn't believe a word I was saying. She was just waiting for me to give first, which I wouldn't.

"So, which one are we watching today?"

There were several to choose from. Alec, which, of course, was the one I was watching. Then there was Craig, my other teammate. Yeah, he was fucking sexy too, but he wasn't the one my panties were getting wet for. Jackson and Chance were also on the course. And then last, but not least, Sinner. The man was every woman's fantasy, but lately, my eyes always drifted from him to Alec and never strayed further.

"Take your pick."

"Oh, I will," she smirked. "If it weren't for Ryan, I'd be all over Alec." My jaw clenched tight and I took a deep breath to keep from losing it. "I'm not sure why I never gave him a chance. He offered up a one night stand when he first started working here. It's a shame I never took him up on it."

"But you *do* have Ryan," I said testily.

"I don't know. Would it really be that bad to give him a shot?"

"Are you fucking kidding me? You already have one man. Now you need another?"

Lola turned to me and smirked, and my mouth dropped open. I had walked right into that and she hadn't even put in any effort.

"I knew it. I thought I saw you watching him more closely lately. If you're not going to make a move, you might want to watch your reactions. When I walked up, you were eyefucking him, and there was no chance you were looking at anyone else."

"Shit," I grumbled.

"How long has it been going on?"

"It's not. Let's just say that one day I woke up and started looking at him as more than a teammate." Quite literally.

"Have you talked to him about it?"

I snorted. "Yeah, because I was hoping to have my inner girl's heart crushed and stomped all over. Oh, and then I could continue to work with him. Yeah, that'd be great. Besides, it's just a little obsession."

"You never know. He might be interested."

"Alec has never looked at me in any way other than the woman that he works with. I'm not even sure he sees me as a woman."

"Well, they *are* a bunch of neanderthals."

"It's so fucking hard in this business. You date a regular guy and the man's a fucking wimp. No offense."

"None taken, but I happened to like that Ryan isn't part of this. It gives me normal, but with my history, that's what I needed."

"I don't want a break from this. I want someone that will fit into my lifestyle. I don't want a man that I have to protect and kick ass for. No offense."

"None taken."

"I want a man that can give as good as he gets. No offense."

"None taken."

"And I need a man that has muscles. Is Ryan ripped?"

"Not like Alec, but he's still got a really nice body."

I sighed as I stared at Alec some more. "I just wish there was a way that I could find out if he was at all attracted to me. I mean, if I knew that he had absolutely no interest, it would be so much easier to move on. Not that I'm looking for more than a good night of fucking," I added quickly.

"Maybe you should write him a note. I'll make sure Cap isn't watching," she grinned.

"I think I'm just destined to watch him from afar."

"You know, the guys are going to The Pub tonight. Why don't we go and you can feel him out?"

"I suppose. What are you gonna tell Ryan?"

"Oh, he'll be going with. There's no way I'm going without him. I don't need men hitting on me and then having to gently break it to them, by smashing their faces into the bar, that I'm taken."

"Fine, but you're not allowed to hint in any way that I'm interested in him. If it's meant to be, something will happen."

"Yeah, sometimes you have to kick fate's ass." Lola strutted away and I watched the swagger that she had. Her confidence seemed even stronger now that she had Ryan. Maybe I didn't need a man in the same field as me. Maybe a regular guy would do. I looked back over at Alec and watched as he wiped down his face and chest with a towel. Yeah, a regular guy just wouldn't do.

God, I was so nervous as I walked into the bar. I must have changed my outfit at least ten times before I got in my truck and headed to the bar. Lola had texted me that they were on the way, so they should be here any minute. What I was about to do would change the way things were between Alec and I. Even one kiss could destroy our relationship. If this was going to work, we both had to be clear that it was just fucking. That is, if he was even interested.

"Florrie!" Craig shouted from across the bar. I smiled and headed over to them. "What are you drinking tonight?"

"Beer."

Craig grinned and headed to the bar, but stopped and turned back to me, looking me up and down. Yeah, I was wearing a skintight black dress and heels. I had left my combat boots at home. "You look good tonight."

"Thanks."

He went to the bar and a warm hand snaked across my shoulders sending shivers down my spine. It was him. I knew based on his scent alone. But his touch was electric to me.

"What's the occasion?"

"Nothing."

He took a seat across from me, his eyes burning a trail of sticky, sweaty lust through my body. "You look fucking sexy. You should dress like this more often."

"Not very many options for ways to carry a gun."

"So, you're not carrying tonight?"

"Of course, I am. I just had to get creative."

His eyes darkened and he swallowed visibly. Score one for me. "I think I'm going to have to check that out, make sure that they're secured properly."

"And what will you do if they're not?" I asked boldly.

"Do you really need me to show you how to use protection? I mean, I'm all up for it, giving you a demonstration, if that's what you need."

I wanted to shout out that yes, that was exactly what I needed. But Craig plopped my beer down in front of me and temporarily broke the mounting tension between Alec and I.

"Damn. It's easy to forget that you're a sexy as fuck woman when we see you at work," Craig grinned. "You should really dress up like this more often. Your body is a lethal weapon."

I tried to think of a response, but Alec's eyes were locked on mine and I couldn't look away. Craig started talking with Alec about some sports team, but I wasn't listening. I was stuck, staring at Alec. He talked with Craig, glancing at him occasionally, but his eyes never strayed far from me for long. I was starting to feel warm, flushed and needy. I needed to step away and get some water before I climbed across the table and mounted Alec.

I drank down my beer and excused myself from the table. I was just about to enter the women's bathroom when a hand wrapped around my waist. Alec pushed me up against the wall, his body too close to mine to not feel how turned on he was.

"Are you trying to tease me tonight?"

"Is that what I was doing? I thought I was making a statement."

"You're making every guy in the room stare at you."

"I was really only aiming for one," I said breathlessly.

His hands skimmed down my body, resting on my hips. "You got my attention and you're making me painfully hard."

"I can tell."

"You were staring at me out there."

"I was watching you watch me."

He leaned forward, his nose skimming along my neck. "Fuck, you smell good."

God, I wanted him to kiss me, put his hands all over me and make me his. But he stepped back, clearing his throat. "I'll see you out there."

I was flushed and my heart was racing. When I felt like I could walk, I pushed through the women's door and splashed some water on my face. The door pushed open and Lola walked in grinning at me. "Hell, I had to come in here to cool myself down after that display in the hallway."

"Shit, I wasn't prepared for that. I mean, I was just going to see how things went. I never thought I would actually get his attention."

"Are you serious? You're wearing a fuck me dress and fuck me shoes. If he didn't go for it, I know Craig would have."

I winced. "I wasn't trying to play them off each other."

"Trust me, they know that. Well, don't just stay in here. Go get him."

I nodded and made my way out of the bathroom only to stop dead in my tracks. Alec was sitting at our table with a woman next to him, his arm wrapped around her shoulder. He was smiling at her as she talked animatedly to him. I was stuck. I couldn't move if I wanted. Lola grabbed my arm and was pulling me out of the bar. I didn't know what the hell was happening, but I couldn't seem to make my body do anything but follow orders.

"What the fuck was that?" Lola asked as she shoved me into her truck.

"I...Did I just imagine that?"

"That Alec practically fucked you up against the wall in the hallway and then was sitting all cozy with Mary Sunshine? No, you didn't imagine that."

"What the hell was I thinking? How could I be so stupid?"

"You weren't being stupid. Alec was being a player. I'm sorry. I never should have suggested that you try to get his attention."

"It's not your fault," I reassured her.

"I should have known better. I mean, come on. We all know how these guys are."

"Not all the guys. Just the one I was after."

Chapter Four

ALEC

Three years ago...

She had to choose now to put the moves on me, when I was already dating someone. When she walked into the bar, it was like all my dreams had come true. She was there, offering herself up to me, looking like the sexy goddess that she was. All thoughts and plans for the night went out the window. I just wanted to have her in my arms. I couldn't stop staring at her. Florrie never dressed up like this unless it was part of a mission. I knew that she liked to, but we just didn't ever get enough down time where she could take advantage.

And then she walked away, and staring at her ass was all I could do. I pushed away from the table and followed her. She practically told me that she was ready to fuck me. It was everything I had been waiting for. But then I came to my senses and remembered that I had a sort of girlfriend and she was meeting me here tonight. I might be a lot of things, but a cheater wasn't one of them. As shitty as it was for me to walk away from Florrie after shoving her up against the wall, I couldn't pretend that I wasn't already committed to someone. That would be worse than walking away.

I knew the moment she walked out of the bathroom. I felt her in the room, felt all the air being sucked out of the room as the scene punched her in the face. I saw Craig visibly stiffen as he walked up to the table and then looked over at Florrie. He had to know I had followed Florrie, but he was probably chalking it up to mistaken lust at this point. Hell, I had my arm around Michelle's shoulders and she was laughing and smiling at me like I was a fucking king. I felt like shit.

I saw Lola lead Florrie out of the bar, but I ignored it. I had a decision to make. I either needed to break things off with Michelle and go after Florrie, or I needed to stick things out with Michelle and see where this went.

It turned out, there was no decision to be made. The next day at work, Florrie pretended like nothing had happened. She didn't treat me like shit like I deserved, and she didn't act hurt either. She was indifferent. I had fucked things up, and now there was no fucking way I would get a chance with her again.

Chapter Five

ALEC

Three months later...

We pulled up to the meet. Florrie was posing as Carrie Hammond, whose daughter Gabby had been kidnapped. Our job was to go in, unarmed, and hand over 'documents' and get Gabby back. Meanwhile, the rest of the teams would be moving in, ready to pull our asses out of there. It was dangerous as fuck. There would be guards and plenty of guns pointed at our heads.

I glanced over at Florrie, praying to God she was ready for this. She was smart and quick on her feet. She had saved my ass a number of times in the field and I knew she was capable. The one problem, she was fucking hot and a distraction to any red-blooded man. She had long, blonde hair that curled slightly in the humidity and killer blue eyes that could bring a man to his knees. They were what always drew me in. Well, that and her amazing rack.

Florrie wasn't shy about showing off her body, though it was never in a sexual way. She just dressed for whatever the occasion was, with no regard for whether or not she was making every man so twisted inside that his balls literally choked him from the inside out. And she had a style that drove me crazy, making me hard in an instant. She could dress up to look like a fucking doll, but underneath, she was loaded with weapons. It was fucking hot.

But I had fucked up any chance of having her three months ago in a bar. I was still seeing Michelle, but things weren't going to work. She was so fucking sweet, too sweet for me. She was the kind of girl you brought home to meet your mother for Sunday dinner. That wasn't me. And we didn't live in fucking Mayberry. I knew it was going to end, but I hadn't had the opportunity to break things off yet. Not that it mattered. Florrie hadn't so much as looked at me with lust in her eyes since that night.

"Eyes forward," I said as we pulled through the gates to the buildings. Men were surrounding the outside, holding automatic weapons. "Remember, our goal is to get Gabby out. Let the guys do their jobs so we can get out safely."

I was mostly concerned about Florrie. It wasn't in her nature to act like a timid and scared woman, and that was exactly the part she needed to play. The guards pulled us out of the car, manhandling Florrie just a little too much for my liking. I tamped down the anger as I held out my arms to be checked for weapons. I couldn't even pack the smallest knife. If I was caught, they would most likely kill me before I even stepped foot inside the building, leaving us one man down. It wasn't worth the risk.

One of the men grabbed Florrie so hard around the arm that I saw her wince and then anger flushed over her face. I shook my head slightly, reminding her to keep her cool. She whimpered, playing the part of the damsel to a T. We were dragged through the hallways, down to the basement and through a long hallway with doors on either side. They took us to the door at the end of the hallway. The trick was going to be whether or not Gabby gave us away. If she did, we were all dead. We just had to pray that she caught on and played her part.

The man shoved Florrie into the room, causing her to stumble and fall to the floor. She looked up right away at Gabby and tried to convey to her to play along. "Gabby, sweetheart, mommy's here now. It's going to be okay."

Gabby looked at her strangely, but didn't give us away either.

"We brought what you asked for," I said, pulling out the envelope before anyone could look too closely at the way Gabby was looking at Florrie.

"Stop," the man said forcefully. "You don't fucking move unless I tell you to."

I held up my hands in submission. The tension in the room was high and I could tell that anything would make these guys snap. A look passed between two of the men and I knew we were fucked. They planned to take the envelope and kill all of us. They didn't care about the life of a little girl.

The man moved forward to take the envelope from me and I moved fast, stepping in front of Gabby as best I could. A weapon was drawn immediately and shoved against my skull. I clenched my jaw in anger, pissed that I was unable to do anything. Craig was in the same position as me, a gun to his head and nothing he could do. Hand to hand combat would only get you so far in a gunfight. If it was just the three of us, I wouldn't hesitate to take the risk, but Gabby was in the room.

He snatched the envelope from my hand and nodded to the man standing next to Florrie. The air prickled and I knew this was it. An awareness washed over me, filling my gut with dread, not only for Gabby, but for my teammates. A flash of Florrie fighting me in the ring flitted through my mind and a sense of longing washed over me. It was Florrie and always had been from the moment I met her. But I had waited too long and now it was too late.

I shoved his gun up and away, yanking his hand back and snapping his wrist. Another man drew his weapon, aiming it right at Florrie. I charged, knowing full well I was about to get a bullet to the chest. The impact was like a freight train. Three bullets pierced my vest and lodged in my chest. At least, I was pretty sure they hadn't gone through. It was strange because it wasn't the type of pain I had expected. It was sort of like tiny pinpricks stabbing me all over the chest and then being doused in hot sauce. And then the burning started and pain enveloped me.

My legs gave out and I fell to the floor. The room was spinning around me and my vision blurred. After what felt like minutes, I sucked in a deep breath, cursing the pain in my chest. I vaguely heard the sound of shouting and gunshots. I felt a hand slip into mine, but I couldn't see anything anymore. Everything was going black. The tang of blood filled my mouth and bubbled up my throat.

Pressure filled my chest, feeling like an elephant was sitting on me. As much as I wanted to stay and see her beautiful face one last time, I was too tired and needed to let go. Her crying was the last thing I heard.

Chapter Six

FLORRIE

No. This couldn't be happening. I kneeled on the ground next to Alec, refusing to believe what I was seeing. How could this be happening? I always thought of Alec as indestructible, but here he was, bleeding out all over the floor. Craig shoved me aside and started taking care of his wounds, something I was too shaken up to do right now. I wanted to hold him and tell him all the things that I felt for him, even though he had been an asshole, but now wasn't the time. Then again, there might never be another time.

Craig lifted him in his arms and carried him outside. Luckily, Alec seemed to have passed out already. Hopefully, he wasn't feeling any pain. I followed them out on autopilot, wiping the tears from my face. I was a professional and I needed to start acting like it.

At the hospital, I waited with everyone else, going through the motions of pretending to hold myself together. Inside, I was shredded. Craig walked over to me and held my hand, squeezing it tight in his. We were a team and like family to each other. They were all I had anymore.

"Do you know if Alec has anyone he would want us to contact?" Cap asked. "He didn't list an emergency contact on his employee records."

I shook my head slightly. "No, I don't think he has any family, or he doesn't speak to them."

"Girlfriend?"

I paused as the air whooshed out of my lungs. Here I was pining away for my teammate and I hadn't even considered the fact that he might be seeing that woman from the bar still.

"He was seeing someone a few months ago. I don't know if they're still together or not," Craig informed him. I felt dizzy, standing there and trying to pretend that a potential girlfriend wasn't the end of the world. Cap pulled out a phone and handed it to Craig.

"Look through his phone. If you find her information, give her a call and find out what's going on."

"What if they're not seeing each other?" I asked almost desperately. "She might show up here thinking that they might get back together or something."

Cap looked at me strangely. "But if they're together, she has a right to know."

I nodded, even though my heart was telling me this was wrong. Craig scrolled through Alec's contacts until he found what he was looking for. "Well, her number is still here, so I'll give her a call."

He walked away and I quickly blinked back tears that were trying to spill over.

"Are you doing okay?"

"Of course," I said stiffly.

"You don't look so good."

"Yeah, well, my teammate was shot. If I looked good right now, you'd probably be asking me the same thing."

Cap nodded and was about to say something more when we were called over by the doctor. It had been hours since Alec was taken into surgery, but I hadn't expected him to be out of surgery so soon. I covered my mouth with my hand as a cry threatened to escape. This had to be bad news. That was the only way he could be done so soon.

"How's he doing?" Cap asked in a rush.

"Mr. Wesley was very lucky. Two of the bullets struck his lungs, but were very close together. It made patching him up a lot easier. The third bullet was lodged in muscle and didn't strike anything else."

"So, he's going to be fine?"

"With time," the doctor smiled. "He'll need about a week in the hospital to recover. We want to make sure that he's on the path to recovery, but he should be just fine."

"Thank you, doctor." Cap shook his hand and continued to talk to him, but all I could think about was the fact that he was going to live.

As soon as the nurse came to get us to see Alec, I was heading down the hallway, completely ignoring anyone else that wanted to see him. As far as I was concerned, Craig and I had first rights. Seeing him lying in that bed almost crippled me. He was so pale and the tired lines on his face made him look older. I walked over to him and gripped his hand in mine, all the while aware of Craig standing on the other side of the bed. I didn't want to let on to how I was feeling about Alec right now, so I took a seat and waited for the moment he woke up. He was out for the rest of the night and half the next day.

Craig was the first to notice him wake up. I had been drifting off, thinking about all the times that I had pretended not to be infatuated with Alec, wondering if there was anything I could have done that night in the bar that would have made a difference. When Craig ran out of the room, I leapt up from my chair and locked eyes with Alec. There was a burning intensity to them that I hadn't noticed before. I wanted to say something, but what did you say to the man that you wanted, had been dreaming over, but just couldn't have?

"Good to see the patient is awake," the doctor said as he walked into the room. I was afraid that my feelings would show through if I didn't step back, and I didn't need everyone in the room knowing exactly what I was thinking. The doctor removed the tube from his throat and examined him, but Alec kept looking at me. He hadn't said a word yet, but I could feel questions drifting off him.

As soon as the doctor left, Craig started in, joking with Alec like he wasn't lying in a hospital bed. I smiled at the appropriate times and pretended that everything was fine, but I was dying inside. I wanted to yell at Craig to get the fuck out of the room and give us some privacy, but then I would give myself away.

"I'm gonna grab some coffee," Craig finally said after what felt like an hour. "You want anything?"

"Sure," I said, happy that he was finally leaving. As the door swung shut, I turned back to Alec and tried to figure out what I should say. I could feel the dried tears on my face and the sweaty stickiness that clung to my body. I was a mess, fidgeting and terrified of facing the man I needed more than life itself.

"You scared us," I finally said, deciding on something neutral.

"All of you?"

"Of course." I could feel the tears building again, and I wiped them away quickly, but not quickly enough. He saw it and he stared like he fucking knew. I was a wreck. I was usually the stoic one, but right now, I just kept seeing him on that floor, bleeding out like I might never see him again.

"I'm fine," he said softly.

"I know, but..." I got all choked up and couldn't get my words out. I wanted him so bad right now, just to hold me and feel his heartbeat. He must have read my mind because he tugged on my hand, telling me to get on the bed with him. I did as he asked and laid down next to him on the bed.

"Didn't realize that I could scare you," he chuckled.

I slapped him on the arm, immediately feeling guilty about it, but he just laughed more, groaning when it obviously hurt him.

"You have no idea what that was like. There was blood everywhere. I thought I had lost you."

"You just don't want Craig to be your team leader," he said gruffly.

I glanced over, seeing his eyes drift shut. "Yeah, that's what I was worried about," I played along. The scruff along his jaw was a stark contrast against his pale skin. He was too pale. Too close to death. I couldn't take it. I stood quickly, needing to be close to him and further away at the same time.

"Where are you going?"

"I just need..." I cleared my throat, fixing my ponytail to keep from fidgeting anymore than I was. "You were almost gone and now you're here."

His eyes burned into mine as he stared me down. It was uncomfortable and that made this so difficult. Nothing had ever been strained between us. He cleared his throat. "It's strange. When I was lying on the floor, I could swear that I heard you crying." His voice was soft and low, but his eyes were knowing. I swallowed hard and then his hand slipped into mine, intertwining with my fingers. "Was I imagining that?"

"You were bleeding out on the floor. Of course I was crying. I'm a girl," I deflected. I wanted to tell him that I needed him, that I wanted him so badly. It was on the tip of my tongue, but I was so scared. I didn't want him to hurt me again.

His eyebrows scrunched and he opened his mouth to say something, but the door swung open and a mess of a woman came running in, shoving me out of the way to get to his side.

"Alec, oh my gosh. When they called, I was so terrified. I was visiting my sister and I couldn't get a flight back until this morning."

She leaned over him, squeezing his body. I saw him tense and realized that she was pushing on his incision.

"You're going to hurt him," I snapped, yanking her off him. I was about to lose my shit with this woman. That is, until she turned to me with those sweet, kind eyes. She had the kind of face that said she was a good girl and a truly caring person. She wasn't being unsympathetic to Alec. She just really was that scared and had overreacted.

"I'm sorry," she smiled shyly. "I'm Michelle."

"I'm Florrie, his teammate."

"It's nice to meet you. I didn't know that he had a female teammate."

She was nice, sweet even in the way that she spoke. I could tell that she wasn't trying to be catty or bitchy. She just genuinely didn't know about me. But I knew about her. This was the same woman from the bar. And if Alec had been with her for a few months, that meant that I really didn't register anywhere on his radar.

I gave her a kind smile and backed up. "Well, I'll give you two some privacy."

I turned and walked out the door before either of them could say anything else. I didn't miss the strained look Alec sent me, but I wasn't going to sit there and decipher it. Alec had her and I had no one. Unfortunately, life was just like that sometimes.

Chapter Seven

ALEC

The week in the hospital sucked. Michelle was by me every single minute of the day. And the whole time, I was wishing she was Florrie. I had meant to break up with Michelle a few days before my mission, but then she told me she was going to her sister's. I had completely forgotten. Now I was in the hospital and she was doing everything she could to take care of me. It was annoying as fuck. Florrie still came by to see me, but she was more guarded around me, like she was trying to keep things strictly professional. I had been about to pour my fucking heart out to her when we were interrupted.

It was that moment in the basement, when my world stood still and priorities shifted. Florrie wasn't just my teammate, never had been. I could feel it like being struck by lightning. She was meant to be mine. Now I just had to figure out how to break up with Michelle and make that happen.

"What's up your ass today?" Craig asked as he walked into my hospital room. I was sitting on the edge of my bed, trying to fucking stand to go take a piss.

"Fuck off."

"Well, it's good to know that you're not discriminating in your assholery."

"What the fuck are you talking about?"

"Cap said he was by earlier and you threw a cup at him." He gave me a crazy look. "It's fucking plastic. What did you think you were going to accomplish?"

"It had water in it."

"Yeah, good one. I'm sure he's quaking in his combat boots."

I groaned as I pushed off the bed. My stitches pulled, but I pushed through. Michelle pushed the door open and rushed over to me.

"What are you doing? You should have asked for help."

"I can fucking do it myself."

"Sure," she snorted.

"I can," I gritted through clenched teeth.

"It won't kill you to lean on someone," she reminded me for the tenth time today.

"I'm taking a piss, not fixing a car."

She stepped away from me, hurt spread across her face. I sighed and shuffled off to the bathroom. I felt like an old man. When I finished in the bathroom, Craig was sitting in a chair, feet up on my bed, and sipping a cup of coffee. Michelle was nowhere to be seen.

"Where'd she go?" I grumbled.

"Said something about needing to run some errands. You're really fucking good at pushing people away, you know that?"

"You don't say."

I lowered myself onto the bed and eased myself back into a comfortable position.

"She seems really nice. Why are you being an asshole?"

I sighed, deciding there was no time like the present to lay it all out on the table. "I was planning on ending things with her. I just didn't have the chance. She went off to visit her sister and then this shit happened."

He snorted in amusement. "So, you're gonna let her continue to show up here every day to take care of your grumpy ass when you have no intention of dating her ever again?"

"What the fuck do you want me to do? You want me to say *thanks for stopping by, but this isn't gonna work?*"

"Why are you ending things, anyway?"

"She's not cut out for this life. Don't get me wrong, she's great. Perfect even. But I can see it on her face every time I talk about work. It scares her. She's even asked me if I would ever consider another job."

"Ooh, that's not good."

"I figured that I would have to end it sooner rather than later. I mean, I could see it on her face when she first got here. She was scared as fuck."

"That's normal though. If she wasn't scared because you got shot, I would say she's not a very good girlfriend."

"But I need someone that can handle this shit. I love my job and there's no fucking way I'm giving it up. She needs a banker or a lawyer."

"Someone boring, you mean," Craig grinned.

"She totally freaked out the first time she saw my gun. She asked me to put it away in the safe for the night," I said incredulously.

"How the fuck do you defend yourself if your gun is locked up? Someone breaks in and you're like *Hold on while I go get my gun from the safe.* Then you enter the wrong password ten fucking times, and by then the burglar already has half your shit and your dick is blowing in the wind."

"I know! Who the fuck doesn't sleep with a gun under their pillow?"

"Crazy people," Craig answered. "That's who. So, when are you gonna do it?"

"I don't know. Soon. I think they're releasing me tomorrow. I have to do it before she decides to move in and take care of me."

"No shit. It's not like you can hide all the guns in your house from her. I mean, the machine gun above the fireplace would be a little hard to hide in the safe."

"And if it's not the guns, it'll be the knives or the cannon."

"You got a cannon?"

I shrugged. "I found one that was from the Civil War. Napoleon cannon. I wanted it. How the hell would I explain that to her?"

"Still working?"

"Of course," I said, looking at him like he was an asshole. "What the fuck would I do with a non-functioning cannon."

"What would you do with a functioning one?" he asked.

"In case there's an attack. Those fuckers are badass."

"They're also really fucking slow to load and fire. When could you possibly need a cannon? Don't get me wrong, I like it. It's a good investment. But in reality, when would you say, *Hmmm, I think I'll use the cannon over the machine gun.*"

"Really? I have one phrase for you. *Leave the gun. Take the cannoli.*"

"Alright, aside from the rare times that you might be able to use *The Godfather* as a reference, even though you didn't use it the right way, when would you actually use a cannon?"

"There are plenty of times. Maybe when I find out the nosy neighbor is actually a spy. The cannonball disintegrates and I could load the shots with everyday shrapnel, making it virtually untraceable."

"Right," Craig nodded. "That is, until someone walks in your house and finds a fucking Napoleon cannon sitting in the middle of your fucking living room."

"It's not in the living room," I grumbled. "It's in my study."

He rolled his eyes as he stood. "Either way, if she doesn't like guns, she's definitely not going to like a cannon in the middle of the house."

"So, how do I break it off with her?"

"Well, you could always just show her the damn thing. If that doesn't send her running, you're fucked."

"Do you want me to get you anything?" Michelle asked as she helped me to my couch.

"No, I told you I'm fine."

"Right, but you don't look fine. I mean, you were shot," she said with a small quiver in her voice. I took her hand in mine and pulled her down to the couch to sit next to me.

"Look, Michelle, I don't think this is going to work between us."

"What?"

I stared into her beautiful eyes, but it just wasn't there. She was great, but there wasn't a spark anymore. Once the excitement of being with me wore off, she started to see the real me. I wasn't even sure why she was still with me.

"Michelle, can you honestly say that you want to be with me?"

"Of course-"

"Seriously. Be honest with yourself and me. Where do you see this going? You're a teacher and I blow shit up for fun."

"That's not what you do," she chastised.

"No, but I like to do it. You can't stand guns and I can't stand to not have one on me at all times." She chewed her lip as she thought it over. "Look, you're great and you're gonna make some guy really happy. I wish that could be me, but we're just too different."

She sighed in relief and looked up at me sheepishly. "I know. I've been thinking that for a while."

"Me too, but then this happened and you were there for me. I didn't want to seem ungrateful."

The front door opened and Florrie walked through like she owned the place, making Michelle extremely uncomfortable based on the way her body tensed up. I took her hand in mine as I spoke to Florrie.

"Florrie, give us a minute," I said harshly, hoping she got the hint to get the fuck out of here. Michelle deserved better than to end our relationship in front of another person.

"Sure," Florrie said, barely glancing at us as she walked toward the kitchen.

Michelle gave a hesitant smile and placed her hand on my cheek. "I hope you get better soon."

I wasn't sure what to say anymore. I didn't want to drag this out and I didn't want to say anything that might make her think we could make this work. So, I smiled at her and kissed her on the cheek.

"Take care of yourself," she said as she stood and walked out the door. I leaned back into the cushions and let my eyes slip closed. I was fucking exhausted and I just wanted to sleep.

"Where'd Mary Sunshine go?"

"Don't be a bitch."

"What? She's very nice. I just didn't picture you with someone so...wholesome."

I glared at her. The problem was, she was absolutely right. Michelle and I were never going to be some great couple. And the fact that Florrie knew it, knew that I really belonged with someone like her, really grated on my nerves. Mostly because Florrie walked out of that hospital when I wanted her to stay more than anything. She had been so fucking worried and then she got spooked and walked out.

"We're not together anymore."

"Oh," she said, genuinely surprised. "Why not?"

"It wasn't going to work."

I needed to end this conversation now. I didn't want to talk about Michelle anymore. I wanted to talk about us and what we could be, but Florrie wasn't ready for that kind of conversation. I could tell by the way she leapt out of my hospital bed.

"I'm tired. I think I'm gonna hit the sack."

"Okay. I'll stick around tonight. Just in case you need anything," she quickly added.

I nodded, wanting to invite her to my bed. I hobbled off to my bedroom, all the while feeling Florrie's stare burning into my back. I just had to give her time.

Chapter Eight

FLORRIE

"Fuck!"

I shot off the couch as fast as I could and headed down to Alec's room. This was the fourth night I had stayed here, needing to be close to him. I told myself that he needed someone to watch out for him and help him out, but the truth was, he didn't really let me do anything. Craig seemed perfectly fine with walking away at the end of the day and leaving Alec on his own. I just couldn't do that.

"What's wrong?" I asked as I rushed into his bedroom. My eyes widened and my jaw dropped. Alec had just gotten out of the shower and his towel was laying in a puddle at his feet. So were his underwear. I had seen him naked before. Of course, I had. But it was never like this, when I had wanted him so bad. He was always my teammate, my friend. But this was just me, one hundred percent woman staring at one hundred percent, hot-blooded, smoking body, sexy-as-hell man.

"Holy shit," I muttered.

He turned and raised an eyebrow at me. I tried to look away, but between the scar running down his chest and the muscles that flexed as he tried to maneuver his body, I just couldn't look away. And it wasn't just his sexy thigh muscles that had me staring at the lower half of his body. There was one muscle in particular that was quite impressive and getting bigger by the moment.

"Florrie," Alec bit out. "Would you mind not staring at my dick? I can't exactly do anything about my current state with you staring at me like that."

"Uh, right, sorry."

I spun around and right into the corner of the door, smashing my face so hard that I had an immediate headache.

"Fuck, that hurt," I cried out. Alec's hands were immediately around me, guiding me over to the bed.

"This is bad. We shouldn't be on your bed."

"Would you rather be on the floor? Because I can walk you over to the door and let you drop."

"Fuck off," I muttered, not happy at all that I had just embarrassed myself. I was Florrie fucking Younge. I didn't get flustered and I never let a man get under my skin like that.

"Let's just call a spade a spade. You saw my dick. You liked it. And now you want a test run."

"A test run? Really? I didn't know you had to have women test you out first. Bad results?"

"Not a single one," he smirked.

"What was the yelling about?" I asked, trying to change the subject from his dick to something more neutral.

"Nothing. I just dropped my underwear. It still fucking hurts to move around, so I was pissed."

"I see."

"Do you? Because your face is swelling up. Let me get you an ice pack."

"Wait," I said, putting my hand on his arm to stop him. "You're the injured one. I can get my own fucking ice pack."

He sighed, rubbing a hand across his face. The stubble had turned into more of a beard at this point. I couldn't help but let my mind think of the feel of it against certain parts of my body.

"You know, I don't need you to stay with me all the time. I can manage."

"I know that." I tried not to let the hurt into my voice. I was so

sick of feeling like I was chasing a man that didn't want me. I knew
that I was halfway in love with him, and if he had any sense, he knew it
too. Yet he hadn't made a move. When he told me he'd broken up with
Michelle, I really fucking tried not to get my hopes up, but then
nothing happened. There wasn't any change in the way he acted
toward me. In fact, it was like he was trying to shove me out the door.
Only, I was the stubborn woman that refused to see the light and
recognize when a man didn't want her.

"Do you? Florrie, you've been staying here, sleeping on the fucking
couch because you think something's going to happen. I'm fine,
though."

Logically, I knew that. I was beating a dead horse here. He was
trying to let me down easy. It was so clear. He was acting like I was
staying here just to make sure he was okay, when in reality, I just
needed to be near him. Desperation was never a good look.

He gripped my hand in his. "I'm fine."

I nodded, but the tears started coming anyway. I swiped them away
angrily. I had never been so emotional in my life. I didn't do crying or
pining away for some guy. Except, Alec wasn't some guy and I had
almost lost him.

His fingers gripped my chin and he forced me to look into the dark
depths of his eyes. "I'm fine," he said slowly. "Stay as long as you need
to so you know it's true. But I'm fine."

I nodded and took his hand when he stood. Handing him his
underwear, he slipped them on and then he led me into the kitchen
and handed me an ice pack out of the freezer. I stayed another two
weeks. I never was very good at taking hints.

I walked into Alec's house, tossing his mail on the table beside him. He
was lying on the couch sleeping, something he did a lot of over the
past few weeks. The scars on his chest were hard for me to see still. In
moments like this, I was able to stare at him unabashedly and think
about what it would be like to have him.

His face was less strained over the past few days. I could tell that his recovery was going better every day. The tense lines on his face had eased and his color had returned to normal. He was moving around better and it didn't look so damn hard for him to do the smallest things.

I leaned over and pressed my lips lightly to his, keeping my eyes on his the whole time in case he woke up. He was so beautiful. Up close, I could see how thick his lashes were. I could imagine what it would be like to wake up this close to him every morning. God, I was a freaking stalker. That's what I had turned into. I pushed myself away from him, running my hands over my head. Pacing away from him, I tried to gain control of my body, but the pull to be near him was too strong. I had to leave before I did something even crazier, like strip him down and suck his cock.

Turning back to him, I looked longingly at him before I left. I needed to stay away for a few days and get my head on straight. Heading into work, I got right into my workout gear and hit the bags. I wanted to let off steam, but I wasn't interested in dealing with anyone else's bullshit right now.

The harder I punched the bag, the angrier I got. Why was I falling apart over a man? Yeah, I liked Alec a lot. Way more than I should. But I knew it could never go anywhere. If anything, it would be a one night stand, maybe two. But we would never be lovers. We worked together and that prevented us from having any kind of lasting sexual escapades. I already resigned myself to the fact that we could never be more than that, so why was I chasing after him like a lost puppy? He had to know that I was crazy about him at this point. I had stayed at his house for almost three weeks while he was recovering and I was still stopping by to see him every day after work. He had to know. Yet he didn't say a word. Not one fucking word.

"Hey, killer. What's got you all worked up today?"

I ignored the guys that walked up behind me. I knew Hunter was there, but I wasn't sure who else was, and frankly, the way I was feeling, they didn't want me to find out.

"Someone must have really pissed her off. I've never seen her hit the bag like that."

Gabe. Fucking perfect. Now that he had Isa, he thought he knew what every woman thought. I hit the bag harder.

"Do you think we should find out what's got her all worked up or walk away?"

"Talk to her. Trust me, when Cara gets like this, there's only one way to deal with her."

Sinner. The man that thought he could fix everything with his charming smile.

"We're not gonna fuck her," Hunter said.

"I wasn't suggesting that," Sinner said. "I was thinking more about talking shit out with her. You know, a woman is like a flower. You have to peel back those petals and get to the pollen. Only then can they blossom."

"Dude....Just shut the fuck up," Hunter said irritatedly. I couldn't agree more. Flowers. What a bunch of bullshit.

"Maybe we should just leave her alone." Rocco. The new guy. "I'm pretty new here, but where I come from, when a woman's pissed, you don't go poke at her."

Finally, someone with some common sense.

"Florrie, what's got you so upset?" Sinner asked. "It's a man, right?"

"Oh, sure. Throw us all under the bus," Hunter grumbled.

"What? Have you met us?" Sinner asked. "We're all a bunch of assholes most of the time."

"Whose team are you on?" Gabe asked.

"I'm on the side of keeping my dick in tact. Finding out why she's so pissed will help me achieve that."

"How do you figure?" Hunter asked.

"Do you want to be the one that gets in the ring with her?"

"Good point. Florrie, sweetie?"

I spun around and glared at Hunter. "Sweetie? Seriously?"

"Uh....I hadn't really thought past that part."

"Yeah, I can see that. But you didn't really think about the whole *sweetie* part either, did you?"

Hunter swallowed and looked at the other guys. "No?"

I snorted and started punching the bag again. "Typical man. Can't make up your mind."

"See, I told you this was about a man," Sinner said. "It's always about a man."

"That's because men only think of themselves," I said as I hit the bag around, feeling slightly maniacal right now. Based on the looks the guys were shooting, I looked it too.

"So," Gabe swallowed hard. "Do you want to tell us about it?"

I saw him close his eyes and cross his fingers. I snorted as I punched the bag again. I didn't need advice from men. They were all idiots that only thought with their dicks. I stopped swinging and looked at each of them staring at me like I was a piranha. On the other hand, they might have some insight into their own species.

"What is it you want?"

"Like now or in general?" Gabe asked.

"In general. What is it that men want?"

Gabe looked at the other guys, wide eyed and terrified. "Does she want a list?" He turned back to me and shrugged hesitantly. "I like pepperoni pizza."

"Are you fucking kidding me? A woman asks you what men want and your answer is pepperoni pizza?"

He shrugged again. "It's good. It's comfort food. I like to feel comforted."

"I'm partial to ice cream," Sinner said.

"We all know that," I spat.

He held up hands and backed up like I would attack. "Sorry, I thought we were sharing."

"I'm talking about what men want in general terms. What makes you tick? What makes you satisfied? What makes you want a woman?"

I cringed as the last one came out. I hadn't meant to say that, but I was on a roll.

"Who is he?" Hunter asked. "Just tell me and I'll kick his ass."

"I think I can do my own ass kicking."

"No. Whoever this asshole is, just tell us and we'll take care of things. We'll make sure you never see him again. If you know what I mean," he continued.

"I know exactly what you mean, and no, you don't need to make him disappear."

"But, that's what we do. We don't know how to solve any other problems," Gabe said, almost in confusion.

Rocco groaned and held up a hand to ward off the guys. "I didn't want to get involved, but it looks like I'm gonna have to. Why don't you tell us about this guy. What's he like?"

"Smart, strong, capable..."

"Sexy?"

"Of course," I huffed. "But he's confusing. I thought that he was into me, but then nothing happened. Is it me? Am I not pretty enough?"

"No," Sinner said, shaking his head sharply.

"Of course not–" Hunter snorted uncomfortably.

"You're beautiful," Rocco said firmly, and the other guys joined in.

"Sexy as hell."

"Nice rack."

"Good ass. Nice and firm."

"You have nice elbows," Sinner said.

"What?" I asked in confusion. Hunter smacked him upside the head.

"I panicked," Sinner said. "You all said *nice rack, good ass.* What else was left?"

"You could have gone with beautiful eyes," I snapped. "Or even nice legs, but nice elbows? Who the fuck says that?"

"Obviously not this guy you're seeing or he'd already be dead," Rocco muttered.

"Did you fuck him?" Hunter asked. "Guys always lose interest after you fuck them."

"No," I sneered. "It's not like I just spread my legs for any guy I come across."

"Did you come right out and tell him you like him?" Rocco asked. "Some guys are fucking stupid and can't take a hint."

"Actually, I wrote him a note and told him that I really liked him and asked if he liked me too."

"Like in the song?" Sinner asked.

"Yeah," I snarked. "Just like in the song. I even drew boxes and asked him to check yes or no."

"Did he answer?"

"No, you idiot! I didn't actually do that. I'm not in second grade."

"Maybe you should," Sinner shot back. "With all your sarcasm, he probably doesn't know if you want to kiss him or kick him in the balls."

"What are you saying?"

"Don't answer that," Hunter coughed.

"I'm saying that you can be a little abrasive," Sinner said, not backing down.

"So, you're saying I should be sweet and gentle?" Gabe snorted and I glared at him. "I could be sweet and gentle."

"No offense, Florrie, but I can't see you interrogating some asshole and being sweet. Remember, I've seen you string a guy up to a tree."

"That's different. That's work."

"That's you," Sinner pointed out. "And that's okay, but not all guys are prepared to deal with all..." He waved his hand up and down my body, "that."

"All what? All of *me*?"

"Well, I didn't want to say that, but yeah. You're a lot of woman to take. And not in the fat way," he quickly clarified.

"So, how do I approach this then? Do I try and be more feminine? I could wear more dresses and try not to drink so much beer."

"Is that really what you want?" Rocco asked. "You want to put on some fake face for a guy that doesn't like you the way you are?"

"See, that's the thing. I think he does like me the way I am, but why isn't he making a move?"

"Maybe he doesn't know what you like," Rocco suggested.

"Trust me, he knows exactly what I like."

"Okay, so maybe he wants to see your softer side. You can do that without turning into some...girl," Sinner added.

"I'm already a girl," I bit out.

"Right, right. We know that," Sinner said placatingly. "We just have to help him see you that way instead of as a ninja warrior."

"Okay, so what kind of stuff?"

"For instance," Gabe said, clearing his throat, "Perhaps you could lose the combat boots. Not all the time," he rushed on. "Just in more social settings. You seem to think they go with everything."

"Because they do. I look badass when I wear these with a dress."

"Right, but he might not be into Goth," Sinner said.

"And maybe try to wear your hair down a little more. You know, ponytails make you look a little too severe," Gabe added.

"And show off your tits more," Rocco said, yanking my shirt down just enough that I looked like I had cleavage. "And don't be afraid to shake that ass."

"Like, when I'm just standing here?"

"When you walk." Sinner started walking away from me, shaking his ass from side to side. "See? It's all in the hips. You have to make that ass more appealing. Plus, if you wear heels, you accentuate the muscles in your calves and lift your ass." He bent over, waving his hand over his calves.

"Ooh." Gabe snapped his fingers and grinned. "Maybe you should try and tell him what you like sexually. You know, things you like in the bedroom. Things you wish you could do to him. Guys love to hear about sexual explorations."

"But not with other dudes," Sinner interjected. "Don't start telling him about some guy's dick and what you did with him."

"But be honest about what you want," Rocco interjected. "Don't say that you like shit you've never tried. If you don't want to be tied to the bed, don't tell him you like BDSM."

"But be adventurous," Hunter added. "No guy likes a woman that just lays there."

"But don't try to control everything either," Sinner said. "I don't mind Cara taking over from time to time, but I'm a guy. I want to have all the control and bring the pleasure."

"Yeah, and don't be clingy. Some guys like a little snuggle-snuggle," Rocco said, "but don't act like you suddenly have bed rights."

"What the hell are bed rights?"

Rocco chuckled and then his face turned serious and he crossed his arms over his chest, leaning in close. "This is important, so listen carefully. There are certain rights that a woman gets in a man's bed. Now, at the beginning, those rights are very limited. We're talking, you might be allowed to spend the night, but you'd better sleep on your own side. Now, after a couple of times in the sack, you might get snuggle rights, but there's a time frame of about ten to twenty minutes. Thirty is really pushing it. And then there's the whole cleaning up rights. Guys in general don't like cleaning you up after sex. I know women have this fantasy that men will take care of their woman, but it's all bullshit. That comes after some very extensive cock sucking."

"Is he serious?" I asked Hunter.

"Deadly."

"Okay, so after a few dates, you might earn breakfast rights, but don't expect anything fancy. I'm talking toast and burnt eggs. If you're lucky and he's already making breakfast for himself, he might think of you. Coffee is your best bet."

"What if I don't drink coffee?"

Gabe hissed in a breath. "Don't turn it down. You turn coffee down, that's like saying you don't need anything for breakfast. Coffee is a man's best friend first thing in the morning. That's all he needs, so he assumes that's what you need."

"What if I make breakfast?"

"Noooo. Definitely not," Sinner said. "At this point, you haven't earned household rights. That falls into the category of making yourself at home in the living room and taking long showers. You just don't have those rights at this point."

"How do you not know any of this?" Rocco asked. "You've been around."

"Yeah, but I don't stick around," I said. "I've never found a guy worth sticking around for. I always leave after sex. I didn't know there was anything about rights."

"Shit, this is worse than I thought," Rocco muttered. "Okay, as far as showering goes. You're allotted about ten minutes in the shower. Anything longer than that when the guy isn't in there fucking you is considered rude and intruding on his time."

He looked at me expectantly and I nodded. "Got it. Ten minutes."

"Good, then we have the whole morning kissing and cuddling rights. That doesn't kick in until well into the second month, if you get that far. And only if the guy initiates. If you have bad morning breath, you'd better get your ass out of bed and into the bathroom to brush that shit out."

"What about him?"

"It's his place," Hunter shrugged. "You don't like it, move on."

"Now," Rocco continued, "as for sex in the morning, most guys don't mind if you initiate, but always start with a good blow job."

"And when you suck cock–" I cut Gabe off right there.

"You know, I'm not sure this is exactly what I was getting at. In fact, I'm not sure saying anything to you guys was the wisest decision. How the hell do you guys get by on the advice from each other?"

"We manage," Hunter shrugged.

"Seriously? With suggestions on bedroom rights and household rights? Is this what you really base a relationship on?"

"Well, the pace of it. I mean, we could go on about dating rights, but I'm getting the feeling you don't want to hear those," Rocco said, eyeing me warily.

"You know, I just came in here to beat the shit out of a bag. I wasn't looking for dating advice or an advice column on sucking cock. I wasn't even planning on getting myself into a relationship," I said exasperatedly. "I just wanted the guy to fucking notice me. Any advice on that?"

The guys all looked at me warily, obviously not wanting to share anymore after my outburst. Fucking useless. I turned and walked away. I was going to have to figure this out for myself.

Chapter Nine

ALEC

Florrie followed me back to my house after poker night with the guys. I had been drinking and she insisted on driving me home. Except, I hadn't really had that much to drink. Unless you count two beers over the course of four hours a lot to drink.

"Florrie, I'm fine. I don't need you to walk me inside."

I really didn't need her to because she looked fucking sexy and I wanted nothing more than to stick my dick in her right now. I needed her to stop following me around all the time. She was much better about it than she had been after I was first released from the hospital. Those first few weeks, she barely left my sight. Even Craig noticed, but he chalked it up to Florrie being an emotional woman. I knew better. I knew that she had a shitload of feelings running through her that she didn't understand. I didn't want to put pressure on her, but I was running out of patience.

"I'm just making sure that you get in okay. I promise I'll leave as soon as I see that you're okay."

I sighed and opened the door to my house. She walked ahead of me, flicking on the lights as she went. I watched her ass sway and groaned when my dick started pressing against my pants. Fuck, I needed her to leave so I could go jack off. I hadn't been with anyone since Michelle, which wasn't all that long ago, but still, a few months for a guy was a long time. I wanted to feel her strong legs wrapped around my waist and feel her heat pressed up against me.

"Okay, I'm going to make something up for the morning for you and I'll be over to make you some dinner tomorrow–"

"Would you stop!"

She looked at me like a deer in the headlights. "What's wrong?"

I chuckled as I stared at the ceiling. "What's wrong? What's wrong is I'm fucking horny and I haven't gotten laid since Michelle. Now you're strutting around my house in those tight pants and I just want to go fuck."

"Oh." Her face filled with confusion for a moment and then cleared. "I thought..." She chewed on her lip for a moment and then looked at me quizzically. "Do you want me to leave so you can call Michelle? Or someone else," she rushed out. "Sorry, I wasn't really thinking about–"

"I'm not fucking calling Michelle. I don't want a fucking booty call. She was great in bed–"

"Then why did you break things off with her?"

I growled in frustration. This wasn't the conversation I wanted to have right now. Everything was coming out all wrong and she was misinterpreting what I was saying. "It wasn't going to work anyway. We're too different. Besides..." She stared at me expectantly and I took a chance. I had a feeling it was now or never with Florrie. "There's someone else."

Disappointment was clear on her face. I just didn't know in what way she was disappointed.

"Found someone else already to warm your bed?"

"Fuck, woman. Would you just shut the fuck up and stop making assumptions?"

"Excuse me, but–"

"No, just fucking stop. It's you and you fucking know it." The look of shock on her face was so real that I began to wonder if she really did know. "You don't know," I said dumbly.

"I didn't know *you* felt that way. I mean, I knew that there was something between us, but I thought it was all one sided."

"Are you fucking serious? I jumped in front of a bullet for you," I said incredulously.

"Yeah, but that could have been because you're a man and thought you had to protect me or something."

"Woman, are you fucking kidding me right now?" I yanked her closer to me, pulling her in by the back of her neck, leaving her nowhere to go. "I've been eye fucking you every day for years. I have to take cold showers to stop myself from mauling you every time I see you."

"Then why did you push me up against the wall and then pull away in the bar? I thought you wanted me then, but you just walked away like I meant nothing."

"Because I was already with Michelle. I'm not that big of an asshole to cheat on Michelle with you. And I would never do that to you. What kind of message does that send about me? Would you ever really trust me?"

"I'm not sure I trust you now."

Ouch. I hadn't been expecting that. I thought that I would tell her why I had backed off that night and she would understand and jump into my arms, ready to fuck me.

"Well, I'm asking you to trust me. I only backed off so I didn't hurt either of you. And I didn't go jump you when I broke things off with Michelle because I knew that I had been an asshole before. I didn't want you to think I was just using you."

"Then why didn't you just tell me that?"

"Because ever since I came home from the hospital, you looked like a scared kitten that would run away if I said anything to you. Besides, we work together."

"We still do," she snapped, trying to pull back, but I pulled her closer, flush against my body. There was no way I was letting her get away anymore.

"Yeah, but you know what? In that basement, something happened. I felt...I felt something that was way beyond anything I felt before. It wasn't lust," I said, bringing my mouth just a breath away from hers. "It was so much more than just wanting to fuck you or feel you beneath me."

Her breath was heavy, mingling with mine in a frenzied pattern. "What was it?"

"It was fucking need." I crashed my lips into hers and shoved my tongue into her mouth just as she opened up to me. Her arms wrapped around my neck and her fingers dug into my scalp. Fire exploded inside me, but it wasn't from the way she was pushing against my healing wounds. It was from the burning need I felt deep inside me. She was mine and that wasn't changing anytime soon.

"You're hurt," she murmured against my lips.

"My dick works just fine," I said, tearing my mouth from hers and shoving her pants down to her ankles. I was fucking desperate.

"Hurry," she panted. "Get them off. I need you."

"Say you want me." I needed to hear that she wanted me just as much, that it wasn't all on me.

"Of course, I want you, asshole. Haven't you noticed that I haven't left your fucking side in weeks."

"Months," I corrected as I ripped open her shirt and pulled at the bra that was covering her small tits. I didn't give a shit how small they were. She was fucking perfect to me. Her fingers fumbled for my jeans as I sucked on her nipples. She moaned and yanked the zipper down, reaching inside to pull me out.

"You'd better not kick me out afterwards," she panted.

"I never would," I gasped as her fingers wrapped around my cock.

"Good, because I'm always the one to walk away."

"Not anymore," I said as I plunged inside her. "You're never fucking walking away from me."

She pulled me tight to her, wrapping herself around me desperately. "Just remember something, when we do this, you're not my boss."

She rolled me over, putting herself on top as she ground her hips down on me. She started circling her hips and rubbing her clit against me so hard that my eyes crossed.

"Right," I bit out. "You can be in charge. Just as long as you don't break my dick with your tight cunt."

"If I break it, I can't use it."

I sat up, fighting against the pain that still burned in my chest and pulled her to me, panting and sweating like I was running a fucking marathon. "Shut the fuck up and fuck me hard. I need you."

"You should have asked a few weeks ago," she panted.

"I would have if I'd have thought you would actually be ready. But now that I know you are, you'll be here more often, sucking my cock and finding out all the ways that we fit together."

"Work," she panted. "I still have to work."

"You can fit me in on your lunch break."

I rolled her over, falling off the couch with her and landing on the floor. I started fucking her hard, clenching my eyes shut, praying that I didn't come yet. I still wanted so much more from her.

"Not when we start working together. Cap will-"

"Fuck Cap. I'll talk to him."

"No," she said so suddenly that I stopped moving. Staring into her eyes, I tried to figure out where her head was at. "If you want to fuck, this stays between us. Nobody else can know."

I stared at her for a moment, sure I had heard her wrong, but the truth of her words was written all over her face. "For now."

And that's all I would give her. Now that I had her, I had to start figuring out a way to make her mine. Forever.

Chapter Ten

FLORRIE

Two years ago...

He slammed into me from behind as I gripped onto the counter in the bathroom. We were in here under the pretense that he was cleaning my wounds. Craig was on guard duty. It was so fucking wrong. We had a client in the other room sleeping and we were supposed to be monitoring the safe house. But when Alec brought me in here to clean me up after we barely escaped a shootout, something carnal took over, and here I was, bent over the counter and still dripping blood.

"Why the fuck did you do that?" Alec growled as he pushed inside me.

"I was doing my job."

"You distracted the shooter."

"So, he didn't fucking shoot you. I thought that was pretty clear."

He pushed down between my shoulder blades, holding me in place, and started fucking me so hard my hips were sore from where they were hitting the counter.

"You shouldn't have done that. You should have done what I told you to."

"But then you'd be dead," I panted. When I saw the men going after him when his cover was blown, I couldn't follow his orders. He was my teammate and my lover. There was no way I could walk away.

"You left yourself exposed. You were fucking shot."

"It was a graze."

"How the hell was I supposed to know that?" He gripped my hair and pulled me back so he could look at my face. "I saw you go down and all I could think about was getting to you. I can't fucking stand the thought of you not being safe."

"Then you need to learn to trust me," I said calmly, trying to soothe the beast inside. Somehow, in the past year, I had gone from lustful to needing Alec so bad I could hardly breathe. Only Alec had gone from lustful to downright possessive. He watched my every move like the ground would swallow me up if I didn't follow in the same steps as him. Whenever he could get me alone, he fucked me harder, proving to me exactly who I belonged to. And I did belong to him. His eyes trapped me and held me to him. All he had to do was look at me and I couldn't resist anything he wanted.

The hard part was keeping it quiet. Over the past year, Alec had gotten more and more attached to me, and if I was honest, I had started to get attached to him also. I just didn't want it interfering at work. We still had a job to do and I just couldn't see how we could make it work if this turned into more than fucking. Or worse, if everyone knew that we were fucking. That led to questions and one very uncomfortable confrontation with Craig.

"Florence," he growled and I bit at the hand that was moving around my neck.

"Don't call me that."

"It's fucking beautiful."

"I hate it."

He gripped my hips and thrust so hard that the cabinet on the walls rattled. His hand slipped around to my face and he covered my mouth just before his other hand slipped to my front and his fingers pinched my clit. I let out a scream so loud and dirty that I knew we would attract attention.

His cum spilled down my legs as he pulled out, but I didn't have time to clean up before I heard the footsteps pounding down the hall. Alec flicked the lock on the door just seconds before Craig stood outside the bathroom door.

"Are you okay?" he shouted through the door.

"Fine," I shouted, trying to sound normal. "This asshole just pressed too hard on my wound."

"Be careful, Alec. Fuck, she was shot trying to save your ass."

Alec growled as he stared me down, but I just shrugged him off. He leaned in, caging me between his arms as he pushed me back against the counter. "Tell him," he said in deep voice against my ear. "Just fucking tell him."

"No." I stared him down, refusing to give in. "Nobody needs to know."

"Why the fuck not?"

"Because, you're already getting too possessive. If you could display that in the open, I would get taken off my team. There's no way Cap will let us work together if your assholery comes out."

He slid his hand around my neck, cupping the back of my head in his hands. His hot breath skimmed across my face and his erection dug into my stomach. "You haven't seen anything yet. You're mine, Florrie. One of these days, we won't be able to hide it anymore."

"It won't last anyway," I said irritatedly. There was no way we could continue like this, and there was no way Cap would let us work on the same team if we were fucking. "We'll get sick of each other or one of us will want out for some reason."

"I'll never want out," he said fiercely. "You're mine."

"I'm not yours. I'm a woman you fuck." His eyes darkened and his grip on my neck tightened. "You know this can't go anywhere. At some point, we'll have to walk away or risk our jobs."

"You're so willing to walk away from me?"

My gaze flicked down so he couldn't see the truth in my eyes. "Eventually, but not yet. Not unless you push me." I looked back into his eyes and steeled myself against his anger. "And if you think you can go behind my back and tell Cap, I'll walk away and you won't ever see me again. You won't even get a goodbye."

He stepped back, giving me my space, then turned and walked out of the bathroom, leaving me to clean up my own cuts. I shook off the nerves racing through me. I couldn't give in. I wouldn't. He was too strong, too powerful compared to me. He would crush me like a bug if I gave him the chance. My heart just couldn't take it.

"Hey, I thought Alec was cleaning you up?" Craig asked as he stared at my cut up arm.

"Yeah," I snorted. "You know he sucks at medical shit. Here," I said, tossing him the first aid kit. "Just patch me up so I can get back on duty."

"She needs to rest." I looked up to see Alec standing in the doorway glaring at me.

"If I needed to rest, then why were you such an asshole in here?"

"Yeah," Craig chimed in, not understanding what I was really saying. "You didn't even clean her up."

"She's out the rest of the night. You and I will take the rest of the watch."

"I'm-"

"I don't give a shit. I'm the team leader and I say you need to sit it out the rest of the night. Besides, we're in a safe house and we're monitoring everything."

He turned and walked away, leaving me even more pissed than before. This was why I couldn't be more with him. He was already walking all over me.

A year and a half ago...

"So, what are we doing tonight?" Craig asked as we walked to the parking garage.

"Um..." I had to think quick. Alec was coming over tonight and Craig most definitely couldn't be there. "I'm watching 50 Shades."

"Really?" Craig grinned at me. "I think I need to be there for that. I've never seen it."

I glanced at Alec with wide eyes, but he just shrugged. What was I supposed to do? "Are you sure you can handle it? There's gonna be a naked guy on screen."

He shrugged. "I'm comfortable in my own skin. I can handle it."

"Alright."

I walked to my truck, cursing myself for suggesting that movie. I thought he would shy away and make other plans. Now I had to watch a movie about dirty sex, which I hadn't actually planned to do, with two guys. One of which I was fucking.

When I got home, I made popcorn and found the stupid movie on tv. Craig sat in an armchair, but Alec sat down right fucking next to me on the couch. At first, it was fine. But then the sex started.

"You look cold," Alec murmured. I looked at him funny, not sure what he was getting at until he stood and walked over to the ottoman, pulling out a blanket from the hidden compartment. He draped it over my lap and sat back down, sliding his hand underneath. Oh God. This was so bad.

His hand slid up my leg, just gently caressing me as Christian Grey took Anna for the first time. His hand slid up to my pussy, his knuckles brushing against me through the fabric of my clothes. My breathing hitched and I glanced over at Craig, sure that he heard me, but he was too busy watching the movie.

His knuckles dug against my clit, the throbbing intensifying by the moment. My breathing was ragged, but drowned out when Alec turned up the volume on the tv. He was lounging back against the couch. His arm slung up on the backside. Craig looked over at us and then shifted uncomfortably. I didn't miss him grabbing and adjusting himself.

But I didn't have time to think about it. Alec's hand moved up under my shirt and then he had my nipple between his fingers and he was rolling it, pinching, and teasing me. I closed my eyes, my body feeling so much, but unable to process everything when I was forbidden from reacting the way I wanted. My body throbbed in desire until I couldn't control anything anymore. My body shook as my orgasm rushed through me. Alec pinched my nipple one final time and then he was shoving his hands down my pants. My wetness soaked his fingers and he smirked as he continued to watch tv.

"Right," Craig said, standing suddenly. Alec didn't even bother to remove his hand from my pants. "That's enough. I think I need to go find a woman."

"Thought you could handle it," Alec teased.

I wanted to smack him. His hand was still in my pants and he was risking drawing attention to us.

"Yeah, I'll see you guys later," he grumbled as he walked out the door.

Alec continued to work his fingers through me as we waited for Craig's truck to leave. The moment it was gone, Alec hauled me off the couch and dragged me back to the bedroom. I spun him around, pushing him up against the wall, dropping to my knees and taking his zipper down along the way. I pulled his length out of his boxers, all the while, his eyes burned through me.

Sucking him into my mouth, he hissed in a breath, his eyes growing darker as I licked and sucked him. I wanted to torture him after what he just did to me. But he didn't let me. He pulled me up slowly, running his hand across my cheek as he stared into my eyes. I could hardly breathe. Leaning forward, he kissed me softly, his lips moving softly across mine. I hadn't been expecting that. I thought this would get heated and nasty, but he took things slowly, kissing me and running his hands over my body until I was tingling everywhere from his burning touch.

Slowly, he pulled my shirt from my body, guiding it over my head and then kissed down my arms and along my collarbone. His arms wrapped around my back, pulling me closer to him. His tongue was all over me, leaving wet trails down my body.

"Shirt off," I mumbled, needing to touch him as well. He pulled his shirt off, his muscles flexing and pulling. He walked me back to the bed, laying me down underneath him, his length rubbing against my stomach. I let my eyes slip closed and just felt. I hadn't imagined ever having this kind of sex with Alec. It was always rough and dirty, but he was making me *feel*.

He slid my pants off me, his hands running up my body as he slowly pushed inside me. My eyes never left his as he thrust inside me, slow and steady. He kissed me hard, his tongue tangling with mine as my fingers dug into his back.

"I love you, Florrie."

I swallowed hard, trying to find the words. I didn't know what to say. I hadn't bothered to examine my feelings for him up to this point. I had flat out chosen to ignore them, in fact. Now he was staring at me, waiting for me to say something, anything, but I just couldn't get anything to come out. I saw the moment the hope died in his eyes and disappointment took over. Then I felt it.

The connection we had was broken. He started fucking me hard and fast, almost ruthlessly. He pinched my clit and pushed me over the edge, and then it was over. He moved to the edge of the bed, leaning on his knees as he caught his breathe. Then he stood and walked to the bathroom, leaving me lying in bed, cold and alone. But it was all my fault.

How had I not seen that he was falling in love with me? I mean, I guess deep down I was aware that I was infatuated with him and that I was on my way to loving him, but other than that, I thought we were just fucking. I had never really thought of his possessiveness as anything other than that. But what I just witnessed in that bed was so far beyond just fucking.

He walked out of the bathroom and over to me, sighing before he leaned down to kiss me. It was forced and there was no heat behind it. He left that night, not bothering to stay like he normally would.

I cringed when the front door slammed shut and rolled over, hugging my pillow to my body. I didn't know what my problem was, but it was preventing me from having a real relationship with Alec, and one of these days, he would walk away and he wouldn't come back.

Chapter Eleven

ALEC

I headed out to the bar with the guys. I wanted to be at home fucking Florrie, but she said that we had to go do things with the guys so nothing was suspicious. I really didn't give a fuck, but I couldn't let Florrie get away. I needed her. I just wished that I had the nerve to tell her exactly how much I needed her. I loved her so much, and I made sure to tell her every chance I got, but it didn't seem to be enough. She still didn't trust me after all this time. I could tell by the way she watched when another woman approached. I knew that was a big reason she was holding back, though she never came out and said so.

"So, what are we looking at tonight?" Craig asked as we walked into the bar. "Blonde, brunette, or redhead?"

I shrugged. I wanted Florrie, but she was over at the bar drinking, completely ignoring me. "I'm not really in the mood."

"Not in the mood for what?"

"This." I waved my hand around the chaotic scene at the bar. Women were dressed in shit that I wouldn't let Florrie out of the house in, and she had the body for it. The more I watched, the more I saw desperate women that would say or do anything to get laid and have the shot at just a little more attention from some asshole that they wouldn't normally look at twice. "Aren't you getting sick of this?"

"What? Women that want to take me home and suck my cock?"

I rolled my eyes at him. "Seriously, is that all you think about?"

"When I'm not at work? Pretty much. Well, that and sports."

"You need a new hobby."

"What's going on with you? You've never not wanted pussy."

I sighed, leaning back in my seat as I looked over discreetly at the bar where Florrie still stood with Lola. "Don't you ever think about what it would be like to have a woman to share things with?"

"You mean, on a permanent basis?"

"Yeah."

He eyed me skeptically. "You've seen what these women are like. I mean, we're the lucky ones. We've escaped the clutches of desperate women everywhere."

"How is that lucky? Don't you want a woman to go home to at night? You know, one woman that will be there and listen to you when you've had a shitty day or who already knows what you want in bed without having to tell her?"

"Who is she?" Craig grinned. "You're already pussy-whipped. So, who's the lucky lady and where did you meet her?"

"There is no woman." And that was partly true, because I didn't really have Florrie. If I did, she wouldn't be running from me all the damn time. "I just look at the guys and I wonder what it would be like to have what they have."

"What they have is a noose around their necks."

"What they have is a woman that chooses to deal with their bull-shit day in and day out."

He stared at me a moment, assessing me, trying to understand me. I kept my face neutral. There was no way that I would let him in on my relationship with Florrie against her wishes.

"Is this some midlife crisis bullshit? Are you feeling old and need to procreate or some shit?"

"Yeah, I don't think that's ever going to happen."

Especially not with Florrie. Having kids was definitely not on her agenda.

"Then what the fuck is going on?"

"I just want...more." I stared off at Florrie, unable to tear my eyes away. "I just want that one woman that makes me feel like I'm the king. You know what I mean?"

I looked back at Craig, but he was staring at me like I was insane. "This is worse than I thought. Hold on, let me get you a whiskey."

I shook my head as he left. He just didn't get it. Over at the bar, Florrie stood and headed for the door. Where the fuck was she going? I didn't hesitate to follow her out the door. When she turned the corner for her truck, I caught up with her, pulling her into the alley and into the shadows.

"What the fuck, Alec?"

I kissed her hard, pressing her into the wall. God, I just needed my hands on her. "You have to stop pushing me away. It's making me crazy."

"That's exactly why I have to push you away. You're getting too possessive."

"You're the one doing this. I have to have you. I need my hands on you all the fucking time."

She tried to push me away, but I caged her in. "Alec..."

"Why? Just tell me why you keep doing this."

She didn't say anything, but I waited. I could do this all fucking night. "I don't want a relationship."

"I don't get it. You were so worried after I got shot, but then as soon as we're together, you push me away. It doesn't make any fucking sense."

"I just...you have to give me space. I love being with you, but you're consuming me. I need space to be myself."

"And I need you."

"See? It's just too much."

"It's not enough, and I think you know it. If you'd just give in, let it happen, you'd see how fucking great this is."

She pushed me back gently and I gave her the space. She didn't say anything, just turned and walked away. I was tempted to punch the wall, but I bit back my anger and flung the door open to the bar. Craig was at the table with a whiskey that I desperately needed now.

"Where'd you go?"

"Thought I saw someone I knew."

"Okay, so what's this really about?"

I debated whether or not to tell him. Really, it's not like he would know anything. He hadn't caught on yet to any of this shit. And I was tired of trying to keep it to myself.

"I've been sort of seeing this woman."

"Sexy?"

"Unbelievably. But she doesn't want a relationship."

He snorted and took a drink of his beer. "Thank your lucky stars."

"This is the real deal." He stopped mid-sip and stared at me.

"Like, *the One* real deal?"

"Exactly."

"But she doesn't want a relationship with you."

"No."

"So, you're just fucking."

"Yes."

He stared at the table in thought, running his hand over his mouth contemplatively. "So, you need a way to catch her. To make her decide that she needs you more than anything."

"I guess," I said slowly, wondering where he was going with this.

"Get her pregnant," he said as I took a sip of whiskey. I spit it out all over the table, choking on my drink.

"Sorry, did you just advise that I go get a woman pregnant to hang onto her?"

"Why not? You said you want a relationship with her."

"Yeah, and I'm pretty sure having a kid is not something that would endear me to her."

"You could always get shot again. I offer to do the honors. Maybe it'll knock some sense into you."

"Why would getting shot give me any kind of leg up?"

"Well, women are emotional creatures. They make rash decisions when the chips are down. Let's say you were to get shot, nothing too life-threatening, but not a graze either. She'd come running and vow to never leave your side."

Seeing as how I had been shot and all that got me was sex with Florrie, I didn't think getting shot again would push her over the edge.

"Not gonna work. I need something else."

Craig drank some more and eyed me speculatively. "What are some reasons that a woman wouldn't want to be in a relationship with you?"

"What? Are we trying to figure out my faults here?"

"You could say that. If we can figure out what it is that turns her off, maybe we can change those things."

"Okay, what are my faults?"

"Well, for one, you have a dangerous job."

"That's not the problem," I chuckled.

"Okay, you haven't had any serious relationships. Maybe she's scared you don't know how to be in one."

"Yeah, but then why would she even stick around?"

"Good sex. Unless you're not..."

"Unless I'm not what?"

He waved at me and spluttered, "You know, something she wants for the rest of her life."

"I think we've already established that she doesn't want me in her life that long."

"I mean, perhaps you're not...satisfying enough for her."

I blinked and then blinked again. "If I wasn't satisfying enough, why would she stick around just to fuck me?"

"I don't know. Maybe you're not quite what she needs, but you'll do for the moment. Do you wax?"

"No, I don't fucking wax, and don't even try to convince me that I should do that."

"Women like it." He leaned forward conspiratorially. "It makes your dick look bigger."

"My dick is big enough."

"Yeah, but is it big enough for her? Maybe that's your problem."

I just stared at him and he leaned back, holding up his hands that he relented the point.

"Okay, what about stamina? On average, how long would you say you last?"

"I don't know. It depends on the occasion."

"Let's just ballpark it."

I shrugged, trying to calculate in my head. "Maybe fifteen-twenty minutes."

"Ooh, that's...not good."

"Why is that not good? I get in and get the job done."

"What about foreplay and...well, the sex?"

"There's plenty of that," I said simply.

"In fifteen minutes?" Craig snorted and then started outright laughing at me.

"What the fuck is your problem?"

"My problem? I don't have one, but I think we just found out why she doesn't want a relationship with you, Mister Fifteen Minute Man."

"Fifteen minutes is plenty of time to satisfy a woman, if you know what you're doing. Besides, some women don't like you to hang out in their pussy for more than that amount of time."

"Sure," he snorted again. "If she wants it to end sooner, that's because it's bad and she wants it to be over."

"If that's true, then explain why she keeps coming back for more."

"I don't know," he laughed, "but I can't wait to tell the guys your new nickname."

"Don't you fucking dare."

"Why? If it's genuinely true that your lady friend likes to keep things short and sweet, then why does it matter?"

"Because you make me sound like a Jiffy Lube oil change."

He leaned forward on the table, his smirk spreading wide across his face. "I can guarantee that even Jiffy Lube takes longer than you."

Chapter Twelve

FLORRIE

One and a half years ago...

Stabbing pain shot through me so sharp that I doubled over in pain on the bathroom floor. I had never had pain like this from a period. Each month over the past six months had gotten progressively worse, but this was just excruciating. I had managed to get through work all the previous months, but there was no way I was going in today.

I quickly changed my tampon and pad. It had only been an hour and I was already bleeding through both. Curling up in bed, I called in to work.

"Reed Security. This is Sebastian speaking."

"Cap, it's Florrie." I bit back a groan as another stabbing pain hit. "I'm not gonna make it in today. I'm not feeling so good."

"Shit. I have you scheduled to go out on a job for a week."

I took a deep breath and blew it out slowly. "Sorry, it's not gonna happen."

"Are you okay? Do you want me to send someone over?"

"No, I'll be fine."

"You don't sound okay. You sound like you're in pain."

I chuckled because it was funny. I had never been in this much pain before, and I could handle pain. "I'll be fine."

"Right."

"Really, I'll be fine. I might be out for a few days."

I started to feel nauseous, so I hung up on Cap and made my way over to the bathroom. That was where Alec and Craig found me just twenty minutes later. I was lying on the floor at this point, curled up in a ball.

"Shit, you don't look so good," Alec grumbled as he knelt down beside me. "Why didn't you tell Cap it was this bad?"

"I'm fine," I mumbled. "Just feel sick."

"Are you in pain?"

"Cramps."

"Cramps? I've never heard of cramps flattening a woman that doesn't even register pain. Hell, it could be your appendix or some shit," Craig said.

I flushed in embarrassment. I didn't want to tell him that it was just my period that was causing me this much pain. "It's not that."

"Fuck that, you're going to the hospital."

"I don't need to go."

"Something that makes you lay on the ground curled up in the ball is something that needs to be checked out. If you don't go, I'll just have Hunter check you over."

There was no fucking way I was having Hunter look me over. There was no way any man was looking at me, bleeding all over the place like that.

"Just take me to Kate."

"If something's wrong, you won't have time to get to the fucking hospital."

He shoved his hands under me and lifted me in the air. Craig shot me a sympathetic look, but I shoved my face against Alec's body, not wanting to have either of them see me in this much pain. We were out the door and down the stairs of my apartment building in no time. Alec didn't bother to set me down in the backseat of his truck. He just hauled me up onto his lap and held onto me the whole way.

I groaned when another stabbing pain hit. I was glad to be in his arms right now. Somehow it made all of this just a little bit less scary. His arms tightened around me and I curled further into him.

"It'll be okay, baby," he whispered in my ear.

I nodded against his neck and then felt a gush of liquid flow down my legs.

"Shit, Florrie, you're bleeding. Where's all this blood coming from?"

The panic in his voice made the embarrassment even worse. "I have my period," I whispered.

"Oh. This much?" He pulled me back and looked down at me. I was covered in blood and now so was he. "This isn't normal."

"It's just really heavy right now."

"Florrie, don't fucking lie to me. This isn't normal."

I shrugged, not knowing what else to say to him. He pulled me against him and held me for the rest of the ride to the hospital. When we arrived, he had me out of the backseat and into the ER in just seconds. He argued with the emergency room staff until they got me right back, but I asked Craig and Alec to leave. How could I possibly explain that I could do this in front of Alec, but not Craig? Besides, this wasn't a topic that I wanted Alec around for.

"Florence-"

"Florrie," I corrected.

The doctor smiled kindly at me. Thank God it was a female doctor. This was embarrassing enough as it was.

"Florrie, what's going on?"

"I got my period this morning, but it's extremely painful. And I know pain, I've been shot. But this is the worst cramping I've ever had. I've been bleeding through a tampon and a pad every hour since I woke up."

"Is this the first time this has happened?"

"No, it's been getting worse over the past six months, but this is definitely the worst."

"Okay, we'll do a pelvic exam and an ultrasound and see what's going on."

The hours of the day drifted by in a haze of pain and tests. The nurse kept asking if I wanted to let my friends back, but there was no way I could let them in here with me. Someone might slip up and say something, and this was not a topic I wanted to discuss with anyone. I sent both Craig and Alec messages that they should go home. I told them I could get a ride, but neither of them would listen.

"Okay, Florrie," the doctor said as she took a seat next to me. It was well past dinner time and I was exhausted. I just wanted to go home and get into bed. The staff had been backed up and the tests had taken forever. "Your tests show that you have endometriosis, which is endometrial tissue that grows outside of the uterus. Normally this tissue is expelled during your period, but this displaced tissue cannot. That's what was causing your pain and your heavy periods."

"What does that mean? Will it go away?"

"No, this is something that we can manage though. I see that you're currently not on birth control. Those hormones will help and I'd like to get you started on them right away."

"Okay." That sounded too simple. "Are there any other side effects? I mean, is this going to affect my job?"

"Well, if we can get it under control with birth control, it shouldn't affect your job. However, endometriosis can make it difficult to conceive. There's an increased risk of ovarian cancer, ovarian cysts, scar tissue and adhesions, inflammation, intestinal and bladder compli-cations-"

"Wait, I might not be able to get pregnant?"

She looked at me sadly. "It could be difficult. There are hormone therapies that you could try and-"

"How would I know if it's going to be a problem? I mean, is there some testing or do I just have to wait until I want to get pregnant and wait for months on end to see if I end up with a baby or not?"

"We could check your Fallopian tubes. That would give us a good idea of how bad your case is."

"Okay, so, let's do that."

"I can set up an appointment for you, but I have to warn you, it's not a pleasant test. You'd probably want to take a few days off work."

I nodded numbly. I couldn't believe what I was hearing. I mean, I hadn't really thought too much about having kids before. I liked my job and the thought of giving that up for a family wasn't the most appealing idea. But to be told that I couldn't produce a child, that I was basically defective, I didn't know how to feel about that.

———————

Craig and Alec stood as soon as I walked through the double doors of the emergency room. They rushed over to me, gripping my arms like I would fall over at any moment.

"Are you okay?"

"What did they say?"

"How bad is it?"

"They're just letting you go? Don't they need to run more tests?"

"Boys!" I held up my hand and they both stopped talking, staring at me with worry. "I'm fine. I just need to rest."

Which was the truth. I was exhausted. The doctor had told me that fatigue was a side effect, and I was feeling it.

"What do you mean? How can you be fine?" Craig asked.

"Yeah, I want a word with this doctor," Alec growled. "There's no way they can hold you all day and then just release you and say you need to rest."

"Well, it's not like you can actually go talk to them. Doctor-patient confidentiality."

"Does that mean something's wrong?" Alec asked. "Oh God, are you dying?"

"No, I'm not dying. Just take me home."

"No, this isn't right," Craig said, running his hand through his short hair. It made him look all scruffy and frazzled. I liked it. "I want to talk with a doctor or a nurse. We need to be sure that everything's okay. What if something's wrong and we miss the signs?"

"Will you guys stop? I'm fine. I had a heavy period."

"That wasn't heavy. That was a fucking flood," Alec retorted. I glared at him, but he just shrugged. "I had to have someone bring me a change of clothes because I looked like someone had been shot and then bled out all over me. That shit's not normal."

"Thank you for that lovely imagery. As you can see, I'm wearing scrubs because my clothes are ruined. So, yes, I'm well aware of what it was like. Now, can you please take me home or should I call a cab?"

Alec and Craig exchanged a look, obviously not comfortable with letting me go home without them talking with someone.

"Go get the truck," Alec said angrily to Craig.

Craig nodded and headed for the door, but I didn't miss the wary look he sent me before he left.

"Tell me what the fuck is really going on," Alec snapped. "You don't just end up in the emergency room all day and then walk out like it's nothing."

"Well, that's just what I'm doing."

"Seriously, don't fuck with me on this. You're mine and I deserve to know what's going on."

"You're mistaken," I snapped. "I'm not yours. We're just fucking."

He clenched his jaw in anger and led me toward the door, his tight grip just a little too much for me right now, but I let it go. When we got back to my apartment, I didn't even bother pretending to care what they did. I just wanted to go to bed. I went to the bathroom and cleaned up, then slipped into bed, completely exhausted.

The bed dipped and I opened my eyes. Alec was lying in bed next to me, staring at me like I was going to suddenly burst into flames.

"What?"

"You didn't really think I was going to let you stay here alone, did you?"

"I'm fine. I just need some sleep."

"Yeah, I recall saying that to you after I was shot, yet you stuck around."

"Well, that was a little different. I'm not dealing with a life-threatening injury."

"I wouldn't know since you refuse to tell me what the fuck that was all about. When are you going to start trusting me?"

His eyes moved back and forth as he stared into mine. I couldn't tell what he was thinking. I knew what he wanted me to say, but it wasn't just about trust. It was about his power over me and the fact that we worked together.

"Alec...this was never supposed to be more."

"I told you I love you. That was months ago and you still haven't acknowledged that. I don't know what the fuck I'm supposed to think. Do you love me too or is this all just fucking to you?"

"It's..." I sighed and closed my eyes. I was tired and this was the last thing I wanted to be doing right now.

"Forget I said anything."

We laid there in silence for a minute before I thought of the fact that Craig and Alec had been in the same vehicle.

"Where's Craig?"

"Taking first watch."

I rolled my eyes. "You can't be serious." He just gave me a funny look, like it wasn't just the most ridiculous thing he'd ever said. "Who exactly is coming to get me?"

"It could be anyone. Let's face it, you're not exactly in the best apartment building. It's not the first time I've told you that. You could be living in my house, but you insist on living in this shit hole."

"And...I don't get it. I've always lived here. So, why are you worried now?"

"Because you're not yourself. Someone could break in here and snap your neck and all you would do is bleed all over them."

"Am I going to hear about this for the rest of my life? Because no girl wants to be reminded how she bled all over some hot guy."

"You think I'm hot?"

I rolled my eyes at him. The tension was gone and now it was just Alec being his playful self. "Of course you're hot. You know that. Don't pretend that I had some sudden epiphany. We've been fucking for over a year. Do you really think I would have stuck around if you were hideous?"

"Would it kill you to tell a guy? Seriously, I'm lucky if I get a pat on the head after sex."

"You know I think you're the sexiest man I work with. Well, maybe."

He raised an eyebrow in challenge. "Fine, who's the best looking guy at Reed Security?"

"You're testing me?"

"It's not a test. I just want to know. From a woman's perspective."

"What? You've gone around asking guys?"

"That's not what I meant."

"I'm surprised you even know I'm a woman. Almost everyone looks at Lola and I like we're men with ponytails and boobs."

He laughed a deep, sexy laugh that I could feel rumbling across the bed and shivering up through my body. "Trust me, none of the guys we work with would get a boner from a man with boobs. Well, except maybe Burg."

"You guys need to stop picking on him," I laughed. "I think the poor guy dealt with enough when he realized he was making out with a woman that had a dick."

He bounced his head from side to side with a sly grin. "Nah, that shit will never get old. So, come on, no dodging. Tell me who's the best looking guy."

I pursed my lips in thought and ran through all the guys I worked with. All of them were sexy in their own right. Trying to classify who was the best looking was practically impossible.

"Really?" he said in shock. "The answer isn't immediately me?"

"I work with a lot of hot men. Did you really think you would be at the top of my list? What if it was Craig? Would you be jealous?"

"Let's see, I'm fucking you and you prefer our teammate. What do you think?"

"Cap," I finally said.

"Our boss? He's an old man."

"He is not. He's like five years older than me. Besides, he's got the perfect body and that smoldering, sexy look to him."

"I could be smoldering," Alec said.

"I know, sweetie. And then there's Cazzo."

"That baboon?"

"He has a nipple ring. I'm not gonna lie. It's fucking hot."

"Sorry, I'm not getting a nipple ring."

"And then there's Knight-"

"Of course," he muttered.

"He's dangerous, dark, sexy-"

"Taken," Alec interrupted. He almost looked like he was pouting and I found it almost charming that he was getting so upset over my assessment.

"And there's something about Hunter's bald head that really gets me going. He looks like The Rock, don't you think?"

"Sure," he grumbled. "He's a fucking beast of a man. The sexiest I've ever seen."

"I'll be sure to tell him you said so."

"I'm surprised you haven't said Sinner. All the ladies seem to flock to him."

"That's true. He is ultimately the classic male embodiment of good looks."

He growled at me and I laughed, a yawn escaping. I couldn't remember ever just sitting around talking with Alec like this. It was nice, and I wasn't ready to go to sleep and go back to normal tomorrow, when I would have to think about what the doctor told me.

"You need to sleep." He ran his hand through my hair, pushing back the strands that had slipped over my shoulder and were laying on my face. "And then tomorrow, when you're better rested and thinking clearly, we can reassess your choices for best male specimen."

I laughed and let my eyes slip closed. I felt him sink further down into my bed and let myself drift off to sleep, thinking about what Alec had said earlier to me about me trusting him. I really needed to get over that, but I also needed to figure out exactly what I felt for Alec. He was being nice to me because I was in the hospital all day, but he wouldn't let it go forever.

Chapter Thirteen

ALEC

I couldn't stop watching her. When I saw her curled up on the floor, I almost said fuck it and let it slip that she was mine. But then I would have had to deal with the fact that Florrie didn't actually want anyone to know about us. It wasn't that I needed everyone to know that she was mine, but I didn't like the secrecy. It felt like we were a dirty secret. But what we were becoming was anything but a dirty secret.

But for some reason, she just couldn't deal with the fact that I was in love with her. I wasn't sure if she even knew how she felt about me. It was like she wouldn't allow herself to think that far ahead. But today was a reminder that I needed her to start thinking ahead. I wanted more than just the time she was giving me now. I wanted the rest of my life with her.

When I sat in that waiting room all fucking day, not being able to be there with her, to hold her hand and know what the fuck was going on, I thought I was going to lose my mind. I sat there with Craig and tried not to show him how fucking scared I was. That much blood was not normal, but if it was life-threatening, they wouldn't have sent her home from the hospital. So, I let it go, thinking she might tell me with time.

I ran my fingers across her cheek, just wanting to touch her. Maybe to tell myself that she really was okay. When she curled up in my arms when I took her from her apartment earlier, something inside my chest tightened painfully. I just wanted to protect her and take care of her. I had never felt that way about a woman before. Then again, I had never loved a woman before. She was the woman that changed my life and made me want things I had never even considered before.

She stirred next to me and rolled to her side, draping her arm over my chest. I held my breath, afraid to move. I didn't want her to wake up. I wanted her to just sleep in my arms for the rest of the night. I needed this with her right now.

"Oh shit."

I didn't open my eyes at her voice. I must have drifted off sometime during the night. She moved out of my arms and I had to struggle not to pull her back. But I knew that with Craig in the apartment, she wouldn't want him to see us like this. I felt her slip out of bed and I finally opened my eyes. The bed was cold without her. Craig walked into the room with a grin on his face.

"You two looked pretty cozy."

"Shut the fuck up. She wasn't feeling well."

His face sobered and I knew I had successfully dodged that conversation. "Is she doing okay this morning?"

"I don't know. She was up before me. She's in the bathroom."

He nodded, glancing at his watch. "I've gotta get home and get a shower before work. I'll make some coffee. Find out if she's coming in today."

"Fuck, no, she's not. She was just in the fucking hospital."

He shrugged. "It was her period."

"She was fucking bleeding all over me. You don't find that odd?"

"Well, yeah, but she said she was fine. What the fuck do you want me to do?"

"You're such a tool."

Florrie shuffled out of the bathroom and got back in bed, completely ignoring us.

"How are you feeling today?"

She grumbled something incoherent and snuggled in deeper.

"Should we stay?"

"No."

I looked at Craig and he jerked his chin for us to head out, but I was still fucking worried.

"Are you sure?"

"Dude, she just fucking said that we could go," Craig said irritatedly.

"Florrie," I said, placing my hand on her shoulder. "Look at me."

She rolled over and looked at me groggily. "What?"

"Are you sure you're okay?"

"I'm fine. Just tell Cap I'm taking a few days off."

"You're sure?"

She nodded and rolled back over. "Sorry about drooling on you last night," she said flippantly. It was so dismissive that it actually kind of hurt. I rubbed at my chest, feeling more than a little unsure of what the hell was going on.

"Alright, call me if you need me."

She grunted in response and I followed Craig out the door. What the hell happened? Was her dismissive attitude because she wasn't feeling well, or because Craig was there? Why couldn't she just admit that she loved me? Was I not good enough for her? And now I was whining like a girl. Fuck, this shit was really messing with my head. I was going to have to get to work and beat the shit out of someone so I could get rid of these girly feelings running through me.

"Hey." I gave Cap a chin lift as I walked into his office. "Where's Florrie?"

We were here for a meeting, but it was only Craig and I in the room.

"She's taking a few days off, maybe the rest of the week," Cap answered, not even bothering to look up at me.

"Why? Is everything okay?"

He shrugged. "She just said she needed a few days off."

"And you didn't think to ask why?"

"You're her teammate. If you want to know, pick up the fucking phone and call her."

"I'm just shocked that you didn't ask. I mean, it's weird, right?"

"Look, you guys all work non-stop. If someone calls off and asks for a few days off, I tend to not think twice about saying yes or butting my nose into your business."

I slumped back in the chair. He had a point, but after Florrie was in the hospital two weeks ago, it seemed odd that she was taking time off already. There had to be something wrong, and I was going to find out.

I sat through the meeting, jittery as hell to get out of there and find out what the hell was going on with my girl. *My woman*. I shouldn't be sitting here in this meeting. I should be with her, finding out what the fuck she was taking time off for. The meeting went on way too long and several times, Cap had to stop and make sure I was paying attention, which I wasn't.

I practically ran out of the room when the meeting was over, and I ignored Craig when he tried to get me to stop so he could catch up. I didn't bother to stop and wait for him. I sped the whole way to Florrie's apartment. Relief poured through me when I saw her truck in the parking lot, but then I worried that I would find her in the same position on the floor as I had two weeks ago.

Banging on the door impatiently, I tried to calm the racing of my heart. I just couldn't stand the thought of something being wrong with her. When she didn't answer immediately, I banged even harder.

"Florrie! Open the fucking door."

The door swung open just as I was about to bang again. Florrie stood there in her pajamas. She had obviously been crying, but she was trying to hide it. I wrapped her up in my arms, squeezing her body to mine.

"Are you okay?"

"Of course. Why are you here?" She pushed me back and tucked her arms around herself, like she was trying to be invisible.

"I'm here because you called off."

"Yeah."

"You never call off. And after what happened two weeks ago, I just thought...fuck, I don't know. But I was scared as hell. Why didn't you call me?"

She looked at me funny and shook her head. "Why would I call you? I'm just taking time off. As you can see, I'm fine."

"But... I don't understand. Why did you take time off?"

"That's my business, isn't it?" she snapped. "Last I checked, we're just fucking. I don't need to run anything past you. If I need time off, I don't owe you a fucking explanation."

I took a step back, keeping my face neutral. It hadn't crossed my mind that Florrie wouldn't want me here. I didn't understand what I had to do to make her see that I wasn't going anywhere. I loved her and I assumed that whatever she was going through, she would want me with her. Apparently, I was wrong.

"I'm sorry. I just assumed that something was wrong and I needed to know that you were alright. "

She huffed out a breath and gripped onto the door handle. "I don't need you coming by to save the day or getting into my business. Believe it or not, just because I'm a woman doesn't mean I can't handle myself."

"Florrie, you know I don't fucking think that way. What the fuck is going on? You've never acted like this before. Since when am I your enemy?"

"Since when is it any of your fucking business what's going on with me? Not everything is about you. I have other things going on in my life that have nothing to do with you. Do me a favor, just leave me the fuck alone."

She slammed the door in my face and I just stood there like a fucking idiot, seething in anger. But I didn't know what I was most pissed about, that she was shutting me out or that I didn't mean nearly as much to her as she meant to me.

I turned and walked away. Fuck, I hadn't been thinking. If I had bothered to pay attention over the last two weeks, I would have seen that Florrie had been distracted. She wasn't thinking about me though. She had other things on her mind. I didn't even factor into her life besides at work. I was such an asshole.

Chapter Fourteen

FLORRIE

I shut the door and slid down to my ass. Tears poured from my eyes and sobs wracked my whole body with pain. I had been so fucking stupid to hope, to think that the doctors were wrong, but they weren't. My tubes were blocked too much, and the chances of getting pregnant weren't good.

I had never cared about having a baby before, so why was this killing me so much? Would it really be that bad to never have a child? Not really. I had never really thought about it all that much. But to be told that there was something fundamentally wrong with me, that would make it nearly impossible to have a baby, made me feel damaged. It was beyond anything I had ever felt before.

I jumped as someone pounded on my door. It had to be Alec, back to give me more shit. I couldn't take any more from him right now. I stood, wiping the tears from my face and flung the door open. But it wasn't Alec on the other side. It was Lola. One look at me and she knew. She walked in and pulled me into a hug. She was the only one that I had told what was happening, the only one I thought I could trust with my secret.

"What happened?"

She guided me over to the couch and sat down with me.

"Blocked. There's surgery and medicine, but..."

"It's not a guarantee."

I shook my head. "Then Alec came by and since I wasn't having a shitty enough day, I decided to take my anger out on him."

"You know, he would understand if you just told him."

"I can't," I shook my head. "Before this happened, he was starting to get serious. He told me he loved me, and I hesitated. Now, I'm glad I hesitated. He deserves better."

"Than what?" she snapped. "What the hell do you think is so wrong with you?"

"I'm defective," I shouted. "The one thing I'm supposed to be able to do, I can't."

"You don't know that he would even care. Alec's never even been in a relationship before you. Has he told you he wants a family?"

"He's told me he wants a future with me. What exactly would that look like?"

"It would look like the future the two of you would have *together*. This isn't the end of the world, Florrie."

I snorted in derision. "Maybe, but you know what I keep thinking?"

"What?"

"You know how the guys make fun of us, say that we're not really women-"

"Florrie, they don't know what they're saying. They're just a bunch of baboons that say stupid shit."

"But it's true," I cried. "The one thing that makes you really feel like a woman, that separates you from the men, are the hormones that run through you. Those hormones give you the ability to produce a child. I've got the hormones, and the ass, and the tits. Hell, I've got the reproductive system, but none of it fucking works. Does that make me still a woman?"

"Do you hear yourself right now? Just because you can't have a baby doesn't make you less of a woman."

I swiped angrily at the tears that continued to pour down my face. "Why did he even bother giving me periods and a uterus? Why didn't he just say *this one's not gonna work*? Why bother make me a woman if I wasn't actually going to be able to be a fucking woman?"

"Florrie, you've got to calm down. This isn't the end of the world. Plenty of women can't have kids, yet they go on to be happy. Cole's wife, Alex, can't have kids either. Maybe you should talk to her. They're perfectly happy, just the two of them."

"Well, fuck. Good for them that they can be happy like that. I didn't fucking ask if I could be happy. I asked why the fuck this had to happen in the first place. Why did this have to happen to me?"

She took a deep breath and blew it out. I could tell she was getting annoyed with me. Hell, I was getting annoyed with me. I stood and walked to the door.

"Just give me some time. My head's not on straight right now, and I just need some time to think."

"I think you need to go beat the shit out of something. Just don't stay away too long."

When she was gone, I crawled into bed after pulling the curtains and stared off into the darkness. She was right, I could live a perfectly happy life, so why was I so fucking sad?

An entire week went by before I went back to work. I didn't know what I was going to say to Alec. Everyone else would pretend like I had just taken some time off, but Alec knew better. I had been crazy with grief when he showed up at my door. Even now, I could hear the things I had told Lola, and while deep down I knew none of it was true, those feelings were still lingering and eating away at me.

But by the end of the week, I knew I couldn't just keep lying in bed and feeling sorry for myself. Life had to go on and I couldn't just ignore my job or my life. I wasn't going to have kids. It was as simple as that. I would enjoy my job and keep going just as I had been, only now with the knowledge of what I could actually do with my life. It wasn't the end of the world. I would move forward and enjoy what I did have. That just wouldn't include Alec anymore. I could never let him stay with me out of pity. And that's what it would be. He was a good man and he wouldn't want to be seen as the coward that walked away from the woman that couldn't give him children.

It wasn't fair to ask him to accept me as I was, and I didn't particularly want to keep thinking about this either. I wanted to forget about everything, and that included Alec. Because he was the one man that I could have seen myself taking that kind of chance with.

I walked into the conference room where Alec, Craig, and Cap all sat. Alec glanced at me, his eyes lit up for just a moment as he looked me over, but then they dimmed and he looked back at the table.

"Hey, slacker," Craig jeered. "I wish you would have told us all you were taking a week off. I would have put in a request myself. We were stuck on security installations while you were gone."

"Sorry, something came up at the last minute," I said as I took my seat.

"We're just her teammates, Craig." Alec glanced up at me, coldness all over him. "She doesn't need to inform us every time she needs a day off."

I took a deep breath, swallowing down my anger. I didn't have any right to be angry with Alec. After he left, I could see that he just cared about me, and I had thrown that in his face, like he didn't matter to me. No matter what I was feeling, Alec didn't deserve the things I had said to him.

"Alright, let's get to it," Cap said.

And off we went. The meeting was long, the job was even longer. Alec wouldn't look at me, but Cap looked at me frequently. I could see the questions in his eyes, wondering if I was ready for this. I knew I didn't look like I was. I still felt drained and shaky from my week of lounging in bed and doing nothing. Based on how tired I felt, I should have told Cap that I wasn't up to this job, but I needed to get back out there. I needed to push aside my feelings and move on with my life. Dwelling on things that couldn't be changed wouldn't help.

When the meeting was over, Alec was out of the room before any of us. I had to chase him down the hall just so I could talk to him.

"Hey," I shouted as I ran up behind him. He didn't turn around. "Alec!"

He opened an office door and pushed inside. I followed, but was slammed up against the wall as soon as I entered. He kicked the door shut and caged me in against the wall, his hands resting on the wall on either side of my head.

"What the fuck do you want?"

My eyes flicked down to his lips and then back up to his hard gaze. "I...I just wanted to apologize."

"For what? We're just fucking. It's not like you mean something to me, right? It's not like I told you exactly how I fucking feel about you. What could you possibly have to be sorry about?"

"Alec," I said shakily, my breath stuttering out of my body and leaving me feeling shaky. "Something happened and...I didn't mean to hurt you. I was upset."

"What happened?"

"I can't tell you."

"Can't or don't want to?"

"Alec, this was never supposed to be more than having some fun."

"But that changed." He moved his hand off the wall and then skimmed his finger down my cheek and across my throat. "I didn't mean to fall in love with you, but I did." His thumb brushed against my jaw and the tender look on his face almost broke me.

"I'm sorry," I said quietly, tears in my eyes. I didn't know why I was crying. It just felt like something was ending that shouldn't be, but I knew that I had to do this.

"Just tell me why you won't let me in. I just need to know why you won't let us happen."

"We work together~"

"Bullshit," he said with deadly calm. "We've been sleeping together for over a year. If you want this to stay a secret, I can do that. I don't want to, but I think at this point, there's not a lot I wouldn't do to have you."

"Alec, I can't give you what you want. I can't give you...I can't return your feelings."

He stepped back like he had been slapped, but then cleared his face of all shock. "If that's what you want."

"So, you want to continue?" I asked hesitantly. "Even knowing that I won't-"

"Please," he said harshly. "If this is going to work, you're going to have to stop reminding me every other sentence that you don't love me and never will. Message received."

He walked out of the room, but nothing felt right. I didn't feel like we were in a good position, and I had obviously hurt Alec very much. I didn't want to keep hurting him, but at the same time, I didn't want to let him go.

Chapter Fifteen

FLORRIE

A few weeks later...

I rolled over in my sleep, only to be stopped suddenly. My wrists and feet were bound to the bed by metal handcuffs. What the fuck? I grunted in frustration. I couldn't believe this was happening again. That asshole had cuffed me to the bed, all because he didn't like the way the mission went. It was getting ridiculous how maniacal he had turned. He had gone from trusting me on missions, to treating me like I was made of crystal.

This was all because of that stupid fucking hospital incident. Ever since then, he acted different around me. It took a good couple of weeks of me telling him that everything was fine for him to let the whole thing go. I tried to let it go, but those feelings of inadequacy still lingered. Logically, I should have walked away. I already had my out, but Alec wasn't someone that I could easily walk away from. So, here I was, handcuffed to the fucking bed.

"Alec, get your ass over here!"

His tall, bulky shadow filled the doorway of my bedroom, but he just stood there watching me. I felt a breeze drift over my body and cursed.

"You undressed me? What the fuck is wrong with you?"

"You wouldn't listen," he said as he stalked toward me. "I fucking told you not to approach that asshole. I told you that he would jump the gun if you made a move."

"Did you see his eyes?" I hissed. "He was deranged. He was going to slit that woman's throat."

Alec knelt down on the bed, skimming his hand up my naked leg, just barely brushing his fingers over my clit before moving up to my stomach.

"He threw a fucking knife at you."

"And I'm still alive," I snapped at him. "I told you this couldn't happen, Alec. You're acting just like Knight. I'm not your fucking possession. You can't treat me like I'm breakable."

"I'm not treating you like you're breakable." His hand continued its path north, cupping my breasts before resting against my neck. He didn't squeeze, but the way it rested heavily against my throat was domineering. Alec wasn't a sadist, but he wanted to feel like he could control my every move to keep me safe. The problem was, I wasn't into all that shit. I didn't want a domineering asshole to act like he could make me submit to him.

"Get your fucking hands off me."

"Not until you realize that you put yourself in danger. You put your team in danger."

"The only thing I did was my job. We all take chances to get the job done, and I did that. Stop treating me like your fuck buddy when we're working."

He moved until he was laying over me, his body resting just above mine. "Can't you see that I'm not capable of that? We're not fuck buddies and there's no way that I could treat you like Craig. You're my woman," he whispered, brushing his lips against mine. "I can't just pretend that you don't mean anything to me, not when every part of me craves you."

His words melted something inside me, and then he was kissing down my body, brushing his tongue over my most sensitive areas. His tongue circled my nipples until they were painfully hard.

"This isn't going to work, Alec. I'm not going to listen to you just because you fuck me."

"That's not the point."

"Then what is?"

His hand slid between my legs, playing with me lightly, teasing me until he pulled the wetness from my body. "To show you that you're everything to me. I need you to see that it's not just my body that needs you."

He moved down my body, his lips brushing against my clit. With one long swipe, he had me groaning and writhing in need. "Alec," I moaned.

"You still act like we're just fucking. But this is so much more." He pulled my clit into his mouth and started fucking me with his tongue.

"You can't use sex against me," I panted. "You just don't get it. I don't want to be owned by you. I'm my own person."

"You're mine," he growled. His phone went off on the nightstand, but he ignored it.

"Don't you see? You're ignoring work just to have your mouth on me, to prove a point."

But he didn't stop kissing me, pushing me higher and higher. His phone rang again, but he ignored it. The metal from the cuffs was digging into my wrists and ankles from me straining to gain some control.

"Come on my face," Alec bit out. I wanted to hold back. I hated that he actually thought he could command me to have an orgasm. But he had me close and there was no way that I could hide that from him. Not when he had me spread eagle and vulnerable.

I screamed as I came, shivering as ripples of pleasure tore through my body. I sighed heavily, trying to calm my body as Alec laid down next to me on the bed. His fingers brushed against my skin as his hot breath crept over my cooled skin. His phone rang again, but he still ignored it.

"You should get that."

"Not interested."

I rolled my eyes, but it was hard to be mad at him when he laid next to me and caressed my skin. God, I wanted so much with him, but I just couldn't do it. I was beginning to sound like a broken record. But that's how he would see me if I told him. Broken. Damaged. That was how I saw myself, so why wouldn't everyone else? He was already taking up so much of my mind that I felt like I was losing myself. If I let him in anymore, I wouldn't have the strength to end things. Deep down, I knew that if I loved him at all, I needed to let him go. When his phone rang again, he rolled over and answered the phone.

"What?" he barked.

"Florrie's place is under attack," I heard Craig shout through the phone. I jerked, but was still restrained and couldn't move.

"What the fuck are you talking about?"

"The sensors went off at her house and audio picked up screaming."

I glared at Alec. "You didn't turn off the sensors?" I mouthed.

"We're pulling in now. Wait, your truck is already here."

"I just got here," Alec said as he pulled on his clothes quickly. "I'm inside. The whole place is quiet."

"Blanket," I whisper-hissed.

He tossed a blanket over my body just as the front door burst in. Alec pulled his gun and moved closer to the bedroom door. "Back here," he shouted.

"What the fuck are you doing?" I hissed.

"Making it look real."

This was so bad. I was gonna beat his ass when everyone left. Six burly men strode into my bedroom, guns raised and looking like they were ready to kill.

"You okay, Florrie," Craig asked as he moved over to the bed. "Fuck, who did this?"

At least it was dark in the room and none of them could actually see my face. That is, until Cap flipped on the light, illuminating the dark room.

"Turn off the damn light," Alec barked. "I don't think she wants all you assholes seeing her like this."

"Would somebody please get me out of these handcuffs," I said irritatedly.

Cap came next to me, leaning down by the bed, looking at me earnestly. "Who did this? Did they hurt you?"

"I'm fine, but I would really like it if I wasn't strapped to a fucking bed."

I glared at Alec, pissed that he put me in this position.

"Hunter," Cap snapped. "Get over here and check on our girl."

"I said I'm fine," I replied angrily.

"Why don't we give Florrie some space," Hunter said as he knelt next to the bed. He placed his hand on my outstretched arm, looking at me with concern. "I'm going to look you over. But stop me if this gets too uncomfortable for you."

"This whole fucking situation is uncomfortable," I said, glaring at Alec.

He smirked and turned to the rest of the guys. "Hey, everyone out. Let's give Florrie some privacy."

I watched as the hulking figures left the room. I hadn't been able to tell who all of them were, but I would find out soon enough, and then I would be killing Alec.

"You too, Alec." Hunter stood crossing his arms over his chest, but Alec just shut the door and raised an eyebrow in challenge.

"Don't make me move you, asshole."

"Would you both just shut up," I said angrily. "Alec, just get out of here so he can get these cuffs off me."

"I'm not leaving you," he said, staring me down with so much lust that I almost just asked him to come over and fuck me, but then my senses came back to me and I realized that this was all a power play. He was worried about Hunter seeing me naked.

"Dude, I know you care about her. She's your teammate. Believe me, I was with Lola for a long time, trying to help her after she was tortured. I know that Florrie's going to need you after this, but you have to give her some space. This is traumatic enough without you making it worse.

I stared so hard at the ceiling that I thought I might actually have a chance at digging a hole in it. The problem was, I didn't know how to get out of this without giving away that Alec and I were sleeping together.

"I think Hunter's right," I said quietly, hoping to sound defeated. "I just need some space right now."

Hunter looked at me sadly, but then Alec stepped forward and blew the whole thing to hell.

"She doesn't need any space. I was over here fucking her and forgot to turn off the sensors."

My nostrils flared in anger. I couldn't believe that he had just outed our relationship. I was gonna kill him when I got free.

Hunter stared at Alec for a moment, then at me, then back to Alec. "*You* tied her to the bed?"

"She wouldn't listen."

He looked back at me and burst out laughing. "Holy fuck. This is great. Really. I mean, we all knew that Alec had a thing for you. I mean, he's always staring at your tits and he always has to shower after training with you. And believe me, he's not just showering, if you know what I mean."

"Yes, I know what you mean. Now, would you please remove the cuffs from me?" I said slowly.

"Does Craig know?" he asked with a laugh.

"No, and you're not going to say anything," I said sternly.

"Sure, sure. Oh my God. This is just great. You two are fucking behind his back. How long has this been going on?"

"Could you take off the handcuffs?" I was getting pissed. Hunter wasn't supposed to know to begin with, let alone laugh about my current predicament.

"And nobody else knows." He threw his head back and barked out a laugh so loud that I thought the others would come back. "Just imagine all the shit I'm gonna get out of this." He rubbed his hands together greedily, his eyes moving back and forth as he planned out his future blackmailing ideas.

"Alec, since Hunter really doesn't give a shit that I'm chained to the fucking bed, why don't you get your ass over here and get me out of these before I decide to end things between us for good."

"I kind of like you like that," he said as he came over and started undoing the handcuffs. "I like it that you can't run away from me."

I hopped up from the bed when he finished and wrapped the blanket completely around me, then stormed into the bathroom. This was ridiculous. I couldn't do this. Now Hunter knew, and there was no way he would keep it a secret. Not unless I could get something good on him.

Chapter Sixteen

ALEC

"Shut it, asshole." I smacked Hunter upside the head, but he only laughed harder. "Are you trying to let everyone in on the fact that this isn't what it seems?"

"What the fuck do you care? It's just fucking, right?" I just stared at him and the smile slipped from his face. "It's not just fucking. Whoa, talk about a total mindfuck. I mean, I'm not surprised, but what the hell? Why are you keeping this from everyone?"

"Because that's the way she wants it."

"What? Is she ashamed of you or something?"

"She's worried it'll affect our jobs."

He nodded in understanding and then gestured to the bed. "So, what was with the handcuffs? You said something about her not listening?"

"I gave her an order on the job and she went her own way. She could have gotten herself killed."

"So you cuffed her to the bed?"

"I was trying to get her to fucking listen to me."

He nodded and then snorted out a laugh. "Sorry, but it's funny that you think you can get Florrie to listen to you."

"I can. I just need to find what works for her."

"Let me ask you this, if it's not just fucking, where do you see this going?"

Where did I see this going? I wasn't sure, not in this business. We probably wouldn't be your average couple, going out to dinner and then tucking the kids in. How would that work? We'd both be gone, working jobs at the same time. The only way it would work is if we were on different teams, and then we wouldn't see each other at all.

"Maybe you need to think about that a little more. Obviously, she's the only one thinking in the long term."

"Fuck," I swore softly.

"Come on. We have bigger things to worry about right now. Like how you're going to explain all this to Cap."

He slapped me on the back and I stopped in my tracks. Fuck, there was no good way to explain this and keep Florrie happy.

I stepped out of the bedroom and followed Hunter into the living room where Cap, Craig, Burg, Chris, and Jackson were all standing.

"How is she?" Cap asked, rushing over to me, obviously distressed.

"She's fine. It's not as bad as it looks."

"She was tied naked to a bed. How could it not be that bad?" Chris practically shouted.

"It's not what you think," Florrie said, emerging from the bedroom. "I had a lover over. We had a bit of a disagreement and I was left chained to the bed."

Well, hell. I didn't really like that explanation, but I guess it was better than nothing.

"So, the sensors went off when he left?" Burg asked.

"Probably."

"No," Hunter interrupted. "The sensors showed someone breaching the property, moving toward the house. It couldn't have been him."

The fucker turned and winked at me.

"It was probably me," I fessed up.

"No, when I called you, you didn't know yet that someone had gotten onto Florrie's property," Craig said. "Wait, how *did* you get here so fast? You beat us here and I was just telling you what happened?"

Staring at all the guys, I went with the only thing that made any sense. "I was already on my way here." Florrie glared at me, but I rushed on. "She told me she was meeting a lover here tonight and I..." Sweat beaded on my forehead as I tried to come up with something, anything that would work. "I was jealous."

"Of what?" Cap asked, confusion in his eyes.

"It's been a while," I muttered. Florrie rolled her eyes. I could see the way her brain worked, wondering why the fuck I couldn't come up with a better excuse.

"So, what was your plan?" Hunter crossed his arms over his chest and grinned at me. "Are you turning into Gabe? Were you going to watch?"

"No," I said quickly, not wanting anyone to think that I was into that shit.

"Wait, you were jealous..." Craig hesitated, "of Florrie or her lover?"

"Whoa," Jackson chuckled, taking a step back. "Are you asking if he's gay? Because we've been through this already with Gabe. Trust me, we would know if he was gay."

He chuckled, glancing around the group, but then his eyes landed on me and he looked me up and down like he was waiting for me to confirm his suggestion. The problem was, if I didn't tell him I was gay, then I was here for Florrie. And then she would kill me. There would be no chance for me to have a future with her because I would be dead. But Florrie saved me.

"For God's sake, it was a woman. My lover is a woman."

"What?" Everyone asked, including me.

"Yeah, I like both guys and girls. I had a woman over and it turns out it's Alec's old girlfriend. When she found out that I worked with Alec, she left me tied to the bed. Apparently, Alec gave her chlamydia and her husband found out that she was sleeping around."

"You were sleeping with a married woman?" Chris asked. "That's such a shitbag move."

Shit, Florrie was making me out to be a manwhore.

"And who were you sleeping with to begin with that gave you chlamydia?" Craig asked.

"Another married woman," Florrie chimed in. "This woman's lover."

"Wait," Cap shook his head. "I'm confused. You were sleeping with a married woman who was lovers with another married woman, whom you were also sleeping with?"

I gritted my teeth together and glared at Florrie. "Apparently."

"So, was this like a big ménage type situation?" Cazzo asked. "Were you sleeping with both of them at the same time?"

"Well, duh, asshole." Burg slapped him on the back of the head. "If it was ménage, of course he was sleeping with both of them at the same time."

"No, I meant, was he the filling in the cookie or was it more of a spectator sport?"

"God," Craig groaned, "Please tell me you were the filling. I've always wanted to do that."

"Maybe you can participate on Alec's next romp," Florrie grinned. "Maybe he'll find a few more women to sleep around with."

"I'm not sure how I feel about this," Burg said.

"Yeah, this coming from the man that slept with a tranie," I shot back.

"Hey, that was unknowingly and it stopped once I saw dick."

"So, how did she find out that you worked with Alec?" Chris asked Florrie.

"Alec walked in on us together."

"You lied?" Craig asked me. "You made it sound like you didn't know what was going on."

"Did you know your old lover was gonna be here?" Cap asked. "Is that why you came over?"

Florrie glared at me and I nodded. "Yeah, I was thinking of starting things up with her again."

"With a Florrie sandwich this time?" Burg asked.

"Can we drop this?" I asked in frustration. "The point is that Florrie's fine and we can all go home now."

"So, are we worried about this lover coming back and stirring shit up?" Cap asked. "Do we need to do a perimeter search?"

"No, she's gone," Florrie interjected. "You can all leave."

"Guess you had the right train of thought, coming over here when you did," Hunter smirked. "Imagine what we could have all walked in on."

"Well, you didn't see anything and you never will. It's over and you can leave," Florrie cut in, glaring at Hunter.

"No, I think we should do a perimeter check still," Hunter said. "You know, make sure this chick isn't still on the property. I mean, the alarms were set off and we need to be sure this chick actually left. We wouldn't want you to end up tied to the bed again."

That asshole was fucking with me hard and I would get my revenge one way or another.

"I agree," Cap nodded. "We're not taking any chances."

"What was this chick wearing?" Jackson asked.

"Nothing," Florrie said quickly.

"She ran out naked?"

"She was in a hurry when she left. She didn't want to see Alec."

"Where are her clothes then?" Cap asked.

"She must have grabbed them on the way out."

"Alec," Cap asked. "Did you see anything to identify her? Do you have a picture?"

"Sorry, I don't keep pictures of old lovers on me."

"Maybe we should get the blue light in here," Hunter suggested. "You know, find out where the samples are."

"Excuse me?" Florrie said harshly.

"What? If we got a sample of her...cum... on file, we would have her DNA."

"Alright, that's enough. I'm fine. There will be no perimeter check. No DNA profiling. And definitely no one staying behind," she said narrowing her eyes at me. "You can all get off my property now."

"Florrie, you're not staying here tonight. We'll have new equipment installed tomorrow, but I don't want you coming back before then." Cap stared her down, waiting for to argue.

"She can stay with me," I piped up.

"I think she should stay with me," Hunter said, raising an eyebrow in challenge. "You know, because of Lucy. You'll have another woman around." Then he glanced at Florrie. "I don't mind watching a little girl on girl action, as long as I get to participate."

"She's my teammate," I bit out.

"She can stay with me too," Craig suggested. He had been unusually quiet that whole time, which now that I thought about it, was very strange for him. Craig always needed answers, so why wasn't he asking any questions? Fuck, he was probably onto us. Florrie was going to kill me.

"She'll stay with both of you. I don't want her out of your sight tonight." Cap handed out orders, including ordering Florrie to pack a bag while Craig and I stood watch. She glared at me the whole fucking time.

"You okay, man?" I asked Craig as we waited.

"Yeah, it's just a lot to take in. How did I not know that Florrie swung both ways? Or that you were banging married women? It just all feels off."

"What part?" I asked, going over our story in my head and trying to figure out what part was wrong.

"The whole thing. I guess I never pictured you as the type to sleep with a married woman. I definitely didn't see Florrie being gay. And how the hell did she let herself get tied up and how did you not catch the chick?"

"Bad timing, I guess. It all took me by surprise."

"I guess. Something's off though. I think we need to keep a close eye on Florrie for a while. It just feels like she's not telling us something."

"I'll see what I can get out of her tonight," I said, grinning to myself.

Chapter Seventeen

ALEC

One year ago...

Stepping out of Chance's house into the dark night, I pulled my gun immediately, ready to take watch for the night. Florrie and Morgan had seemed to bond inside while I was the odd man out. Craig wasn't along this time around, leaving us short one man, but we'd be fine. The chance that Wes "The Broker" Hughes knew where we were hiding Morgan was slim.

"I'm going on a perimeter check," I told Florrie. She nodded and took up her position in front of the door. I had just gotten halfway down the driveway when the hairs on the back of my neck stood to attention. Squinting into the darkness, I couldn't make out anything. I glanced at my watch, noting that no sensors were signaling any problems. But that didn't mean jack shit right now. Something was wrong and I was positive that we had to get the fuck out of here now.

"Florrie," I said in my coms as I turned and headed up the driveway. She didn't answer. "Florrie," I tried again, but still nothing. My heart pounded in my chest as I raced up the long driveway. I stopped in my tracks when I reached the garage. Gathered around the front of the house were at least a dozen men, two of them holding onto Florrie. She had blood dripping down her face and her arm was wrenched up behind her back painfully. How had they moved in without us knowing, without alerting the sensors?

"Put the gun down or I put a bullet in her head."

I held my gun steady. It wasn't in me to surrender. Florrie knew this, glaring at me, telling me that I better not put down my fucking gun. Still, she knew that I wouldn't risk her life. I glanced around quickly at the other men. There was no way we were getting out of this. There were too many of them and Florrie was already incapacitated.

"You don't have a fucking choice. Do it now or I'll put a bullet in her," the man said, leaving me no options. I slowly lowered my weapon, but I didn't give away that I had three other guns on me. Not that they couldn't figure that out. What I needed was a plan. It was better to comply for now and give myself the chance to come up with something, anything to get us out of this clusterfuck.

"Don't-ah!" Florrie shouted as they wrenched her arm.

"Stop," I shouted. "I'm doing what you asked."

"Tell us the codes for the house."

"No fucking way." I might put down my gun, but I wasn't allowing them access to the house just like that. I needed to find a way to get ahold of Cap, but with coms down, they weren't getting any of this.

A man stepped up behind me, slamming his gun down on the back of my head. The darkness spun all around me as pain ripped through my skull. I fell to my knees, catching myself before I fell completely and passed out on the ground. I willed myself to stay alert. I could vaguely hear Florrie screaming, but it was muffled. I looked up through blurry eyes to see Florrie's face contorted in pain. They were gagging her so her screams were silenced. I shook off the pain and blinked rapidly, but I couldn't clear my vision.

"Tell us the fucking code!"

"Fuck you," Florrie spat and then whimpered in pain. The man grabbed my arms and yanked me to my feet. I was barely able to stand. He gripped my jaw, forcing me to look at Florrie.

"You want to see her killed?"

I blocked everything out as best I could, but it wasn't enough. I still saw Florrie lying in my bed, her blonde hair spread out on my pillow. I saw her smile and felt her touch. I thought I could think rationally on the job, but not when they were hurting her. Anger ripped through me so fiercely that I lost it and tore myself from the man's grip.

A blinding rage took over as I swung around, jabbing the man in the throat with my fist. He fell to the ground, clutching his throat. A second man came toward me and I pulled a knife, whipping it into his chest. They kept coming and I tried to fight, but with every fist to my face, every kick to my chest, I faltered just a little. The final blow to my head had me falling to my knees and then dropping to the ground.

Through drooping eyes, I saw Florrie drop to the ground just as I had. She was out. I saw a man in a suit approach the door and knock. I prayed that Morgan wouldn't answer. My fingers moved down my vest, trying to find my phone, but a boot to the face had blackness creeping over me. The last thing I saw was Florrie passed out on the ground.

———

Heat burned at my skin. I peeled my eyes open against my better judgement. My head was pounding and I was seeing double everywhere I looked. I knew I had a concussion immediately, which wasn't a surprise. But what shocked the hell out of me were the flames coming out of Chance's house. I tried to sit up, but immediately fell back when a wave of dizziness hit hard.

"Don't move." I glanced over and saw Cap's face twice.

"What the fuck happened?"

"You don't remember?"

I scrambled through my memories and then it hit hard. "Florrie."

"She's okay. Just woke up and has a bit of a headache, but I'd say she's okay."

"Her arm," I grunted out.

"Yeah, it's in a sling. Fuckers dislocated her shoulder, but she's more pissed that they got the drop on her."

"What about Morgan?"

Cap's face turned somber. "Died in the fire."

"Fuck." My head thunked on the ground and I closed my eyes. I had never lost someone I was protecting, but this was worse. I had lost a teammate's girl.

"It's not your fault. We should have had more people on her."

"Yeah, try telling Chance that."

I couldn't just lie around on my ass. I pushed up, even though I felt like I was just gonna fall over again.

"Whoa, maybe you should stay down."

"Maybe you should fuck off."

I stood on shaky legs and stumbled over to where Florrie was sitting at the back of an ambulance. She was holding her arm awkwardly in a sling and staring off into space.

"Florrie." Her name whooshed out of me like a dying wish. Her eyes locked on mine and then she practically collapsed into my arms. I had to steady myself against the floor of the ambulance so I didn't fall over. I held her close to me, running my hands over her back and feeling the weight of her body against mine. She was really here and she was okay.

"You shouldn't have done that," she said after a moment. "Why did you fight them like that? They could have killed you."

"They were going to anyway. They were hurting you. I just couldn't stand there. What the fuck did you expect me to do?"

"I expected you to not make the situation worse," she bit out.

"You wanted me to stand by while they tried to rip your arm off?"

"You should have tried to get help. We were outnumbered. There was no way we were going to win that one."

"I did try. Coms were down. I couldn't get to my phone," I explained, but she just shook her head.

"I knew we should have ended things. If you were thinking rationally, you would have put the job first. But you put me first."

My jaw clenched in anger. She was pissed at me for trying to protect her in an impossible situation. "We were outnumbered. What the fuck did you expect me to do? Was I supposed to not try and get to you?"

She pulled back and stepped down from the ambulance. "Morgan's gone. She died in that fire and she was our responsibility."

"I know," I bit out. "You think I don't realize how bad I fucked up?"

"How bad *we* fucked up. We were both responsible for her."

I was about to argue, but Cap walked up and Florrie pulled away even more. "We need to head back to the office. Chance took off with some of the guys to get more information. You two need to head over to the hospital-"

"I'm not going to the hospital. I'm fine."

"Florrie needs her shoulder checked out," Cap argued.

"Hunter can set it. I don't need the hospital," Florrie said.

Cap sighed, obviously tired and ready for this night to end. Well, that made two of us. "Fine, let's head back, but the two of you are getting checked out by Hunter or Rocco and you're staying in the panic room tonight. Nobody's going anywhere after what just happened."

Florrie and I rode back with Cap in silence. She wouldn't even fucking look at me. When we got back, I got cleared by Rocco, while Hunter set Florrie's shoulder. She tried to sneak away from me, but I snatched her hand and yanked her with me down the hall to an empty room.

I shoved her up against the wall and molded my body to hers. "You can be pissed all you want about the job, but I did what I had to. They were hurting you."

"I'm a big girl."

"I fucking know that, but you're mine and seeing those men hurting you tore my fucking heart to shreds."

"They did worse to you."

I breathed in her scent, running my nose along hers. God, I needed her, but not for sex. I just needed to hold her in my arms and know that she was mine. Even if it was only for a short time. I couldn't let her go yet.

"I can handle a lot of shit, but I can't handle watching you get hurt. It fucking scared the shit out of me to see you in pain. Please, just stay with me. I need you right now."

Chapter Eighteen

FLORRIE

I let him lead me over to the couch. This room was a sort of lounge area, so there were no beds. This couch was the most comfort we would be getting anytime soon. I was still pissed at Alec for putting his gun down. He did that for me and he shouldn't have. It went against everything we were supposed to be doing, protecting the client. And now she was dead.

"Alec, this is over. We both fucked up tonight. We should have been-"

"Don't even fucking tell me that we weren't doing our jobs. We were outnumbered. We did everything right."

"Except that you tried to save me. What good did that do?"

"Florrie, look at this from another angle, the one where we aren't a couple."

"I thought that was what I was doing," I snapped.

"Really?" He hiked his knee up on the couch and turned to face me. "So, tell me how the fuck I was supposed to defend our client if you were dead? It was fucking twelve men against the two of us. If they killed you, it would just be me. I fought to get to you and they still overpowered me. I didn't stand a fucking chance. So, you tell me how you being dead would have helped anything."

I sat there for a moment, because he was right. He was trying to save his teammate, and romantic relationship or not, it wouldn't have done any good for me to be dead right now. Morgan would have still burned in that house and Alec would have been dead. I knew that for a fact, because if they had killed me, Alec would have gone insane, trying to kill anyone in his path.

"You're right."

"I don't understand why the fuck they left us alive. It doesn't make any sense."

"It was Wes," I said quietly. "He knew that he could walk right up to the door and get Morgan. He was trying to send a message, that he could get to her no matter what, that he didn't even have to kill anyone to get past us."

I could tell that I should have kept my mouth shut. Alec's face turned hard and cold. No man wanted to be told that he was let go because he wasn't a threat. And Alec was a proud man. He was a protector. Knowing that he had been beaten was bad enough, but to be told you weren't even worth killing was so much worse.

He leaned back against the couch and shut his eyes. I could tell he was in pain. The lines around his face were drawn tight and he was squeezing his eyes shut in pain. I wanted to comfort him, but I knew there was something else I had to do. I had to end things. This had gone on long enough. And no matter what Alec said, I saw the way he looked at me when those men had me. We couldn't afford for him to think of me in that way.

"Alec."

He looked at me, his eyes sad. He knew it was true as much as I did.

"Don't. Not tonight."

"We both know we can't do this anymore. Who's it going to be next time? Maybe tonight was inevitable and us not being together wouldn't have changed anything, but what about next time? We can't afford for you to be thinking about me on a job."

"And what about you?" he said angrily. "Do I really mean so little to you that you don't worry about me?"

"I do, but the difference is that I trust your abilities."

"I trust-"

"No, you don't," I said matter of factly. "You used to, but every-thing's changed. You worry about me in ways that you never have before. You used to think of me as one of the team, but now you think of me as your girlfriend first and your teammate second."

He stared at me for a moment, then lifted his hand and ran it across my cheek. "You know, that's the first time you've referred to yourself as my girlfriend."

His touch was so gentle that I wanted to curl up next to him and just be his, but there were too many things against us right now. I had led him on for two years, making him believe that the only thing holding me back was us working together. And while tonight proved that it could be a huge issue, deep down, I knew that wasn't the only problem. We could work out the issue of being on the same team with one sit down talk with Cap. It would be hard, but we could make it work.

But if we did that, I wouldn't be able to hide my real reasons for pushing him away anymore. He would see through me and know that I was hiding something much bigger. Something that would make him look at me completely different. Better to be looked at as a heartless bitch that cared more about her job than to be looked at with pity. As the incomplete woman that failed at the simplest things human nature had made me for.

So, instead of telling him any of the things that I felt deep inside, I curled into him and let him hold me. If only for tonight. We could deal with the rest in the morning, but for now, I wanted to enjoy the feel of his arms around me one last time. In the morning, I would have to make sure he knew this was over.

I startled awake sometime later. I hadn't even realized that I had fallen asleep. Alec was still asleep on the couch. I rubbed the sleep from my eyes, trying to figure out what had woken me. And then I heard it. Gunfire. A blast shook the building and I jumped to my feet, immedi-ately grabbing my weapon.

"What's going on?" Alec stood and wobbled on his feet. He was in no condition to fight right now. I knew he had a concussion, but I could tell that he wasn't even seeing straight based on the way he was looking at me.

"Stay here."

"What the fuck are you talking about?"

"Something's going down, but you're not in shape to fight. You're not even seeing straight."

He clenched his jaw and pulled me into him, flush against his body. "Don't tell me what I can and can't do."

"But you're-"

"Shut the fuck up." More gunfire erupted, but his eyes never left mine. "We do this together."

He kissed me hard, but pulled away quickly, gripping my hand in his, and led me to the door. I pulled away, needing to have my one good arm free. I wasn't some damsel in distress that needed his guidance.

I nodded to him when I got in position by the door. He opened it and I went low while he went high. Down the hallway, chaos reigned down on the rest of our teams. Smoke filled the hallways in a gray blanket that made it impossible to easily make out targets. I hugged the wall as I made my way down the long passageway. In the conference room, hell had broken out. There were men lying on the ground and blood splattered all over the walls. A hand shot out and I grabbed it with my right hand, not thinking twice as I wrenched it back, snapping the wrist and making the gun drop that was cradled in it. I spun, kicking out as I felt someone else approach. I connected with a stomach and ducked just as a knife was thrown in my direction. I could see Alec fighting another man out of the corner of my eye, but I didn't have time to stop and see if he was okay.

Arms wrapped around me from behind, cutting off my air supply. I dropped my weight, adding more pressure to my throat, but putting him in a bad position. My shoulder pulled sharply, practically taking what remaining air I had in my lungs. I flung my elbow back and air whooshed out on my neck as the man gasped for air. I pulled my knife and slammed it in his throat. He dropped the ground, eyes wide in disbelief. I didn't even bat an eye at it. The fucker could gurgle in his blood on the ground for all I cared.

I caught sight of Alec struggling with a man on the ground. I ran for him, but a spray of bullets had me flinging myself on the ground. I groaned in pain as I landed on my bad shoulder. I rolled to my other side and brought my gun up just in time to shoot a man that was charging me. I pushed myself to my feet, stumbling into the wall as black spots filled my vision. Leaning against it heavily, I sucked in deep breaths, trying to battle the pain coursing through my body. Fuck, this was bad.

"Florrie!"

I looked up just as Alec flung himself in front of me. His body jerked back and into me as a bullet tore into him.

"Fuck, fuck, fuck," I said as I caught him as he fell into me. He shot several times and I barely registered another man dropping in front of us. I lowered Alec to the ground, completely ignoring everything around us. Tears threatened, but I sucked them back and cleared my head. Assess the damage.

I looked up for any more assailants, but most of them were gone by now. "What the fuck were you thinking?" I shouted at him. He groaned and pushed off the floor. "Stop moving."

"It's not that bad. Through and through," he said through gritted teeth. "The guy was a piss poor shot."

I shoved his shirt aside and saw that Alec was right. The shot most likely didn't cause any damage. I tore off a piece of his shirt and pressed it to his wound. Fuck, we were in a bad position here. I only had one good arm and he was injured. This was really fucking bad. I kept my eyes trained on the chaos around us, but the smoke was getting too thick to stay here. We had to make a run for it.

"We need to move," I said urgently.

"What about Craig?"

"I haven't seen him. I see Cap. Let's get over to him."

I helped Alec to his feet, but he slumped against the wall once he was standing. Shaking his head slightly, I saw him blinking rapidly. His head had to be killing him right now. Lola ran up to us and I thanked God that she appeared alright.

"Can you help Alec outside?"

She nodded and hauled one shoulder under Alec to help prop him up. I was useless. We quickly worked through the smoke and made our way to the emergency stairs at the back. Cazzo met us on the stairs and took over for Lola.

"I have to get back. Ice is still in there with Chris."

"I've got this," Cazzo nodded.

By the time we were out of the building, we were all coughing and gasping for air. We watched as the last of the teams made their way out of the building, and then we watched as the building crumpled to the ground.

Chapter Nineteen

ALEC

9 months ago....

It was finally out in the open. Hunter had outed us in the middle of an argument all of us were having. Florrie was pissed, but I didn't really care too much right now. We were together and fuck anyone that didn't like it. It took a few days for Florrie to calm down about the whole thing. For an entire day, she refused to speak to me, even went so far as to walk away when I was in the same room just so she didn't have to see me. But slowly, she came to the realization that things were out in the open and we had to talk about it.

I went looking for her to try and hash things out with her, but I couldn't find her anywhere. If she wasn't training with everyone else, that left her bedroom. I made my way down to her room and knocked, but she didn't answer. Rocco came down the hallway, whistling and giving me a wink as he walked past.

"Don't forget to wrap that shit up. Florrie will kick your ass if you get her pregnant."

"Shut the fuck up," I growled, but he just laughed and moved on. I pounded on her door again and this time she answered.

"Hey, I was thinking we could talk." She nodded and moved further into her room. She looked a little pale and she was holding her stomach. "Are you okay?"

She smiled hesitantly and nodded. "I actually have something I need to talk to you about."

"Okay. Is this about us?"

"Yes."

"Good, because I was thinking, now that our relationship is out in the open, maybe we should talk with Cap and see what he plans to do about our team."

She grimaced and sat down on the edge of the bed.

"Unless you don't want to talk to Cap," I said, realizing that this probably didn't change the way she felt about our relationship. She still hadn't told me she loved me and there really wasn't any difference in the way we were together.

"I think we need to talk about things first. There are things that you need to know before we decide if we're going to really do this."

Hope filled me, but then she doubled over in pain and let out a piercing scream that replaced hope with terror. I rushed to her side and caught her right before she fell to the floor. Her face was twisted in pain and she clutched her stomach so tight that it was like she was trying to claw her way out of her own body.

"Florrie," I said, my voice filled with panic. "What's wrong? What do I need to do?"

"Something's wrong," her voice quivered.

"I can see that," I said, practically shouting at her. I laid her down on the floor, but she curled into a ball. And that was when I saw it. Blood. A fuck ton of blood. Just like before. "What the fuck is going on, Florrie?"

"I'm pregnant," she cried as she squeezed her eyes closed.

My heart hammered out of control and a rush of wind filled my ears so much that it was like a freight train going by. She was pregnant, but she was fucking bleeding.

"I'll be right back."

"No! Don't leave."

I gripped her hand in mine, cradling her face in my other. She looked so fucking scared, her face all red and tears rolling down her cheeks. "I have to get help. We have to get you to the hospital." I kissed her and then raced out of the room. Rocco had just been here. He could help.

"Rocco!"

I raced down the hall, pushing open doors and yelling out his name. I rounded the corner and slammed right into him.

"What's going on?" he asked, then looked down at me and his eyes widened. "What the fuck happened?"

I looked down for the first time and saw the blood staining my hands and parts of my shirt. It wasn't a lot, but it was enough to know that something was wrong. I couldn't speak as I stared down at Florrie's blood on me.

"Hey, talk to me. Who's hurt?"

"Florrie." I just barely whispered it and then he was racing down the hall toward Florrie's room. My brain came back online and I ran down the hall, coming to a halt when I saw Rocco leaning over Florrie, listening as Florrie whispered to him.

"She's pregnant," I spluttered out. "She's....why is she bleeding?"

"She has endometriosis," he said as he shoved his hands under body and hauled her up against him. "We have to get her to the hospital. It's probably an ectopic pregnancy."

He ran past me out the door and down the hall. "What does that mean?"

"It means that she can't carry the baby to term. The egg is probably lodged in her fallopian tubes. I'm guessing the tube ruptured. That's why she's bleeding."

I pulled my phone and dialed Cap.

"Cap, I need to get Florrie to the hospital now. Rocco's taking her to the truck."

"What's wrong?" he asked urgently. "You know we can't just show up at the hospital without giving away our identities."

"I'll explain on the way. But she needs a hospital, Cap."

"I'll meet you at the SUV."

He hung up and I caught up to Rocco. "Why does this house have to be so fucking big?" he grumbled. "Run ahead and bring the SUV by the door so we can hit the road."

I took off, not wanting to leave Florrie behind, but she was in the best possible hands at the moment. I was pulling the SUV around just as Cap was running toward me from a different entrance in the garage. Rocco burst through the other door with Florrie, and Cap had the back door open for them. I threw the SUV in park and raced around to the other side.

"You're driving," I practically yelled at Rocco. I needed to hold Florrie right now. I had no fucking clue what was happening, but I knew she was scared and I was going to be there for her. I jumped into the back seat and pulled her limp body into my arms. She was pale and her skin was clammy. Her eyes were huge.

"She's losing too much blood, Rocco."

"Raise her feet. There should be a blanket in the back. Wrap her up in it, but not too tight."

I quickly found the blanket and wrapped it around her. Her teeth were chattering and her breathing was becoming shallow. I propped her feet up and then knelt down on the floor just as Rocco took a turn too fast. I caught myself and gripped onto Florrie's hand.

"It's gonna be okay, baby. Just hang on."

"I didn't know," she whispered.

"You didn't know what?"

"I thought I couldn't get pregnant," she mumbled. Her words were starting to slur and she was having trouble focusing on me.

"It doesn't matter now."

A tear slipped down her cheek and she squeezed my hand harder. "I'm sorry I pushed you away."

The SUV squealed to a stop and Cap was there before I could ask her anything else. Her eyes fluttered and then rolled back. Hauling her out of the SUV, I ran into the hospital to the waiting gurney. Rocco started spouting off information to them while I stood there, staring at the woman I loved going into shock and bleeding out on the gurney.

"Sir, you need to wait here."

"But I'm-"

"Sir, we need to go," the doctor insisted. I let go of her hand and then they were pushing her through the double doors. Cap's strong grip on my shoulder had me glancing over at him. Worry and pity marred his face and that was when I felt it. A pain so deep inside me that I thought I would be ripped in two.

I sat in the waiting room, my elbows resting on my knees, and stared at my bloodied hands. It was dry now, but I couldn't bring myself to wash it off yet. I just brushed my fingers together, feeling her blood on me. I had been on the brink of a breakdown since we brought her here, but I was holding it together as best I could.

Rocco sat down next to me with a sigh. "You didn't know."

I shook my head and continued to rub the dried blood around on my hands.

"Did you know she was pregnant?"

I shook my head again. I felt his hand come to rest on my shoulder briefly and I closed my eyes, needing that contact right now, to remind me that I couldn't lose my shit. I needed to be strong for Florrie.

"You said she had endometriosis. What is that?"

"It's when endometrial tissue builds up outside the uterus, but it doesn't shed like normal tissue."

"And that causes problems?"

"Yeah, she would have had symptoms."

"Like what?"

"Fatigue, nausea, severe cramping-"

"Extremely heavy periods," I said, looking up at him. He stared at me and nodded slightly. "Like a little over a year ago when I took her to the hospital and she fucking bled all over me?"

He nodded again in understanding. "She didn't say anything."

I shook my head. "So, what does this have to do with her being pregnant?"

I knew he had already explained it to me, but so much was going on and I wasn't really retaining anything he said.

"Basically, endometriosis makes it more difficult to conceive. What

I'm guessing happened is that she had an ectopic pregnancy. That's when the egg attaches itself outside the uterus. It's usually in the fallopian tubes. The egg starts to grow and eventually, if not caught in time, the tube ruptures."

"What does that mean for her?"

"Honestly, I'm not sure. I know very little about this stuff. This is all basic information."

"So, you can't tell me if she's going to be okay."

"With that amount of blood, I don't want to scare you, but that was serious."

I nodded numbly. My hands started to shake as reality set in. This was really fucking serious. I could lose her. I could feel the tears building and I brushed a hand over my face, wiping at my eyes. The last thing I needed to do was start crying.

"So," I cleared my throat and blinked back the remaining tears. "She would have known that pregnancy wasn't very likely."

"It would have been something her doctor talked to her about."

I laughed lightly. "It makes so much fucking sense now."

"What does?"

"It was a little over a year ago that she really started pushing me away. She almost succeeded. She kept telling me that she could never love me. The thing is, I know she fucking loves me. I can see it every time I look at her. But I couldn't figure out why she didn't want to admit it."

"Finding out stuff like that makes people think irrational thoughts."

I knew he was right, but that didn't make it any harder to hear.

"You have to think of it from her point of view. She just found out she probably wouldn't be able to have kids. She's seen how everyone reacts to having kids at Reed Security."

"Like it would have fucking mattered to me," I hissed.

"It doesn't matter that you wouldn't have cared. She would have always been thinking that you were just saying that to make her feel better."

"I thought you didn't know anything about this."

"I know human nature. I've seen men push their wives away

because they've lost a leg or an arm. The worse the injury, the more that person feels inadequate."

"But she's not injured."

"Isn't she?" Rocco asked. "Some of the worst scars are the ones we carry around on the inside."

Chapter Twenty

FLORRIE

A steady beeping woke me up. The white room was fuzzy, but one thing I could clearly make out was Alec sitting beside me. He leaned forward to rest on his knees when he saw me and blew out a deep breath.

"What's going on?" I asked. My throat felt dry, but it was nothing compared to the pain I was starting to notice in my stomach.

"You had to have surgery."

"For what? Was I shot?"

He shook his head, but his eyes never left mine. They looked sad and red, like he had been crying. But that couldn't be right. Alec never cried.

"Florrie...you were pregnant."

Flashes of me looking at a pregnancy test flitted through my mind. I remembered feeling happy, overjoyed, that I was pregnant. I was excited because they had told me it would be very difficult. I smiled at Alec, but he didn't return the smile.

"You're not happy. I figured you might not be. I'm sorry. It was never...I didn't think it could happen."

"Florrie," he said quietly, almost brokenly.

"Wait, you said I *was* pregnant." A sad, lonely feeling filled my chest and that was when I knew I had lost the baby. Alec's eyes confirmed it. There was no baby anymore.

"I'm so fucking sorry, Florrie."

Pain so sharp and agonizing filled my heart, it felt like I was literally being ripped apart. An ugly, desperate sob tore from the depths of my soul, pulling all the anger and frustration of my situation along with it. Alec was out of his chair the next second and holding me in bed. I gripped onto his shirt and let the tears flow. I had been hiding it for so long, the desire to have a baby that I wasn't supposed to have. I had that dream in my grasp and just like that it was gone.

"This wasn't supposed to happen," I cried. "This was my chance."

Alec ran his hand up and down my back, trying to calm me down, but I was too lost to calm down.

"Why did this happen? I wasn't supposed to be able to get pregnant and then it happened. Why did he take it away?"

Anger built inside me and I lashed out at Alec, slamming my fist into his chest over and over again. He gripped my wrists in one hand and his other hand came up to cup my face to keep me still. He looked right into my eyes and I could see that he was in pain too.

"This isn't the end, Florrie. We'll get through this. I swear."

"I can't do it," I cried. "I can't..."

I dropped my head to his chest and just cried. It was so unfair. Why would he give me a baby only to rip it away from me? Why would he even give me the hope of something I could never have? It was cruel and he wasn't supposed to be cruel. Was this because of me? Was I not a good enough person? Did I not deserve a baby? If it was never meant to be, I wished that I had never had the chance to even feel like it was going to happen. I wished that baby had never existed to begin with. That would be better than having it ripped away right after I found out.

At some point, Alec leaned back with me in the bed and just held me, running his hand up and down my arm to soothe me. I felt like he was my lifeline, the last thing to hold onto to feel sane. I could feel myself unraveling and he was the only thing that could keep me together right now.

"Everyone wants to see you. They're worried about you."

"No," I said as I dried my tears. "I don't want to see anyone."

"Not even Lola? She said that she knew about this."

I thought I detected a hint of anger in his voice, but then his hand started moving again and I forgot about all of it.

"I don't want to see anyone," I repeated. "I just want to sleep and forget about all of this."

I felt his lips on my forehead and I let myself slip into the comfort of his arms and drift off.

For three days, Alec asked me if I wanted to see anyone, and all three days I told him no. I was supposed to be discharged today and all I could think about was getting home and away from this hospital. The hospital where my baby had been taken from me. At some point on the second day, I had lost it and asked to see my baby, but they told me there was nothing to see. The baby hadn't even really been developed yet. It was just a bundle of cells at that point. There was nothing to say goodbye to.

The doctor had to sedate me so that I didn't tear apart the room looking for my child. When I came out of the fog of the sedative, Alec explained it to me again and this time it made sense. I was embarrassed that I had overreacted, but the doctor had assured me that I wasn't the first mother to grieve in such a way. After that, I just laid there. I didn't think about a whole lot. I just stared off in space and tried to feel numb to everything.

I ignored the nurses when they came in to check on my incision. I didn't want to see it or be reminded of why I was here in the first place. And now today, it was time to go home and recover. Except, I wasn't going home. I was going to Knight's house in Colorado because we were on the run. It pissed me off even more that I couldn't even go back to my own place and wallow in peace. There were going to be people stopping by to check on me constantly and that just pissed me off.

"Are you ready to go home?"

I nodded and stood slowly, holding the pillow to my stomach to help ease the pain. Moving to the wheelchair, I sat down and closed my eyes. I hadn't even argued when Alec brought it in. There was no point, and I was in no mood to argue with anyone. When he wheeled me out of the room, I was relieved when I saw no one was there. I half expected half of Reed Security to be there, and that would have just pissed me off. This was because of Alec.

"Thank you...for telling everyone to stay away."

"Well, I think if they didn't get the hint before that you didn't want to see anyone, they know now."

It wasn't that I was ashamed to see everyone. I couldn't help what had happened. But the thought of sitting there with everyone as they asked me how I was doing and if there was anything I needed, was all too much. Both of those questions were completely insane. Of course, I wasn't doing okay. And the only thing that anyone could give me was the child that I was supposed to be carrying.

Craig was waiting by the truck, staring off into the parking lot. I looked up at Alec and scowled. He was the last person I wanted to see.

"What? He's your teammate and you've refused to see him. What the fuck did you want me to say to him?"

"That I needed space?"

"You're going to have to face them all at some point. Just let Craig make sure you're alright and the others will be satisfied for a while."

I turned back around and had to look away when Craig caught my eye. He opened the door for me and I pushed up from the wheelchair, taking his hand only because I needed it to get into the truck.

"At some point, we're going to have a talk about all the secrets you've been keeping." Craig was staring me down, but there was no anger on his face. He was right. Between Alec and my medical diagnosis, I had really kept him in the dark. Alec sat in the back on the way home and I couldn't deny that I wanted him next to me. It was awkward sitting here next to Craig, knowing that he had so many questions, but he wasn't saying a word.

After sneaking into Knight's house as best I could, I shuffled off to my room to sit in peace. Craig followed me in, but Alec hung back by the door.

"So, are you going to tell me what's going on?"

"Don't you know?"

"Only what I've been told. I want to know why you didn't say anything to us."

He stood in front of me, arms crossed and a don't fuck with me look on his face. I looked away. I wasn't ready to talk about all this. It was all too fresh and I just couldn't bring myself to talk to him yet. Craig leaned down in front of me on his haunches, taking my hands in his.

"You don't have to be so fucking strong all the time. I'm more than just your teammate. You can trust me with your secrets. When you're ready."

I turned to him, tears brimming my eyes, and nodded. He wrapped me up in a hug, and I didn't push him away. It felt good to accept his comfort. When he pulled back, I swiped at my eyes and put a smile on my face. He talked to Alec for a few minutes and I couldn't hear what they were saying, but I wasn't interested anyway. I just wanted to slip back into my state of ignorance and pretend no one else existed.

Chapter Twenty-One

ALEC

Florrie had been home for two days and we still hadn't talked about how she ended up in that hospital. I couldn't ignore it anymore. I needed to clear the air with her. I knew that it was the wrong time, but then, it seemed that it had always been the wrong time for Florrie to talk about it.

She was laying in bed, looking like a fucking angel, but when I looked at her right now, I saw my angel that had lied to me for over a year. I sat down next to her and ran my fingers through her long, blonde strands. Her eyes fluttered open and after a moment of recognition, sadness overtook them.

"We need to talk," I said. She nodded and shifted until she could sit up in bed. "Why didn't you tell me?"

"Alec, we weren't supposed to be anything-"

"No, I don't want some bullshit excuse from you. We had been together for a year when you found out. It was when I took you to the hospital. And then two weeks later, you snapped at me and told me to leave you the fuck alone. That's when you found out about the endometriosis, right?"

"Yes."

"And instead of talking to me about it, you acted like I was nothing to you."

"You know, it wasn't like this was all a fairytale for me or something. Can you put yourself in my shoes? I had just found out that I couldn't have kids. Do you know what that was like for me?"

"No, because you decided to keep me in the dark. You kept pushing me away, no matter how much I tried to get you to open up to me."

"It's not that easy for me, Alec. We were just having fun. I went into this thinking that we were just messing around. I never expected you to start to feel more."

"And you're telling me you never felt more? Because I call bullshit on that."

"Of course I felt something for you, but there was so much to think about at the time. It just seemed like too much risk. I didn't see a future for us, and then there was the fact that we had no clue what would happen if Cap found out about us. There was no point in sharing and dragging you into something that...that..."

"That what? I told you I loved you. I waited for you to say it back. I fucking prayed that one day you would open up to me. I practically begged you to say it back. So, you tell me why you didn't say anything for a fucking year about what was going on with you. When you knew that I was in love with you. When you knew that I would have done anything for you."

"That's exactly why I didn't tell you."

"I don't understand," I said in frustration. I stood and paced the room. I was feeling antsy and ready to detonate if she told me one more fucking time that she was trying to save me.

"You would have done anything for me. Including stay with me when you knew I couldn't ever give you a family."

"You must think I'm a real shitbag if you think I would stay with you out of pity. You should have fucking talked to me."

"Would it have made a difference?" she asked after a moment.

I huffed out a laugh. "Are you serious right now? Of course it would have made a difference. To know that you were going through that and to understand what was going on in your head would have made a lot of things a lot fucking clearer."

"It wasn't your business."

"Is that what we're going with right now? It wasn't my business? What's next? You're going to tell me that I was just a good fuck, but now that everything's in the open, it's better if we just end this?"

She looked down at her hands and it became really fucking clear that that's exactly what she intended to happen.

"What about our baby?"

"We never really had a baby. It wasn't planned or wanted by either of us."

"How the fuck would you know? You seem to be making a lot of assumptions about me lately. You're not even giving me a chance to talk about any of this with you."

"Look, if you didn't want it, then it doesn't matter because it's gone. If you did want it, then you know now that's something I can never give you. It seems pretty clear to me that we just don't work."

"Wow, you just glazed over a whole bunch of shit like it didn't matter. It's not just you that's dealing with this. It was my baby too. It was you that almost died because of it, and you mean everything to me. Why can't you see that? Why can't you see what's right in front of you?"

"Alec," she said, tears clogging her voice. "It's not going to happen between us. I can't give you kids. I can't give you what every other guy at Reed Security has. That'll never be the life you'll have with me."

"And what if I don't care? You didn't even bother to fucking ask me. You lied to me for over a year. You made me think that you didn't love me."

"I don't," she said harshly. "For some reason, even though I keep telling you that, you just don't believe me. I don't know what I can do to prove that to you."

"You can stop looking at me like I'm your whole fucking world. Do you think that I don't see you staring at me? Do you think that I don't feel you snuggling up to me at night and holding on tight? You can lie to me all you want, but eventually, you'll have to admit it to yourself."

Her eyes dropped and she turned away.

"So, that's it. It's over because you say so and I don't get a choice in the matter?"

"If I could make this right, I would. But I can't and I don't want to keep fighting over this. I just want to be on my own for a while, without the pressure of..."

"Of what?"

"Of life," she shouted. "I can't do this anymore. I just need some time to sort through this, and I can't do that with you constantly pressuring me!"

"No fucking problem. You want space? I'll give you all the fucking space you want."

I walked out the door and that was it. The pressure in my chest caved and I fucking broke. Because the woman I loved was hurting, but she didn't want me to help heal her. She didn't want anything to do with me.

"Dude, how long are you gonna beat the shit out of that bag?"

Sweat poured down my face, but I wasn't even close to being exhausted. I hadn't been able to sleep in weeks. Ever since Florrie kicked me out of her life, I was a fucking mess. I spent most of my time in the gym, and when I wasn't in the gym, I was drinking until I passed out.

I hadn't seen her since that day. As far as I knew, she was doing okay. I had gone to see her the next day because I just couldn't manage to stay away, but Lola had been coming out of her room. She suggested that I give Florrie space to figure shit out. In other words, stay the fuck away until Florrie was ready to talk.

"This isn't good for you," Craig said from behind me. "See, this is why you don't get involved with women. You're here, beating the shit out of a bag, and from what I can tell, she's the one that fucked up."

I turned around and wiped the sweat from my face. "Look, I get that you want to be here for me and everything, but I really don't need it."

"You know, I'm your friend too. And after you and Florrie snuck around behind my back for the past year, the least you could do is allow me to help when you need it."

"Seriously? You sound like a chick right now."

"Well, maybe my feelings are hurt."

I sighed and took off my gloves. "Fine. What do you want to talk about?"

"I actually want to take you out, you know, get your mind off things."

"Fine. Let me shower and I'll meet you out front in twenty."

He grinned and smacked me on the shoulder. "I'll grab a few of the guys to go with us."

I showered quickly and got dressed. Hopefully we were going to a bar. If not, a strip club would do. Anything to not feel like such a pussy right now.

"Hey," I said as I approached Craig. No one else was around. "I thought you said you were getting more guys."

"Cap is coming and so is Ryan."

"Ryan?"

Craig shrugged. "The guy is here with women all day. I figured if anyone needed a day out, it was him."

I nodded. It made sense. And I liked Ryan, but I didn't really know him that well. Hunter came walking up with Knight, which shocked the hell out of me.

"Whoa, I thought you said we were going for a beer," Knight said to Hunter.

"Suck it up. You can hang out with the rest of us for one fucking day."

"You're lucky that I need to get out of here. I'm starting to feel like my sanctuary is being taken over. It makes my skin crawl."

"Tough shit," Cap said, walking up to us and slapping me on the back. Yeah, it was the man slap, the one that said, *sorry your life is so fucked up right now. I'm here to drink with you.* "Let's hit the road. Maggie's on my ass about hanging out with the kids, but I told her that you were feeling pretty low and needed some cheering up, so she let me go out."

"She let you go out?" I laughed. "That woman has you by the balls."

"Says the man that's been drinking himself into a stupor every night," Cap retorted. "So, where are we going?"

Craig grinned. "I found a place a few weeks back. It's just what we need for today."

"Please tell me there are women," I begged. "I'd give anything to see any woman on her knees for me today."

"Whoa, I thought you were just giving Florrie space," Cap said. "Now you're going out to get pussy?"

"I'm not talking about touching. I just want to see a woman, maybe dancing for me, and imagine that she actually likes me. I've forgotten what it's like to have a woman look at me with something other than hate."

"Florrie doesn't hate you," Hunter chastised. "She just needs space. See, women, especially strong ones like Florrie, need time to process shit, just like us."

"Well, thank you, Freud. I'm so glad I had you to explain that shit to me." I turned to Craig, a little irritated now that he had invited everyone else out. "So, are we going to see women or not?"

"Trust me," he grinned, "there will definitely be women on their knees for you."

"This is a strip mall," I pointed out.

Craig rubbed his hand along the back of his neck and grimaced. "Now, don't say no. This is just what you need."

"What is just what I need?" I said warily.

"Just come inside and see. I've had the place cleared out just for us. I swear, this is gonna change your life."

I looked at the other guys and they looked just as wary as I did.

"Let's get this over with," Cap said, pushing past me and through the door where he stopped dead in his tracks. "What the fuck? Hell no. You may be into this shit, but I'm not. This is not happening."

"What?" I walked in and stopped. "Hell no. Why the fuck would you bring me here?"

"You need this. This is amazing."

"What the hell is wrong with you?" Cap asked Craig. "What in the world would make you think that any of us would want to take part in this? We have reputations to uphold."

"I actually think this is a great idea," Hunter chimed in. "I could use a little spa treatment."

"Of course you would," I grumbled. "You wax."

"And I'm not afraid to admit that's true. Now," he said rubbing his hands together. "Where do we get started?"

Craig walked up to the counter and grinned at the woman. "We're the Devereux party, here for the full day spa treatment."

"All day? What the fuck? I thought we would just be in and out," Ryan said. Then he turned to Cap. "What the fuck do you guys get into? I thought you were all masculine and shit, but waxing and spa treatments?"

"Don't worry, guys," Craig said excitedly. "I've got beer and pretzels for us, and they've got a big sandwich bar for us halfway through."

"No," Knight said angrily. "I'm not doing this shit. You said beer," he accused Hunter. "You said hanging out with the guys. You didn't say shit about fucking spa treatments."

"Would you relax?" Hunter sighed. "It's not that fucking bad. We'll probably get a massage and just relax today. It'll be fine."

"Isn't that what the woman that waxed you the first time said?" Cap asked.

"Alright, gentlemen. If you'll follow me, we'll get started. Now, are you all wearing underwear that can get dirty?"

I looked at the other guys. What the fuck was going on here?

"It's just that we'll be giving you a full body mask and your underwear might get the mask on it. It's not easily cleaned out of clothing. If not, we have disposable underwear, which would probably be for the best because if you're not wearing briefs, we won't be able to do the whole mask."

"Whoa, you want us to wear pasties or some shit?" I asked. The lady smiled and walked away. "What the fuck was that? What does that mean? Craig, what the fuck did you get us into?"

"Gentlemen?" the lady said, quirking her finger at us.

I followed, even though I knew I shouldn't, but there was a

commotion and when I turned around to see what it was, I saw Knight fighting to get out.

"No, I'm not fucking going in there. You can't make me!"

"You'll go in there or I'll tell all the guys about that time with Wakefield."

Knight froze and jerked his hands down, pulling his jacket straight. "Fine," he bit out.

"Wait, what's Wakefield. I think we should hear this story," I said, but Knight just pushed past me. "Oh come on! You can't tease us like that!"

Chapter Twenty-Two

REED SECURITY

Knight

"Here's some underwear to change into. We're going to do a mask on your entire body that will leave you feeling refreshed and recharged."

Her grin was too fucking wide and her happy demeanor was just too fucking much for me. People shouldn't be that happy. Especially not at work. Well, unless they had my job and got to beat the shit out of people.

The lady walked out of the room and I quickly changed, feeling like a fucking fruitcake when I pulled up the faux underwear. I got on the table and pulled the sheet over me. This was so fucking weird. I couldn't believe I was doing this, but there was no way I was letting Hunter tell everyone the story about Wakefield.

"Are we all set here?"

"Sure."

"Oh, someone's grumpy today."

She walked around the room, heating up shit and flicking switches. I watched her like a hawk. "This is my everyday mood."

"Hmmm. Well, by the time you're done here, you'll be ready to put that smile on your face and you'll be laughing and happy."

"Obviously you don't know me."

"Oh, turn that frown upside down." And then she fucking giggled. I was ready to pull my gun out right then and shoot her.

"Alright. I'm going to apply a mask to your body that will leave you feeling completely refreshed! Then, we'll let that soak in and do some other fun things."

"Fucking fantastic."

She started spreading what looked like mud all over my body. At first, I watched her every move. I didn't fucking trust her. But then I started to relax when the warmth of the mud spread over me. This really wasn't too bad.

"I'm going to give you a scalp massage. Just relax into it."

I let my eyes drift closed. She was right. The scalp massage really was helping me relax. I'd have to look into hiring a full time masseuse for Reed Security. I must have drifted off because the next thing I felt was pain being ripped from my body by my dick. I shot upright, reaching to the table on my right side where my gun was lying. I grabbed it and pointed it at the woman that was holding a strip of some kind. I squinted, shaking the sleep from my eyes and looked closer. There was hair on the strip. My fucking hair. Looking down quickly, I saw that I was missing a whole fucking strip of hair from my groin.

"What the fuck did you do?" I shouted at her.

"They told me that you needed this, but to wait until you were really relaxed. I thought...did I not do it right?"

"Do what right? Who the fuck told you to do this?"

The door burst open and Pappy walked in, staring at me covered in mud and my dick blowing in the wind.

"When the fuck did you take off my panties?"

"Panties?" Hunter snorted in laughter.

"That underwear shit. When did you do it?" I shouted, still pointing the gun at her.

"I'm sorry," she cried. "He told me to do it. I thought you wanted it."

I swung the gun in Pappy's direction. "You told her to wax me?"

"It's all good, man. It was just some fun. You know, to get you to loosen up."

"Were you fucking relaxed when they ripped the hairs from your body? What the fuck?"

"Hey, I've been laying around for the last few months recovering. I needed something to laugh at. Surely you can understand."

"Surely you can understand that I'm gonna put another fucking bullet in you now!"

"Don't call me Shirley," he grinned. "See? Isn't this fun?"

I growled at him and his smile dropped. The woman ran out of the room, crying and practically in hysterics.

"You didn't have to point a gun at her."

"You're lucky I didn't shoot her. What the fuck were you thinking, sending her in here to do that. You had to know how I would react."

"Fine, maybe it wasn't the smartest idea, but I wanted you to loosen up a little. You're so tense."

"How the fuck do I get all this shit off me?"

"Hold on, I'll go ask her to come back."

Pappy walked out of the room and I snatched a towel, tying it around my waist. This was a fucking nightmare. I'd never make the mistake of coming out with him again.

"She says she won't come back in," Pappy said, walking back into the room with a bottle of something.

"Make her. Point a gun at her and make her get back in here."

He cringed. "Yeah, she took off. She's not coming back. But hey, she gave me the solution and told me how to get it off you."

I glared at him and he shrugged. "It's me or no one. That mud's gonna get awfully uncomfortable when it completely dries."

"Fine," I bit out. "But you don't tell anyone about this."

"Just like Wakefield. My lips are sealed."

"They better fucking be."

I laid back down on the table while Hunter got to work. It was fucking uncomfortable. I took over for him where I could, but I couldn't reach all the different areas effectively. I was rolled over on my stomach and he was wiping down my upper thighs when the door swung open. Cap ducked his head and turned to go, murmuring that he was sorry, but then stopped and looked back in the room.

He shook his head. "I knew this was going to happen. Knight, I expected more from you."

"I expected not to get my dick waxed, but shit happens," I snapped.

He nodded and turned back for the door, but then stopped. "You're not gonna tip him, are you?"

I pulled my gun and he slammed the door just as my bullets hit the wood.

Ryan

I had seen some weird shit in my time. Hell, I had done some weird shit. There was the time that we all got shit faced and the women painted our nails as payback. That wasn't exactly the most pleasant experience, but not the worst either. Hanging out with the women day in and day out was definitely a transition for me. I was used to seeing my friends, going out to The Pub for a beer and just bitching about our lives. And poker night, that was the thing I missed the most. These guys played Go Fish, but still called it poker. It was fucking weird.

I didn't regret being with Lola. Not for one second. But I was beginning to wonder about the guys she worked with. Plus, I saw a new side to Sebastian that I hadn't seen before. Sebastian was one tough bastard, which I knew all along, but now I was seeing it up close and personal. I had been there when he was in work mode, getting us all transported to Knight's house. He was another scary bastard, but for some reason, was super nice to me. Maybe it was because of Lola. She had told me that he really helped her with her PTSD issues.

Yet, here I was, on the run with my kickass wife and her crazy work crew, but we were getting a fucking spa day. When Sebastian told me we were going to hang out with the guys, I practically pissed myself in excitement. I pictured lots of alcohol, a pool table, and maybe some hot wings. But I was sitting in a chair after having a mud treatment, and I was getting a fucking pedicure.

"This wasn't really what I had in mind when you said we were gonna hang out with the guys."

Sebastian turned to me with the same irritated expression. "Trust me, pedicures wasn't on my list of fun things to do. Not to mention seeing one guy wipe another guy down," he muttered to himself.

"What's that?"

"Nothing. Forget I said anything."

"How long does it look like we'll be..." I looked down at the lady washing my feet and then back to Sebastian. "Gone?"

He sighed and leaned back and sighed. "I have no fucking clue. We're falling apart here."

"So, this is what you guys do to bond and shit? How you get back on track?"

"Not exactly the idea of male bonding you had in mind, is it?"

"Even Lola doesn't do this shit. It's weird."

Alec and Craig walked in and sat down in their own seats. "See? Isn't this relaxing?" Craig asked.

"Craig, I'm sitting here, in a fucking spa chair, with mud stuck in places that I don't want to even mention. No, this isn't fucking relaxing," Alec bit out.

"You know, after all the shit I put up with since finding out about you and Florrie, the least you could do is pretend to enjoy this day that I've put together for you."

A woman walked into the room with a tray of drinks and handed one to Craig. When she walked over to me, I grimaced. "I thought you said beer? What the hell is this?"

"It's a Sex on the Beach," the woman supplied.

"Great. I'm sitting around, drinking Sex on the Beach with a bunch of guys as I get my feet pampered," Alec growled. "Fucking fantastic."

"Well, I'm enjoying this. Doesn't your skin feel softer?" Craig asked.

"I guess," Alec grumbled.

"You know," I leaned closer to them and lowered my voice. I wasn't proud to admit this. "I'm actually surprised at how much softer my elbows and knees are. I get dry patches, but this stuff just worked all that shit out."

"Forget your elbows," Sebastian scoffed. "Did you get the scalp massage? I never knew a woman's hands could do that shit."

"The hot stone therapy was pretty good," Alec admitted. "But I'll fucking shoot anyone that repeats that."

"Whoa," I said, pushing up in my chair as the woman at my feet pulled out a pair of scissors. "What the fuck do you think you're doing with those?"

"Sir, you have the start of an ingrown toenail and the skin around your toes is rough and needs to be removed. I promise, you'll feel better when I'm done."

"Trust her," Craig grinned. "I'm telling you, it'll change your life."

"Fine." I sat back and watched in fascination as she scraped away what looked like years of dirt and dead skin and a ton of other shit. It was amazing. I didn't even know it was there. "My toe doesn't hurt anymore," I said in wonderment. "It's amazing."

"Told you it would change your life," Craig smirked.

"What else do you have?"

"Well, the package was only for–"

"I'll pay anything. Show me whatcha got."

"Well, we have an ultimate healing pedicure. We combine oils and a hint of vanilla to revitalize your feet. That would probably be our ultimate package. Then there's also a foot massage and we also have manicure options."

I looked at my hands in confusion. "What exactly would you do to my hands?"

"We have a dip, well, it's basically hot wax. But when you peel it off, your hands will feel completely different."

"You want me to willingly dip my hands in hot wax."

"You're a big, tough guy. I'm sure you could handle it," she grinned. And not wanting to look like a pussy in front of all the other badass guys from Reed Security, I agreed.

"If I'm doing it, so are the rest of them."

Alec actually growled at me, but then he shoved his hand in the wax and waited for it to dry.

"Wow," Hunter grinned. "This is amazing. My hands are so smooth."

"It's like a baby's bottom," I said in awe. "Not that I caress babies bottoms," I quickly added.

Knight groaned from the chair at the end and I looked down. The woman at his feet was massaging the bottoms of his feet. It looked awesome.

"Just wait," my lady grinned. "You'll get that too."

"Another Sex on the Beach?" the woman handing out drinks asked.

"Yeah," I said, eagerly taking the drink. "You know, it's not bad. It's a nice change from the bitter taste of beer. I think I like this."

"But only here," Craig stressed. "You don't ever get this shit in front of a woman."

"Of course." Because, what sane guy would drink a frou-frou drink in front of a woman they were sleeping with, married or not.

"Can you do something about my cuticles?" Sebastian asked his lady. "They feel like they're getting too long."

"Yes, I'll trim them when I start your manicure."

I stared at him in shock. He looked like he was actually enjoying himself. Which, if I was being honest with myself, I was too. There was something to be said for pampering yourself. But then he turned to me with a glare.

"Friend or not, I'll put a bullet in you if you tell anyone about this."

Craig

"Now that I have you where I want you, how about you tell me what the fuck is going on with you and Florrie."

He sighed and shifted his hand as the woman started on his manicure. "What do you want me to say? We started fucking one day and then I fell in love with her."

"And what about her?"

"Let's just say she was more interested in keeping our relationship private. She doesn't love me, or so she says."

"Okay, I know I've only known for a little while, but I've seen the way she looks at you. I always thought she had a thing for you, I just didn't know you were fucking her."

He laughed and looked over at me. "There were so many times that we were fucking with you in the other room."

"Really? Like when?"

"The Carson job, the twins job, the gala in Chicago-"

"Wait. The gala?" Something niggled at the back of my brain. "You were the couple in the bathroom?"

He chuckled slightly. "Not my proudest moment, but you saw the dress she was wearing. I was hard most of the night. It was embarrassing."

"Oh my God! The cruise. That wasn't Marco and his mistress, was it?"

He threw his head back in laughter. "He wanted to switch rooms. He didn't like the view. So, Florrie and I took advantage."

"I was in the next fucking room. The pictures fell off the walls. I heard things that scarred me for life!"

"And then Marco decided he'd rather have the shitty view than the shitty room and we switched back."

"And that's why I never fucking knew."

He shrugged. "It worked out for the best."

I sat there in astonishment. I couldn't believe all the times that they had fucked when I was there. And then something crossed my mind. "Please tell me that wasn't you two..." I closed my eyes and said a quick prayer.

"In the Caribbean? Yeah, that was a good time."

This was so bad. I had heard them and it had fucking turned me on. I had dreams about that night. Hell, I had jacked off along with them because it was so fucking hot.

"I'm never speaking to you again. We'll have to switch teams or something."

"Oh, come on. All over a little innocent fucking?"

"You don't get it. I heard that shit. I can't just unhear it and then go on working with you."

"Don't be a pussy. It's sex. You've had it and you will in the future."

"Yeah, but..." There was nothing more I could say without giving myself away, so I kept my mouth shut. "So, what are you gonna do about Florrie?"

"Hell if I know."

"But, you two are gonna get back together, right?"

"Honestly?" He sighed and then held out his hand to look at the job the woman had done. Then he lifted it to his mouth and blew on his finger nails. Fucking weirdo. "I'm not sure that we can make it work."

"She'll come around."

"It's not just her. She lied to me for a fucking year. She left out some pretty major shit that affected me. I don't know how we come back from that. And even after she came home from the hospital, I tried to talk to her, but she didn't want to talk to me or admit that what she did was fucking selfish."

"So, this is the end?"

"I don't know. The more distance I get from the situation, I think maybe she was right. Maybe it was never going to work between us."

I sat there and thought about it for a minute. I didn't want them to break up. I could see that they were good for each other, but Alec had a point. On the other hand, if they kept fucking, there were way too many chances that I was going to get caught up in it.

"Just do me a favor, if you're going to have hate sex or whatever, make sure I'm not around."

Cap

I groaned and leaned back in the chair. "Oh, this so much better than sex."

"Really?" Ryan asked from beside me. "Things getting a little stale?"

"No, but Maggie's not exactly giving it right now. She's still pissed about the last time I knocked her up." I scoffed and thought about all the shit I had to deal with right now. "She actually hid knives in the diaper bag. We took Gunner in for a check up and I had to explain why the fuck she had knives with the baby bottle."

"It could be worse," Ryan shrugged. "When Lola and I took James off to college, she set an unlabeled bottle on his desk in front of his roommate. She told James that if anyone was bothering him, just to slip them one of those pills and call her to come collect the body."

"You're joking," I laughed.

"Dead fucking serious. I thought his roommate was gonna shit his pants," he laughed.

"What was in the bottle?"

"Tylenol."

I sat there laughing with Ryan, just like old times. Except, now we weren't just friends. He was a part of the Reed Security family, and that meant he was in on how the crazy worked.

"So, how's Maggie gonna react when she realizes that you went for a spa day when she was at home with the kids?"

"Oh, I'm gonna pay for this. The only way I'll get out of this is if we bring Alec back home, drunk and unable to hold himself up."

"Well, the way he's pounding those Sex on the Beach drinks, that's entirely possible."

"I gotta tell you, I didn't think I would like this. But it's very relaxing. We should take a day every month and do something like this. You know, treat ourselves. We deserve it."

"Yeah, I could see that going over really well with the ladies. We'll be off getting our hair done, while you tell them that it's too dangerous to leave Knight's house."

"It is. For them. Maggie attracts trouble wherever she goes. I swear, she could just be walking down the street, and suddenly it's like she's in a backyard brawl."

"That's because you don't have a hold on your woman."

I snorted and shook my head. "You know that Lola has you by the balls, right? I mean, let's face it. If anyone is protecting anyone, it's her protecting you. You'd be curled up in the corner while she was off shooting all the bad guys and snapping their necks."

"I'm man enough to admit that's true. I know my weakness, and strength is my weakness."

"So, what attracts her to you?"

"Sex. I may be a pansy-assed wimp, but I can fuck her better than anyone. And that includes Hunter." Ryan looked past me to Hunter, who was talking with Knight. "She doesn't think that I know about them, but I'm not stupid."

"Then how do you know that you're better in bed?"

"I did the test," he said like I was stupid.

"What test?"

"You know, the one where you ask about previous lovers."

I shifted in my chair so I could get a better look at him. "Okay, I don't know about this test, but I'm curious. Tell me how this works."

He smirked at me. "Gonna use it on Maggie?"

"No need," I shook my head. "I just keep getting her pregnant. That's my strategy. She can't leave me if she's always knocked up."

"You're gonna end up dead."

"I'll take my chances."

"Alright, so the test is that you casually ask about her worst sexual experience."

"That's easy. It's usually the first time."

"Well, yeah, but then, you ask about her best. If the answer isn't immediately you, you're fucked."

I stared at him in confusion. "That doesn't mean jack shit. How do you know she's not lying?"

"Well....because she's not."

"Ryan, I hate to tell you this, but if she immediately says you, it's not you."

"How do you figure?"

"Come on, man. If she's that quick to respond, it's because it's an automated response."

"So, I'm a pity choice?"

I shrugged.

"You mean, he was better than me?"

The poor fucker, he was completely clueless. "I'm not saying that he was for sure, but it's not looking too good for you right now." He slumped back in his seat, looking depressed as hell. "Hey, if it makes you feel any better, she chose you."

"Well, that makes me feel a fuck ton better. I'm not the best she's ever had, but hell, at least I'm a good, stable guy to settle down with." He snapped at the woman walking around with drinks. "Get me another Sex on the Beach!" He snatched it out of her hand and scoffed. "Probably the only sex on the beach I'll ever get."

Shit, this wasn't the response I was thinking I would get. Now I felt like shit. "Ryan, it doesn't mean she prefers him. It's just a stupid theory. I'm probably wrong. You were probably right in your assessment. What the fuck do I know? Hell, I called Maggie fat when she was pregnant. I'm the last person in the world that should be handing out advice."

He sniffled and he actually looked like he might cry. I couldn't handle him crying. "So, I'm not a pity choice?"

"Hell no."

"And she does like fucking me?"

"Do you have sex at least once a week?"

"At least three times."

"Trust me, she likes fucking you."

"And I'm the best sex she's ever had?"

I rolled my eyes, but played along. Anything to get off this subject. "More than she can take. You're probably her Goliath."

"I'm not sure if that's a good thing," he said.

"I'm not either, but I'm hoping it's enough to end this uncomfortable line of questioning."

He raised an eyebrow at me. "I want to hear you say it."

"Say what?"

"I want to hear you say that I'm better in bed than Hunter."

"What? Why the fuck would I say that? And how the hell would I know?"

"Please? Do it for me, man. I'm feeling low. Please tell me that Lola isn't with me out of pity because of my dead wife."

I narrowed my eyes at him. "That's fucking low."

He sighed and took a sip of his drink. "I suppose I could just ask her myself if she only wants me because she pities me. I might need somewhere to stay for a few days. She might not react too well to that question." He looked at me, blinking his eyes like a fucking puppy dog.

"Fine," I growled. "You're better in bed than Hunter."

"Can you say it with more confidence. I'm not feeling it."

"You're a better fuck than Hunter," I said again.

"It just feels like you're saying that to shut me up now."

"You're a better fucking lay than Hunter," I shouted.

The talking stopped all around me and Ryan burst out laughing. The rest of the guys were staring at me and Hunter was looking at me strangely. "He fucking made me do it," I said, pointing at Ryan.

"Do we want to know how you know that Ryan is better in bed than Hunter?" Alec asked.

"Fuck off," I said, standing up from my foot bath and sloshing water all over the floor.

Hunter

"Okay, boys. We're going to give you your facials now while you relax into the last part of your pedicure."

My woman stood behind me and applied a lavender mask to my face, giving me cucumbers to put over my eyes. I sighed and relaxed back into the seat. This was the most relaxed I had been since getting out of the fucking hospital. Lucy had been riding my ass every chance she got. I just needed some downtime that didn't include being lectured about what I was doing.

I felt something wiggling between my toes and I peeled off one of the cucumbers. "What are you doing?"

The woman was putting a white thing with toe spreaders on my feet. "I'm applying a nail cream to your toes. It'll help revitalize and strengthen the nails."

"Is it going to stay on or does it soak in?"

"It'll soak in," she said hesitantly.

"But will it go away?"

"Well, you'll be able to tell that it's on there, but I swear, it's good for the health of your nails."

"You're putting fucking nail polish on me. Just say that."

"It's not nail polish. It's a-"

"Yeah, whatever." I replaced the cucumber and dozed as she finished applying the 'cream' to my nails. Screaming from the front had me jumping up in my chair. I tightened the belt on my robe and stood quickly, moving as fast as I could with fucking toe spreaders on. The other guys were right along beside me, masks and all, as we headed up front with our guns drawn. We rounded the corner and skidded to a halt.

"I fucking knew it!" Maggie said, holding her hands up in victory.

"How did you know where we were?" Cap asked.

Kate held up her phone. "You know that tracker that Knight insisted on injecting into his family? Well, I might have knocked him out one night and inserted one in him."

"You did what?" Knight growled. I stepped back, hoping to slip from the room, but I wasn't fast enough.

"Hunter helped me," Kate grinned. Knight turned on me and swung, his fist connecting with the mask on my face.

"Hey, that wasn't done drying yet," I said indignantly.

"Really? Sorry about that." And then he swung again and we were on the ground, wrestling in our bathrobes. I felt the toe spreader come out of one foot and then the other.

"Hey, asshole. You're messing up the cream on my toes."

"It's fucking nail polish," Knight growled.

"What?" Alec said in outrage. "She told me it was a special cream!"

"It's fucking nail polish," I heard Cap say.

"Don't you dare take any pictures," Craig said. "You're going to ruin our sanctuary."

"But that's such a nice picture of Hunter's ass," Maggie said with a smile in her voice.

"Garrick Knight," Kate reprimanded. "What is that under your robe? Did you...did you wax?"

Knight jumped off me and straightened his bathrobe. "It's not what you think. I was waxed against my will."

"By who?"

"Hunter," he snarled.

"Hunter waxed you?" Kate asked in shock.

"Not him personally, but-"

"Wait, you let another woman touch you there?"

"It would have been better if it was Hunter?"

"He's your best friend," she said incredulously. "Of course it would have been better."

"Whoa, let's not get any ideas here. It wasn't like I wanted to wipe the mud from his body or anything," I said, trying to ease the tension in the room.

"You did what?" Ryan asked.

"Besides, it's not like I let anyone stare at my wax job or touch my dick to make it fit in a thong. Let's face it, this is not the strangest thing you've ever heard."

"This isn't the first time you've done this sort of thing?" one of the ladies that ran the spa asked.

"Professionally, it is," I answered.

"So, you just go around waxing and doing things to each other? For fun?"

I stared at the other guys, but I was alone on this one. They hadn't been in on any of these shenanigans before.

"I don't know how this shit happens. One minute, we're just discussing your basic grooming shit, and the next, someone's dick is out and waxing is happening. Shit happens, right?"

Ryan shook his head and snatched a towel, wiping the mask from his face. "This is the last time I go anywhere with you guys. Next thing, you're going to tell me that you all sit around and pretend that you're superheroes."

Cap leaned in close and cleared his throat before lowering his voice. "It was just the one time for a wedding.

Ryan rolled his eyes. "I should have fucking known."

Chapter Twenty-Three

FLORRIE

Alec walked back through the door after his day out with the guys. I had planned to talk with him today, but when I went looking for him, he was already gone. He looked like he had been drinking, but then, he was doing a lot of that lately.

"Alec, can I talk to you?"

"Is it about us?"

I nodded, smiling, letting him know that I was finally ready to put this behind us.

"Too fucking bad. I don't want to talk."

"What? But I thought–" Something caught my eye and I leaned in closer to look at his face. "Do you have something purple on your face?"

"It's alien blood. Yeah, I went and slaughtered me some aliens today."

"Don't aliens have green blood?"

"Does it fucking matter?" he shouted.

"Well, I just think it's really weird that you come home shitfaced and you're telling me you fought aliens that have purple blood."

"Lady, what I do isn't your business anymore. You threw me out of your life, remember? I'm not good enough to know your deepest, darkest secrets, then you're not good enough to know about the aliens I slaughtered."

I quirked an eyebrow at him. "That doesn't even make sense."

"Well..." He looked off in the distance and swayed on his feet slightly. "You broke my fucking heart. So suck it!"

He stumbled past me and I put a hand out to stop Craig. "What the hell did you guys do? Why does he have purple shit on him?"

"I'll never tell. What happens in Little Springs stays in Little Springs."

"They went to a spa," Maggie said as she walked past.

I crossed my arms over my chest and stared Craig down. "It was one of the best days of my life."

"Really?"

"Dead serious." He looked off in the distance fondly. "Best bonding experience of my life."

"I thought we weren't saying shit about what happened today?" Cap grumbled. "None of you can hold your fucking liquor."

Knight stalked by, a scowl worse than any I had seen before on his face. "Training tomorrow, and that goes for you too, Florrie. This is your fucking fault. I expect you in the training center at seven in the morning."

"But I haven't been cleared for training yet," I shouted after him. He turned around slowly and glared at me. "I've had my dick waxed. I've had a tracker implanted in me. I've had fucking mud stuck in places that I won't tell any lady. If I say you're going to start training tomorrow, you'll get your ass there or I'll drag you out of bed myself. Are we clear?"

I wanted to laugh at him, but I was pretty sure that wouldn't help the situation. Besides, getting a wax was never fun. He'd probably be grouchy for a few days. Sometimes it was best not to poke the bear.

"Fine." He turned to walk away, but stopped. "And have an actual conversation with Alec this time. He needs to get his head on straight, and he can't do that when you're jerking him around."

It wasn't as bad as I thought it would be. Knight pushed me hard, but it was all within the guidelines of what my doctor was comfortable with. Now that I had showered, I needed to find Alec. I had a feeling that I had hurt him more than I had ever imagined, but I would make it right. Or, at least, I would try.

Shaking off my nerves, I knocked on his door and waited for him to answer. When he pulled the door open, he looked more pulled together, more in control of his emotions than he was yesterday. He leaned lazily against the door, like he was telling me he didn't give a fuck about what was going on.

"I was wondering if we could talk."

He pulled the door open wider and motioned for me to enter. He was acting pretty cold and distant, and I supposed I deserved that. I wasn't sure if I should sit down. Even though he let me in, he wasn't acting all that welcoming right now.

"You wanted to talk, so talk," he practically snapped at me.

"I wanted to talk about what happened. With what you found out..."

"You mean when I had to rush you off to the hospital because you were bleeding out all over the fucking place because you have a disease I didn't know about. The same disease that prevented you from having our baby. The same disease that almost took you from me and I didn't have a fucking clue."

I cleared my throat uncomfortably. "Yes, that one."

"So, what more is there to talk about? It's all pretty fucking clear now why you pushed me away. I know now, so what more is there to say?"

God, it was like he was reading my mind. Only, in my head, I was going to delicately broach the subject and then explain to him my reasons. But he seemed to have gotten the gist of it.

"When I found out, I didn't think our relationship was going anywhere anyway. It just seemed like-"

"Don't you dare fucking patronize me. You fucking well knew that I loved you. I told you. So, don't act like I was pretending like we were just fucking."

"You're right. *I* was assuming that it wasn't going anywhere. I know you told me you loved me, but in my mind, that was never on the table between us."

"So, it was perfectly okay for you to hide something that important from me. Because we were never *supposed* to be more in *your* mind, it was okay to continue fucking me when you knew that you would never try for more with me."

I narrowed my eyes at him in anger. I could be accused of a lot of things, but I had always been honest with him. "Don't act like I led you on. I told you that I wasn't in love with you. I told you that I didn't want more. You're the one that told me you would take whatever you could get. You led yourself on."

"I suppose that makes it all better, right?"

I sighed in frustration. This wasn't going to get us anywhere. "Look, I get that you feel I wronged you in some way. I hate that you found out the way you did, and I'm sorry about the baby-"

"The baby is just the icing on the cake, Florrie. It was never meant to be, and I've accepted that. My problem is that you didn't trust me. Craig and I were there with you at the hospital when you first found out. We would have been there for you, to support you. I was sleeping with you! No matter what you thought we had together, did you really think so little of us that you assumed you couldn't talk to me?"

"It had nothing to do with you. It was my life, my decision."

"And I just didn't factor in."

"Look, that's not what I'm trying to say. Do you know what it's like to find out that you can't do the one thing that you're supposed to be able to as a woman? Imagine if you were sterile and couldn't get a woman pregnant. How would that make you feel?"

He stood there glaring at me.

"I knew how you felt about me, and since I didn't feel the same, I didn't think there was any point in having the conversation. I knew we were never going to get married and have that life. And-"

"Would you just shut the fuck up?" he shouted. "Do you even hear yourself? You keep making excuses why things wouldn't work out. You decided for me. You didn't explain why you didn't want to try a relationship. I would have at least fucking understood you better if you had told me. You can lie to yourself all you want, but don't fucking lie to me. After all that's happened, I don't deserve any more of your lies."

He was right. I had been thinking this way for so long that I didn't even really know what the truth was anymore. The truth was wrapped up inside me in a box where I couldn't actually feel anything. And since this was over anyway, he did deserve the truth. It was the least I could give him.

"The truth is that I didn't want to love you. I didn't want to feel so consumed by a man that it took over my life. I didn't want to worry that one day you would want me to leave my job to start a family. Lola gave up everything for Ryan, and maybe that worked for them, but I'm not Lola. Maybe someday I would have wanted kids, but I didn't want to feel pressured to make that decision prematurely. I wanted to make it for myself, and frankly, you're too overbearing. You push in and demand your own way, with no regard for my thoughts or feelings. You were treating me like I didn't know how to take care of myself and it was interfering with our work. So, when I found out that I couldn't have kids, that seemed to end any kind of relationship we could have had. Whether you want to believe it or not, having that option taken away is a punch to the gut. Even if you had been fine with it, it would have changed our relationship in some way. So, yes, I figured it was easier my way, and I took control of my life and went with it."

"And the baby? When were you going to tell me about that?" he snapped.

"I had just found out that day. I was coming to tell you. I thought... I thought that maybe things could be different. I thought that maybe we could have the relationship that you wanted."

"So, let me get this straight, you were finally willing to have a relationship, because you were pregnant, but the moment you lost that baby, I just wasn't good enough for you anymore."

"That's not what I said."

"No, but you sure did push me out the door, didn't you? It fucking amazes me how your warped mind works. I would have fucking been there for you in any way. If you didn't want kids, that would have been fine with me. I wouldn't have tried to push you into that. Frankly, I never even fucking wanted kids. If you had decided you wanted them,

I would have gone along with it. I wanted you, Florrie. You're all I've ever wanted. But I can't be with someone that takes every option out of my hands. I can't be with someone who would lie to me for a fucking year because it was for my own good."

"I'm not asking you to," I said quietly.

He laughed for just a moment and stepped back. "Wow. You're still controlling everything. Here I am, thinking I'm giving you the fuck off speech and you're already out the door. I guess you were right, we never would have worked. I was prepared to give you everything, and you were prepared to give me nothing." He nodded and walked to the door, opening it for me. "Just remember," he said as I stepped outside his door, "it's gonna get awfully fucking lonely up there on your perch. Don't come asking me for a friendly fuck. It ain't gonna happen."

Then he slammed the door in my face and I stood there staring at the door like a fucking idiot. I had done it. I had successfully cleared the air between us. I had what I wanted. I was no longer restricted by what I thought Alec wanted or what might happen between us. I had my wish. So, why did it feel like the biggest mistake of my life?

Chapter Twenty-Four

ALEC

"So, that's it?" Craig asked next to me. We had gone to town for a supply run and we were driving back to Knight's compound.

"What's it?"

"You and Florrie. It's been weeks and you still haven't forgiven each other."

"You mean, I haven't forgiven her. I'm not sure she has anything to forgive me for."

"Well, you did-"

"I did what?" I snapped. "Please tell me how any of this is my fault. Maybe then I would understand how her lying to me for a fucking year could be blamed on me. Or how she didn't want to see me after she lost the baby. Yeah, I could definitely see that as being my fault."

"I'm just saying that you take over and push her around. I mean, looking back on the time that you two were screwing around behind my back, I knew you were acting differently toward her. You were so protective of her and you acted like an ass to her. It was like you didn't trust her."

"Of course, I fucking trusted her."

"Really? Because you did handcuff her to a bed for doing her fucking job. I mean, had I been in her position during that mission, I would have done the same fucking thing. And I'm pretty sure you wouldn't have chained me to the bed."

I glared at him.

"Okay, maybe I'm wrong, in which case, that would have made things really fucking awkward between us."

"Look, I loved her. I wanted to take care of her. Maybe I did get a little out of control with her, but I couldn't help myself. When I was around her and she was in danger, I wanted to burn the whole fucking world and anyone that tried to take her from me."

"But she doesn't need that from you. She's always been able to take care of herself." He continued talking, but I wasn't listening anymore. Up ahead, there was Florrie, running along the side of the road. I pulled out the scope from the backseat and zoomed in on her. Yep, just as I thought. She was running with both earbuds in, and knowing Florrie, the music was blaring. It was so fucking unsafe. Someone could attack her and she would never know. She would be long gone before anyone knew she was missing.

"Pull over," I snapped at Craig.

"Why?"

"Just do it."

He pulled over and I opened the door. "What the fuck are you doing?" Craig asked.

"I'm going to teach her a lesson. Do you see her? She's gonna get herself killed. She's not paying attention to her surroundings at all. And look at what she's wearing."

"She's wearing what she's always wearing, a sports bra and running pants."

"And she'll attract every rapist in the area."

"Yeah, all the rapists in the middle of Bumfuck Nowhere, Colorado. On Knight's property, none the less."

"She needs to be more careful. See, this is the reason that I always tried to protect her," I said, shutting the door quietly.

He rolled down the window and shook his head at me. "I'm pretty sure this is what she was talking about, you know, with you not trusting her and all."

"Just stay here for a minute. I have a feeling I'm going to be dragging her ass back here in a minute."

"This is not a good idea, man. This is what we were just talking about." But I ignored him and kept walking. "A pissed off Florrie is never a good thing!"

I snuck up behind her, making sure to stay where she couldn't see me. The grass was tall on the side of the road, making the perfect place for someone to hide and then snatch her and drag her off. Which was exactly what I was going to do. I got in position behind her, but just before I went to grab her, she spun around and kicked me in the stomach. Shocked, I fell to my knees. She kicked me again, in the fucking face. I flew sideways, blood spewing from my mouth where my teeth cut my lips and cheek.

I shuffled to my feet, but she was already behind me, putting me in a headlock and cutting off my air supply. I tried to break the headlock, but she countered me and then punched me in the kidneys. Where the hell was the injured woman from just a little over two months ago? Hell, I was gonna be pissing blood for a week with that last hit.

I finally got ahold of her and tossed her to the ground, but the woman pulled a fucking knife and threw it at me, imbedding it in my side. I stared down at the knife and then looked back at her in confusion. "What the fuck?"

"Trying to teach me a lesson?"

I nodded.

"Next time, make sure I don't have a gun. The next time you pull that shit, I'll put a fucking bullet in you."

Anger surged through me and I charged. This woman was going to be the death of me. I dug my shoulder into her stomach and hauled her up in the air, but she just gripped the knife from behind me and twisted. Groaning, I fell to my knees. She ripped the knife out and stuck it to my throat.

"Are we still doing this? Because I thought I made myself pretty fucking clear."

I set her down and spit out the blood that was pooling in my mouth. Reaching down, I pressed against my knife wound and grimaced. Craig pulled up in the truck, grinning like a fool.

"I see you taught her that lesson you were talking about. Florrie, you wanna throw his ass in the truck so I can get him to Rocco?"

"Why should I?"

"Because he's your teammate."

"He just tried to take me down."

"And clearly he failed."

"I'm right fucking here," I bit out.

"Shush, the adults are talking," Craig said. "Come on, the stupid fucker is in love with you and you stomped all over his poor, pitiful heart. The least you could do after handing him his ass is put him in the truck."

"Fine, but I'm not helping him inside. He can pass out in the truck for all I care."

"How did I not see the she-devil in you before?" I asked.

"You always underestimated me."

"Trust me, I won't do that again."

Chapter Twenty-Five

FLORRIE

"How long are the two of you going to continue to glare at each other?" Lola asked.

"I'm not glaring at him."

"Right. I'm pretty sure what you've developed over the past six months is called resting bitch face."

Now that we were back at Reed Security, things were even more tense between us. We were back where it all began and that only seemed to intensify the pull that was still between us.

"I can't help it. He's always watching me, even after all this time. You'd think he would hate the sight of me by now."

"Um...I'm pretty sure he does," Lola said.

"Then why is he watching me all the time?"

I kept my gaze trained on Alec from across the dining room table. He stared me down as he stabbed his steak with a fork and then sawed into it until he was scraping the plate with his knife. He shoved the steak in his mouth and growled at me as he chewed.

"Yeah, I'm not sure what that's about."

"It's like he thinks I'm the steak and he can chew me up and spit me out or something."

"I wish Ryan would chew his steak like that."

"No, you don't. If I was that steak, Alec would have killed me with his incisors."

"Yeah, but you don't want a guy to be too soft either. I mean, if you were to sleep with Alec right now, imagine all the anger and hate that would be involved. It would be so fucking hot."

"I don't think that would be a good idea. I mean, after everything that happened between us, that's like asking for trouble."

"I'm not saying you should do that. It would be a very bad idea." I nodded, but couldn't take my eyes off Alec's dark eyes. "Bad ideas are so much fun, though."

———

"I need your help."

Sinner looked up from his paperwork in confusion. "Help with what?"

"Do you remember when you offered your help about a certain man in my life?"

He thought for a moment. "Yeah, the guy that..." It dawned on him who I was talking about and he quickly rose to his feet, gathering his paperwork in a pile. "You know, I don't think I'm the right person to help you out with this."

"Yes, you are," I said, slamming my hands down on the pile of papers.

"It's not gonna happen. I gave you advice and you were fucking Alec. I shouldn't have been involved."

"Technically, I wasn't fucking him at the time."

"And I would have told you then to leave it alone had I known it was him. Mixing business and pleasure is never a good idea. Plus, no offense, but I saw what you did to that man. I haven't seen many men brought to their knees by a woman, but you really fucked with his head." He looked around and then leaned in, lowering his voice. "And I mean that as a compliment. There aren't many women that wield that kind of power over a man."

"Look, I'm not trying to suck you into the drama of it all, and I'm not trying to rekindle a relationship with Alec. Technically, we never had one. But..."

"But you miss the big D and you want a second go at it."

"Well, it's a lot more than the second time. I mean, when you think of all the missions and different places where we fucked-"

"Alright, alright, alright," he said, pinning his fingers in his ears. "I don't need to know about it."

"So, you'll help me?"

He cringed, but finally nodded. "Wait, I take that back. There's one thing that I want to know and you have to answer if you want my help."

"Fine."

"When you were cuffed to the bed, was there really a woman there that night?"

"No."

His face dropped, along with his shoulders. "So, you're not gay?"

"Not even a little."

"Man, that totally kills a few fantasies."

———————

"Are you sure about this?" I asked Sinner. He was on the other end of my earpiece, back at the Reed Security compound. I was in the parking lot at The Pub where Sinner found out Alec would be tonight. His big plan was that I pick up another guy. Only, I didn't know how to pick up another guy without actually taking him home. I only knew how to go tell them I wanted to fuck. We would leave and that was the end of it. *This,* actually talking to the man first, was so much harder.

"Why can't I just wear my fuck me dress like I did last time?"

"Because last time he wanted to fuck you. This time, he's going to do anything he can to resist you. He doesn't want to want you."

"I don't know how you think this is going to work. I don't know how to flirt. Especially with someone that I have no interest in."

"Well, you're going to have to find the best looking guy in the place and go for it. Otherwise, he's not going to believe it."

"He's not gonna believe it anyway. You forget how well he knows me."

"Just do what I tell you to and you should be fine."

I opened the car and got out. I could work a dress with the best of them, but flirting was definitely not my strong suit. I straightened my shoulders and headed inside. Looking around, I found what I wanted immediately. I noted that Alec was sitting in the corner of the bar with Craig, chatting away as if I didn't exist. But I saw the looks he shot me when I walked in. If I could burst into flames from his looks, I would have been on fire as soon as I walked in the door.

There was a man standing at the bar, waiting for a drink. I headed over there and leaned against the bar, letting him know that I was available for conversation. But then I just stood there waiting on Sinner.

"Just say hi," Sinner coaxed.

"Hello," I said, putting on my most charming smile. The man turned to me and I about dropped to my knees. Talk about one sexy hunk of a man. He wasn't Alec, but he was damn fine. He had short blonde hair and the most beautiful blue eyes. I was temporarily stunned into silence, but then Sinner spoke in my ear.

"Okay, you can't be this bad. Just tell him your name."

I stuck my hand out for him to shake. "Florrie."

"Logan."

"It's nice to meet you."

"You too," he said warily.

"So, do you come here often?"

"Uh, yeah, I'm here pretty often."

"I don't get a chance to come around a lot. I'm out of town for work a lot."

"Oh yeah? What do you do?"

"Lie," Sinner hissed in my ear.

"Uh...Liposuction."

"You do liposuction." he said slowly.

"Yep. I'm a doctor...who...sucks the fat out of people."

"And that's a traveling gig?"

I giggled nervously, placing my hand on his arm. "Well, you gotta go where the fat people are."

"My God, you're terrible at this," Sinner laughed. "Where do you come up with this shit?"

"Right," Logan smiled. He glanced down at my hand that was still on his arm and cleared his throat. I tried to do a smooth transition from his arm to his pecs, but my ring, that I hardly ever wore, snagged on his shirt.

"Um..." I tried to retract my hand, but one of the prongs was stuck on a thread from his shirt.

"So, good at removing fat, but not rings," he said uncomfortably.

"What is it you do?" I tried to make conversation as I focused in on his shirt.

"Architect."

"Uh...Florrie, I think you need to get out of there," Sinner said in my ear.

"Shut up," I whispered under my breath.

"Excuse me?"

"Florrie, I'm serious. You need to get the fuck away from this guy."

"Uh, I was just swearing that I can't get my ring off your shirt. This is so...weird."

"You have no idea," Logan muttered. "Uh, maybe you should let me try."

And as if things couldn't get any worse, Cap walked up. "Hey, Florrie. Logan," he said more sternly. "What's going on here?"

"Uh, I was just talking with Florrie when her ring snagged on my shirt," Logan laughed uncomfortably.

"Wait, you know him?" I asked Cap.

"Yeah, we go way back."

"I'm sorry, but maybe you should just take off your shirt," I said in irritation. "I can't get my ring off like this." I started undoing the buttons on his shirt, getting a really nice look at the body underneath. "Holy hell. Is it hot in here?" I said, fanning my face. I started tearing the shirt off one of his shoulders, all the while, he was trying to pull it back on.

"Hey," he laughed uncomfortably. "Maybe you should not just rip a man's clothes off in a bar."

"Don't be such a pussy. I'm just getting my ring off your shirt. Not inviting you home for sex."

"Which is actually what you're supposed to be doing," Sinner muttered in my ear. "Just give him his shirt back and get the fuck out of there."

I started ripping the ring harder, just wanting to get it off his shirt so he could put it back on and stop whining.

"Florrie, I don't know if you're aware, but Logan is actually a good friend of mine," Cap said. "One that's married."

My head shot up to meet Cap's gaze and then over to Logan's. "Oh my God." And then I noticed that there was something familiar about him. "You're the guy from the meeting!"

"Yeah, I thought I recognized you, but there were a lot of people there that day."

"Yeah," Cap snapped. "And your wife is about to lose her shit over there. Maybe you want to hurry this along?"

"Sinner, why the fuck didn't you say anything?"

"Sinner?" Cap questioned. "Is he on coms with you?"

"Don't answer that," Sinner said quickly.

"Hmm?" I said innocently to Cap. He reached into my ear and yanked out the earbud.

"Sinner, you're a dead man. Maggie's gonna kick your ass for this. In fact, I'd watch out for a grenade in your bed tonight."

"Can I ask what you're doing with my husband's shirt in your hands?"

I turned to the woman in irritation. This was getting a little ridiculous. "Look, I was fake hitting on your husband to get my ex-boyfriend's attention. I wasn't actually trying to take him home. But, I don't actually know how to flirt, so I ended up snagging my ring on his shirt, and now all I want is to get the damn thing off so I can get out of here."

The woman looked at me curiously for a moment and then grinned. "I'm Cece." Then she turned to her husband. "You should kiss her."

"What?" Logan and I both said at the same time.

"You should kiss her. Think of it as doing a favor for all womankind. She's just trying to get her boyfriend back." And then she turned to me. "Am I right?"

"Well, yes. I just wanted him to see what he was missing."

"Oh, hell, we can help you with that."

"Now, wait a minute, Cece. I'm not a stallion that you can pass around for all the mares to play with."

"Oh, come on, Logan. You were a player once. Don't you want to see if you've still got it?"

"This is a trap," Logan muttered.

"It's not. This woman is a friend of Cap's. I'm sure he can vouch for her."

We all turned to Cap and he shook his head, completely puzzled. "Yeah, she's...Florrie. She's only got eyes for Alec."

"Dark and mysterious? Glaring daggers into you right now?" she asked.

I nodded, "Yeah, that would be him."

"See?" she said to Logan.

"And you're not going to kick me in the balls when we get home tonight?"

"If you wait any longer, he's going to just come over here and kill you for even being near her," Cece said.

Logan looked at me and awkwardly wrapped an arm around my waist. "I'm going to hell for this."

"Maybe we should-" But Cap's statement was interrupted by Logan's lips pressing tightly against mine. I could tell that he didn't want this anymore than I did. It was the worst kiss of my life, at best. Logan pulled back and shivered slightly.

"Yeah, I didn't like it either," I muttered.

"But you should see the look on your man's face," Cece grinned.

"Angry?"

"Um...Well, I guess, maybe now he looks more like he's laughing?" She turned to Cap. "Is that him laughing?"

"Yeah," Cap sighed.

"Ah!" I held up my hand. "But at least I got my ring back."

Logan shrugged his shirt back on and I immediately tried to help. "Sorry about that. Let me just..."

"I've got it." He turned to Cece and glared. "I get two of last night and I'm collecting tonight!"

Cece flushed red, but tucked herself into Logan's arms. Cap and I stood there awkwardly as they walked away. "So..."

"So..." Cap mimicked.

"Can we not speak of this ever again?"

"Oh, thank God. I thought you were going to want to talk it out and ask what it all meant or something."

"Only girls do that. I mean, I'm a girl, but... well, you know what I mean."

"Right, so I'll see you at the office."

"Good." I held out my hand for him to shake and he just shook his head. "No, Maggie wouldn't be quite as forgiving as Cece."

Chapter Twenty-Six

ALEC

"The look on your face was priceless," Craig laughed.

I added more weights to the barbell and stretched my arms for my workout. "There was no look. I noticed she walked in, but that was it."

"Why can't you just admit that you still want her?"

"Because I don't."

"Right. That's why you were ready to leap up out of your chair at the bar and go snatch her away from Logan."

"If I had known it was Logan, I wouldn't have been worried. She puts herself in danger."

"So, you finally admit it. You still worry about Florrie."

I huffed out a huge breath. "She's our teammate. Of course I still worry."

"You worry about her because you love her. Just admit it. Shout it from the rooftops. You're in love!"

"Would you keep it down? You're embarrassing me."

I looked around the room and saw that the other guys were shooting me strange looks. The last thing I needed was to be the center of attention around here.

"Look, we just got back," Craig said. "Maybe after we've been back a few weeks, you'll both adjust back to normal. Besides-"

He stopped talking and I looked up. Florrie had just walked into the weight room, acting like she didn't have a care in the world. Like she hadn't just gone to a bar to pretend to pick up some guy last night.

I scoffed and laid down on the bench. "Did she really think she could make me jealous?"

"Maybe she wasn't so much trying to make you jealous as make you see what you're missing."

"That's the same fucking thing."

"You two were made for each other. Seriously, I've never met a couple that hated to admit how much they wanted each other."

"Were you not around for most of our relationship?"

"Actually, no."

I rolled my eyes, but he had a point. "I was the one always professing my undying love and she was the one always walking away."

"And now you're both trying to outdo each other to get attention."

"Put another fifty pounds on the barbell," I said, still staring at Florrie.

"What?" he laughed. "You're joking, right?" When I didn't laugh along with him, his face sobered. "You *are* joking, right? Come on, man. Don't be stupid. You already bench press more than most of us. You're gonna hurt yourself."

"You're right. Make it seventy-five pounds."

"I swear, it's like I'm standing here talking to myself."

"Look at her," I jerked my head in her direction. "She's showing off for everyone."

"Yeah, and you're not doing the same," he muttered as he loaded the bar.

"Did you know she went to Sinner for help?"

"I wish someone would ask me for help. Oh, wait. You did and I offered advice, but yet, here you are, attempting to lift more than you can. You would think you would just say, *Thank you, Craig. You're so smart, Craig. I'm amazed by your forethought, Craig.*"

"I'm amazed by your forethought," I deadpanned, then laid down on the bench and blew out a long breath, preparing to lift more than I ever had. "Move away. She needs to see how strong I am."

"Oh, you want me to stand over here?" He pointed to a spot

further away. "Yeah, that sounds like a good idea. Sure, I'll just stand over here while you drop the whole fucking bar on yourself."

"Whatever, the extra weight is like carrying half of Florrie. I can handle that."

"I'll be sure to let her know that you think she weighs one hundred and fifty pounds. I'm sure that will endear you to her."

I lifted the weights off the bar and brought them down, then raised them up. "See?" My voice was strained, but I pushed on. The second time down, my elbows locked and the bar stuck right above my chest. "Oh, fuck," I grunted. "Craig, a little help here."

"Hmm?" he asked as he examined his nails. "I'm sorry, did you ask for help?"

"Get over here," I barely got out. My voice was strained and sounded like a little girls.

"What?" he leaned over, cupping his ear. "My hearing is getting bad in my old age."

"You fucker, I'm gonna kick your ass," I wheezed.

"Yeah, not if you're stuck under that barbell. Looks like you're gonna have to do the old roll to get it off you."

"Fuck you. You'll pay for this."

He laughed, but didn't move any closer. "I'd like to see the day."

Fuck, I couldn't stay like this too much longer and he wasn't making a move to help. I couldn't really see around the rest of the room, but I was sure the other guys were staring at me. Slowly, I rolled the barbell down my chest. It hurt so fucking much, but it was the only way to get the fucking thing off me. I just prayed that Florrie wasn't watching. When the barbell passed my hips, I sat up and glanced around the room. Florrie was running on the treadmill and completely oblivious. The guys were all standing around fucking laughing at me.

"Fuck off," I said, getting myself the rest of the way out from under the barbells. My arms were sore and my chest hurt, but I hadn't gotten my workout in. I rolled the barbell back toward the bar and unloaded the extra weights, and then a few more. I was fucking exhausted.

"Did you need help?" Craig asked.

"*Now* you want to help?"

"It looks like you're going to lift weights. Need a spotter?"

"Need a-" I grumbled under my breath for a moment and then gave a stiff nod. It didn't matter. He would get his one day. I laid down on the bench and prepared myself again. Craig spotted me as I lifted the barbell and brought it down to my chest again. This time, I didn't make the mistake of locking my elbows. After a few times, my left arm started to slack. It was my weaker arm. I had been trying to strengthen it for the past year, but it still just wasn't as strong. My right arm went higher and I felt the slide.

"You fucker. You didn't put the clips on," I shouted at Craig.

The barbell tilted all the way down on the left and the weights slid right off the bar. I knew what was coming, but I had no choice but to hold on. My right arm collapsed under the pressure and the other weights slid off the right side.

"Incoming," I shouted as the barbell catapulted out of my hands. Forty pounds of bar went flying across the room and shattered a mirror. I sat up slowly, taking in all the damage. I felt someone come up next to me and shut my eyes. Damn, she just had to see that.

"I thought you were a professional? Only an amateur forgets to put on the clips."

I turned to Craig as she walked away, but he was already running from me. He'd better run, because when I caught up to him, I was gonna beat his ass.

Chapter Twenty-Seven

FLORRIE

I was getting out of the showers in the locker room when I walked smack dab into Alec. He was carrying a caddy with all his shower supplies and had a towel draped over his shoulder. I rolled my eyes. It was so cliche that he was trying to run into me. He was obviously wanting to start things up between us again and thought this would be a good introduction to the conversation. Both of us wet. Both of us horny. Both of us not able to look away from the other's body. Yeah, he was playing a dangerous game here.

"I saw that you were having some trouble in the weight room today."

"Yeah, it's tough to find a good spotter."

I quirked an eyebrow. "Typical male, blaming someone else."

"Well, since he didn't put the clips on, I would say it was his fault."

Sure, he could think whatever he wanted, but the truth was, he had been too distracted and he was the one that forgot to put the clips on. Yeah, Craig saw it and did nothing, but it was Alec's fault.

"Well, it's been nice talking, but I need to get dressed." I stepped past him, but slipped on the wet floor. I slid sideways, almost hitting the wall, but he dropped his caddy and wrapped an arm around me, pulling me into his body before I could hit the wall. We stood there, staring into each other's eyes at the entrance to the showers. I couldn't hear anything over the heavy breathing that mingled between us.

My eyes dropped to his lips. They were so kissable and the heavy stubble on his jaw had me sighing with need.

"Don't," he growled.

"What?" I asked, completely missing what he said.

"Don't," he said again. I took a step back, shaking my head.

"You're right." I pulled the towel tighter and took another step back, but stepped on one of his bottles that had fallen from the caddy. My arms cartwheeled in the air as I tried to catch myself, but it was no use. I was going down. His arms reached for me again and I gripped onto his hand, but when he stepped forward, he slipped and we both went crashing to the ground.

"Ow," I laughed as I pulled a bottle out from underneath me. Liquid poured out of the bottle and all over me. Alec's eyes watched as the liquid dripped down between my breasts. And then his fingers were removing the towel from where I had tucked it.

"Fucking gorgeous," he murmured as he spread the liquid over my breasts and down over my stomach. "I want to fuck these tits."

"Be still my heart," I mocked.

His eyes snapped up to mine and he narrowed them in anger. "I don't recall your heart ever having anything to do with us fucking."

He was right. "Then don't let it get in the way."

He smashed his lips against mine, his teeth hitting my lips and drawing blood. He sucked it into his mouth and licked my bruised lips as his hand trailed down my body and reached for my pussy. It had been too long without Alec and I needed him. I shoved his pants down far enough that he could maneuver out of them, and then he was pushing inside me.

"Oh, God," I shouted. "It's been too long."

I gripped what I could of his short hair and pulled hard. "If you weren't such a selfish bitch, we would still be fucking all the time."

"If you hadn't gone and brought love into it, I wouldn't have been a selfish bitch."

He thrust harder and we slid across the floor with the water and soap foaming up bubbles underneath us. "We should just hate fuck," he growled. "I'd rather fuck your pussy than watch you give it away to some other asshole."

"I'd rather you shut the fuck up," I panted. "I'd rather you fuck me than yell at me for being a bitch."

He got up to his knees and spread my legs wide, but when he went to fuck me, he slipped and ended up on top of me again. "Fuck, maybe if I fuck you hard enough, I could actually stand to see your fucking face."

"Is that why you watch me every minute of the day?" He slammed into me harder, like he was trying to deny the truth. "Just admit that you still need me as much as I need you."

"Of course, I fucking need you."

He leaned forward and bit me, fucking bit me on the shoulder until I screamed. I clawed at his back, scratching him until I could feel blood oozing from the cuts. "God, you frustrate me so much."

"I fucking hate you," he growled. And then he was fucking me so hard that it actually hurt. His dick felt like he was hitting right up against my heart.

"I love fucking you," I panted. He gripped my hair and pulled as he shouted out and came inside me.

"Fuck," he sighed, dropping his head to my chest. "I really fucking needed that. It's hard to be so fucking angry at you all the time when I really just want to fuck you up against a wall."

"The shower works too," I panted.

"Maybe next time, we'll leave out the shower gel. I'm feeling extra clean right now."

"I'm good with that. Say, tonight? The trampoline in the training center?"

"Hey, I fucking use that," a voice said from behind us.

"What did I miss?"

My head snapped up with Alec's and we saw Gabe, Jackson, and Hunter staring at us.

"You missed one hell of a show," Gabe grinned. "There were lots of bubbles and some good hate-fuck talk. And if I'm not mistaken, there was some ass play." He turned to Hunter. "Her, not him."

"Wait," Hunter said, "Her playing with his ass or him playing with her ass?"

"Hey!" I snapped. "Would you mind?"

"No, go ahead and continue," Gabe said, turning back to Hunter. "Does it matter?" Gabe asked Hunter.

"Well, yeah, I'm not sure I want to see her playing with his ass. Now, her on the other hand-"

"Hey, assholes," Alec snapped. "Would you mind giving the lady a little privacy?"

Jackson snorted. "That's no lady. We saw what the two of you did. Besides, no one walked away when I was in this position."

"Damn, I have a feeling that I missed out on some of the same shit that I would have seen when she was tied to the bed. Missed it by just this much," Hunter said, holding his finger and thumb just an inch apart.

"Since when are you all a bunch of voyeurs?" I asked. "Usually people don't *want* to watch others having sex."

"Gabe's a bad influence," Hunter said as he continued to stare at us.

"Getting a nice view of Alec's ass? See something you like?" I asked.

Hunter turned red and tried to turn around quickly, but slipped in the soap and fell down, his face landing right on Alec's ass.

"What is that between my ass cheeks?" Alec shouted. "Get it the fuck off me!"

"It's my nose," Hunter said, struggling to get up. He put his hand on my leg to help himself up.

"Don't touch me!"

"Get your fucking hands off her right now!"

He moved, placing his hand on Alec's ass, cringing and pulling it away quickly.

"What the fuck are you doing?" Alec shouted. "Stop fucking touching me!"

"Hey, it was fucking worse for me. My nose touched something between your ass cheeks. I'm not into motor boating!"

"Then maybe you shouldn't be watching us fucking!" Alec shouted. "All of you get out!"

"Alright, alright, don't get your balls in a twist," Gabe laughed. "We're going."

"You need a hand, Alec?" Jackson asked. "I'm sure Hunter could help you out."

"Get out!" Alec and I both yelled at the same time.

Chapter Twenty-Eight

FLORRIE

"I'll go in and cause a distraction," I said confidently outside the biker bar. Our target was inside and we needed to get him out before he got himself killed. There were only so many things that would distract men when they had their sights set on something, and pussy was one of them. I had the body to pull off this job, so it only made sense that I be the one to do this.

"No. You're not walking in there dressed like that."

Alec's eyes wandered over me, and even though I knew he appreciated my body, his look was anything but appreciative right now.

"I wasn't planning to," I said, pulling my jacket over my head and handing it off to Craig. He took it without a word, knowing that when my mind was made up, there was nothing to say about it. Besides, he knew that speaking right now would only make things worse. I took off my shoulder holster and pulled out the gun at the small of my back. It wouldn't do any good to let the men think I was armed.

"What the hell are you doing?" Alec spat. "I'm the team leader and I said we're not fucking doing it this way."

"I'm getting undressed. Like you said, I can't walk in there looking like a woman that knows how to use a gun."

"Taking off your clothes isn't the way to go either," he growled.

"Don't worry," I said, patting his cheek playfully. "I'm only taking them off for you."

"And me," Craig said from beside me. I raised an eyebrow, wondering why he was being so unhelpful. "What? Don't expect me to just automatically side with you. I have to deal with his grouchy ass too."

I yanked my t-shirt off, revealing my white tank top that showed off my tanned skin and toned body. Being in shape definitely had its advantages when we needed a distraction.

"There's no fucking way I'm allowing you to walk into that bar dressed like that."

I glared at Alec. "Just wait. I'm not even finished yet." I turned to Craig with a jerk of my chin, "Hand me my bag."

Craig tossed it at me and I dug through the contents. I always kept a change of clothes on me just in case, a pair of shorts that happened to be one of my favorite pair. They were short and sexy, cutting off just below my ass cheeks. They would be perfect for the occasion.

"No," Alec said furiously, eyeing the teeny tiny shorts. "No fucking way."

I grinned and unbuttoned my pants. Craig, being the smart man that he was, quickly turned away as I yanked down my pants.

"It's like you're just begging for me to get my ass kicked," he grumbled.

"Aw, don't worry. I'm here to protect you from the big, bad wolf."

"Yeah?" Craig turned back as I yanked up my shorts, knowing he caught a glimpse of the thong I was wearing. "What are you going to do when I'm not around you?"

Alec growled behind me and I turned just in time to see him smack Craig across the back of the head. He had been staring at my ass. I yanked my boots back on, admiring the way my tank top and shorts showed off my body, but the boots really brought it all together. It was a fact that men in these biker bars were driven by tits and ass. Since I had that, it made sense that I use it to my advantage. Plus, the boots I had added to the wild woman look. It was perfect.

"How do you expect me to stay outside when you're in there looking like a slut?"

As I checked my ankle holster, I studied the stubble along Alec's jaw. Every time I saw him with stubble, I was reminded of his head between my thighs as he ate my pussy and made me come harder than I ever had before. I shook the thought from my head, because it wasn't helpful right now.

"Is that what you think of me? I seem to recall you not being able to keep your hands off me for the past three years. And you never thought I looked slutty before."

"You were never going to walk into a bar dressed like that before."

"So, it's okay for me to dress like this around you, but not around other men. Are you worried I'll be swayed by one of them or that I won't be able to fight off their advances?"

He stood and yanked me into his body. "I'm worried that I'll get so fucking jealous watching other men looking at what's mine that I'll ruin the whole fucking operation and kill every fucking man that dared to even glance in your direction."

And here we were again with the possessive jealousy. We'd only been fucking, but it was already overwhelming.

"Look, the best way to get the attention off our guy is for me to walk in and stir up some trouble. You know that. Don't be stupid."

"It's not necessary for you to-"

"Just stop," I said forcefully. "This is ridiculous. We work together. You can't prevent me from doing my job just because you're fucking me."

"Fucking you?" he snarled.

"Oh, shit," Craig muttered.

"I think that's what people call it when you stick your dick in my pussy and pound into me until I'm barely able to walk."

"Obviously, I haven't fucked you hard enough to pound the stupid out of you."

"Why me?" Craig muttered again as he started shoving my gear into a bag. "I just signed up for a job. *'It'll be fine,'* Cap said. *'They're professionals and it hasn't been a problem so far,'* he promised me. Yeah, we're getting along really fucking great right now. My two teammates are fucking and I didn't know about it for two fucking years. You would have thought that I would be one of the first to know, but no. I find out along with everyone else. And even better, now I have to find a way to work with a man that can't see past his own obsession and a woman that's too stubborn to realize that the fucker loves her."

Craig looked up and saw Alec and I staring at him. Glancing at Alec, I almost laughed at his lethal expression. He apparently didn't enjoy Craig's running commentary.

"What?" Craig huffed. "You have no fucking clue what it's like for me. I've been playing referee since we started working again."

"My obsession is just fine, and she knows exactly how I feel about her," Alec snapped.

"I know and that's the problem."

"You've known all along how I felt. Don't pretend like I just started telling you."

"Loving me wasn't part of the deal. I swear, if I have to deal with this possessive shit anymore, we're done fucking."

Alec narrowed his eyes at me, but this wasn't the time to deal with this. I strapped my knife across the lower part of my back, under my shorts, and slung my bag over my shoulder. Luckily, it was black leather and perfect for what I needed.

"Whoa," Craig stopped me. "You can't go in there with your hair in a fucking bun. It ruins the whole look you have going."

"Really? And how should I be wearing it?"

Craig sighed and walked up behind me, pulling my hair out of my ponytail holder. "If you ever fucking mention this, I'll kill you."

I waited as Craig worked his fingers through my hair, braiding it from one side, around the back, and down the other side. He pulled out his knife and I looked in the gleaming metal at the inverted braid he had put in my hair.

"Where did you learn to do this?"

"I'm not fucking talking about it." He bent over and grabbed his bag, slinging it over his shoulder and stomping around the building. Alec grabbed my upper arm and dragged me back to him.

"I'm fucking telling you not to do this."

"And I'm fucking telling you that this is my job. If you can't deal with this, then we have nothing to talk about."

I yanked my arm from his grasp and turned to the bar. I just didn't understand why he couldn't live with the fact that I didn't want a relationship. We fucked and it was good. He already tried the relationship thing with me and it failed. He just had to let it go.

Chapter Twenty-Nine

ALEC

"I'm done."

I rolled my eyes in annoyance as we all sat in Cap's office. She was overreacting. Again. Typical woman, she couldn't see that I was protecting her in that bar. That was my job as her man, or the man fucking her, and there was no way I was letting anything happen on my watch.

"She's being dramatic," I told Cap. "Everything's fine."

"I'm being dramatic?" she asked incredulously. "You blew our job-"

"We got the client out," I pointed out.

"Here we go again," Craig muttered beside us.

Cap turned his gaze on Craig with raised eyebrows. "Is there something you want to add?"

"I don't know. Would it matter? Would you believe me?"

Yeah, there was still a lot of tension between Craig and Cap over what had gone down over the past year. Being accused of being a traitor kind of sours a relationship, and I completely had Craig's back, but at some point, they needed to work their shit out. The tension wasn't good for the Reed Security family.

"Look, the point is that we can't work together anymore," Florrie said, crossing her arms over her chest defiantly.

"There's nothing wrong with us working together. You just need to listen to me when I tell you what to fucking do. I *am* your team leader, after all."

"Oh, fuck you and your team leader bullshit. You were acting like a caveman because you didn't like the way another man had his hands on me."

"Here we go again. Same shit, different day," Craig sighed. "I'm your man. You do as I say." He made his voice high to mimic Florrie. "I'm perfectly capable of taking care of myself. I don't need your bullshit." And then he dropped it low. "I'll kill any motherfucker who dares to put his hands on you. You're my woman and I protect you." And then high again. "Do I look like I need you to protect me? Does my vagina render me incapable somehow?"

He was about to go on, but Cap interrupted him. "Are you done?"

"With the team or giving the play by play of my life nowadays?"

"Both."

"Do you see what I'm dealing with?" he asked Cap almost painfully. "Every fucking job is a nightmare now that we all know. And I'm never really sure what the fuck is going on. Are they together? Are they just fucking? I want to go back to *don't ask, don't tell.*"

"That was about gays in the military. Doesn't apply here," I said.

Cap tapped his pen against his desk as he stared at us thoughtfully. "I think the only way this is going to work is if you go to counseling."

Craig burst out laughing and I shot a glare in his direction. "What? It's fucking hilarious. If you had just stuck to fucking and it never came out, you wouldn't be going to a shrink. Finally! I might actually be able to get some sleep without having nightmares about the two of you."

"You have nightmares?" Cap asked.

Craig leaned forward, all too eager to spill his guts to Cap. "Are you fucking kidding me? You know how some teams have flashbacks to traumatic events?" He shook his head. "Not me. I'm traumatized by every look that these two shared, wondering if they were fucking when I was in the same room sleeping." He glanced over at me and then leaned in closer to Cap. "You know how it is, dreams have a way of manifesting from reality. What if...you know...they were fucking and it worked its way into my dream? It'd be like fucking my teammates. Which wouldn't be bad if it was just Florrie..."

The thought of him even remotely thinking about Florrie naked had my stomach churning in anger. I almost got up and snapped his neck just for even mentioning her like that, but then he continued.

"But with Alec...Don't get me wrong, he's a handsome man. I mean, he's strong and virile. He's obviously great in bed based on the fact that Florrie's putting up with his bullshit. And then there's the fact that he has that smoldering gaze going on-"

"Craig, are you trying to tell us that you're gay and have a thing for Alec or that you've had dreams about him and now you're worried how they're affecting you?" Cap cut in. I raised an eyebrow in surprise. I obviously had overlooked a very strange aspect to our new team dynamic. Craig turned bright red and started stammering, confusing me even further.

"Hey-they were dreams and I never said that they were about him. That was all your assumption. And even if I had, there's nothing wrong with being gay-which I'm not. There's nothing wrong with it. I'm just not. And having sexual dreams about other dudes doesn't mean that-you know, dreams don't even necessarily mean anything. They're just dreams."

It was quiet for a moment as Cap and I stared at Craig, trying to figure out what the hell he was trying to say. And Florrie, damn, she was just sitting next to us laughing her ass off. Apparently, this was all funny to her.

Cap cleared his throat uncomfortably. "Well, obviously, anything that happens in your group remains between the three of you. If you choose to have a...ménage-type situation, that's completely up to you-"

"Wait a minute," I cut in, but Cap continued.

"Just as long as it doesn't interfere with your work."

"Hold the fuck on," I said angrily. "Not that I don't reciprocate Craig's admiration, he too is a handsome man, but there was never any talk of Florrie and I having relations with another person. And if there was, it would be with a woman."

"Why a woman?" Florrie asked testily. "So, I'm supposed to share you with another woman and give you pleasure in ways that you'll never give me?"

"You want to share Craig?" I asked incredulously. "I'm a dude. There are parts that men do NOT share."

"Craig," Cap asked. "How do you feel about all this?"

"I'm...I'm thinking."

"You're thinking?" I shouted, jumping from my seat. "I'm never gonna fucking share Florrie. She's mine."

"Hey, it's a lot to take in! One minute we're talking about you two going to counseling and now we're talking about having a three-some. Give a guy a chance to catch a breath."

"No, there's no fucking breathing, because there's no chance in hell that I'm sharing Florrie with you."

"Sharing Florrie?" She stood and got in my face. "I'm not exclusively yours. What if I want to try Craig out, see where this could go?"

I clenched my jaw in anger. This was bullshit, but if I pushed too much, she'd just walk away. And there was no fucking way I was letting her walk away. Even if we were just fucking.

"Whoa," Craig cut in. "I'm not some piece of meat that can be passed around for personal use. If I'm getting involved in this, it's because someone wants me for more than my body."

"Would you shut the fuck up," I said irritatedly. "Look at you. You're basically a bodybuilder with a salami hanging off the front."

Craig crossed his arms over his chest and glared at me. "I have a brain, you know."

"I think what you need is some team building," Cap finally said.

"No," I cut in angrily. "The last time you had everyone do team building, we were fighting each other with wooden swords."

"I'm going to send you all to a therapist I recently met. She's really good with this shit."

"Whoa, why do I have to go see a therapist?" Craig asked. "I'm not part of this relationship."

"You're part of the team, and obviously, there are some unresolved issues that need to be dealt with," Cap clarified. "It's either you all go to a therapist or the team breaks up."

"We break up," Florrie said instantly.

"Not a fucking chance in hell," I grumbled. "Someone's gotta watch your ass."

"Nobody has to watch my ass," she shot back. "Why do you always do this?"

"What? Protect you?"

"Jump in the line of danger because you think I can't take care of myself."

"You can't," I said before I could think better of it. The look of fury on her face had me scrambling for something romantic as fuck to say, but it was too late. I was fucked.

"You were the one that got yourself shot when we rescued that girl that was taken hostage. You were the one that got yourself stabbed in the leg because you thought I needed saving because I had an injured arm. And today, you almost got yourself killed by a gang of bikers because one of them grabbed my ass. You've been injured more than I have," she seethed. "If you would just let me do my job, you would see that I'm perfectly capable of fighting off any asshole that comes my way."

"You know what I don't get," Craig said. "Why now? We've worked together for years and now that you're fucking, you think she can't do her job?"

Florrie crossed her arms and glared at me, like he was actually making fucking sense.

"You can't be seriously considering all this bullshit, can you?" I asked her incredulously.

"What I can't believe is that you actually think I would continue to work with you, let alone fuck you, when you act like I can't handle myself. Something has to change and if you can't trust me on the job, I will leave the team."

"And what about us?"

She looked away, which gave me my answer. This was her ultimatum, go to counseling with her or we were over. Well, shit. I sighed and sat back down in my chair, knowing I had lost. I couldn't fight her on this. This might have started up again as fucking, but she was mine and

I would do anything to hang onto her. And if this was what it took to recognize what was right in front of her, then I had to do it.

"I guess we're going to counseling."

Chapter Thirty

FLORRIE

"I still think this is fucking ridiculous," Craig grumbled as we walked toward the brick building in front of us. We were on our way to our first therapy appointment and Craig was especially pissed off that he had been lumped into this little gathering.

"Suck it up and deal with it." Alec was no more happy about this than Craig. "If I have to do this, then so do you."

"You don't *have to* do anything," I sassed. "I told you that we should split up. It's not a good idea for us to work together. And based on how you're handling this, it just proves my point."

Alec put a hand on my arm, stopping me where I was. "I do have to do this. You didn't give me a choice. If I want to stick with you, this is my only option."

"Saying that you are obligated to do something doesn't make the effort very sincere," I sneered.

"It's just one thing after another," Craig sighed. "I tried to tell him. I told him it was a bad idea and that nothing good would come of this, but nobody ever listens to me. Of course, why would they? I'm a traitor."

"You really need to let that go," Alec shot to Craig. "I'm on your side, but you walk around like it's your own personal crown of thorns."

I couldn't believe that Alec had just said that to him. He had no fucking clue how much Craig had been hurt by that or what it did to him. I couldn't stand to be around him anymore, so I turned and headed for the building. When I opened the door and walked over to the door labeled Psychiatry, I heard a chuckle from behind me.

"Oh, this is too good. Delilah Sunshine?" Craig snorted and then broke out into full on laughter. I rolled my eyes and opened the door. If she was good enough for Cap, then she was good enough for me. I checked in at the front and took my seat while Alec and Craig bickered about a sports magazine.

"Hey, isn't Sunshine the name you used to call Alec's old girlfriend?"

I glared at him. "Way to make things uncomfortable by bringing up past girlfriends."

His grin dropped and he leaned back in his chair. "Oh." He cleared his throat and nodded, staring at the wall opposite him. "How about those Raiders?"

"What about them?" Alec asked.

"Uh...Go football," he cheered.

"Craig, what the fuck are you talking about?"

"Hell, I'm just trying to ease the tension."

"Alec, Florrie, and Craig?" the receptionist called.

"Thank fucking God," Craig muttered. "Never thought I'd be so happy to go see a therapist."

We walked back into the therapist's office and I immediately took the single chair and left the couch for the guys. Alec and Craig both looked at the love seat and then sat down, both being careful not to touch each other.

"Hi, I'm Dr. Sunshine, but you can call me Delilah if it makes you more comfortable."

"Yes," Alec looked to me, "it would, Delilah."

"Alright," she smiled uncomfortably. "So, why are we here today?"

"Alec's a possessive asshole," I started.

"Florrie can't admit that she loves me. Apparently, we're just supposed to go on fucking the rest of our lives."

"I'm not gay," Craig said. "I just want to make that clear from the start."

"Okay," Delilah said slowly. "Um...gosh, where to start...This sounds like it's going to be loads of fun," she muttered to herself. "Okay, let's start off by telling me how you all know each other and what your relationship is. Other than the f-fucking."

"We're all on the same team at Reed Security," I informed her. "Alec is our team leader, but he seems to think that he can tell anyone what they should do at any given time, on or off the job."

"Florrie is my lover, and yes, I'm her team leader, but I'd like to be more, if she could just get her head out of her ass and admit that we have something good. See, I like to protect the people I care about, but Florrie sees that as a bad thing."

"That's because I already know how to take care of myself," I said through gritted teeth.

"And you?" Delilah asked Craig.

"I'm the third man out. I just found out about a year ago that they'd been screwing behind my back for two years. There were so many times that they were fucking right in the other room and I didn't have a fucking clue. Now, I'm left wondering if things that I dreamt about are some kind of twisted mind fuck or not. And on top of that, I have to constantly listen to them fighting. Seriously, it's worse than anything I've ever heard. I don't know how they manage to listen to each other argue."

"Right." Delilah looked at the three of us and then back down at her notepad. "Let's start with Alec and Florrie. Where do you see this f-fucking going?"

"Nowhere," I answered quickly.

"See?" Alec said. "She speaks for both of us, I guess."

"Mhmm," Delilah nodded. "Florrie can you tell me why you don't want a relationship?"

"We don't need one. We're just fucking."

"All the fucking time," Craig muttered.

"Are you around for this?" Delilah asked.

"Oh, yeah. You have no idea. There were so many times I was right fucking there."

"And they just kept going?" Delilah asked in shock.

"Hell yeah."

"And they knew you were there?"

Craig glanced to Alec, who grinned. "All the fucking time."

"Perhaps…" Delilah cleared her throat and straightened in her chair. "Perhaps we should talk about what kind of relationship the three of you have as a whole."

"We're just teammates," I said quickly.

"It's good," Craig answered. "I mean, we all get along well. We're really close, you know, like the three musketeers."

"I wouldn't say we're that close," Alec said, his gaze narrowing in on Craig.

"What? Am I no longer part of the group because the two of you are fucking?"

"Maybe you should consider ways that you can expand your relationship," Delilah suggested. "I get the feeling that Craig is feeling left out of this threesome."

"Damn right, I am," Craig muttered.

"Would you like to expand on that?"

"Well, it's like, they have their things they do together that I'm not part of. I'm just the third man out, the twig to their berries."

"And you'd like your twig to be more cohesive with their berries?" Delilah asked.

"Well, it'd be nice."

Delilah nodded and Alec and I exchanged looks. I had a feeling that Craig and Delilah were not at all on the same page.

"I think I have a solution for your problems," Delilah said, leaning forward. "I think the three of you should take some time to spend together, really get to know each other from a new dynamic."

"Like, go to the movies and stuff?" Craig asked.

"Well, to start. You could do things that other…groups like you do."

Craig turned to Alec. "Yeah, would it kill you to take me out to dinner once in a while?"

"Craig, I don't think you're understanding what she's saying."

"She's suggesting we get to know each other in a new way," Craig said. "I'm down with that."

"No," Alec bit out. "That's not quite what she's saying. She thinks that we're more of a different kind of team."

"Well, we are. None of the other teams have a couple and a third man out. I think she's onto something. We should mix things up. I wouldn't mind seeing this side to Florrie that you see."

"That's not gonna fucking happen," Alec growled.

"Do you see what I'm working with?" Craig asked. "It could be so good between us if they'd just open up a little."

"I agree. I think your assignment for this week will be that you do more things together. As a group. I'll make sure that Mr. Reed follows up with you and makes sure you're completing your assignments."

Craig nodded along happily, but he didn't get it. I was going to have to make this clear for him. "Just how much time would you like us to spend together?"

"A few hours every night. I think you should get adequate...knowledge of each other in that time."

"And would you suggest any specific things we should do?"

"Well," Delilah cleared her throat again, pulling down her skirt like she was trying to hide herself from us. "If you and Mr. Wesley engage in any acts of a sexual nature, perhaps you should include Mr.-"

"Whoa!" Craig jumped up from his seat and stared at Delilah, completely flabbergasted. "You want us to do what?"

"Well, you said that you wanted to feel more connected. A great way to feel connected is through touch. I don't know what exactly the mingling of the twigs and berries would look like, but I'm sure there are websites that could help. Perhaps that would even...liven things up between the three of you. Plenty of couples that enjoy a more...diverse relationship also enjoy engaging in pornographic film watching."

Alec and I smirked at each other, but Craig looked like he wanted to shrink into the seats.

"Thank you, Ms. Sunshine. We'll see you next week."

I stood and Alec quickly followed me to the door.

"You're a sick woman," Craig said before he exited behind us.

Chapter Thirty-One

ALEC, FLORRIE, CRAIG

Alec

"So, are you shoving me aside for the night or do I get the honor of your company?" I asked as I walked into Florrie's room.

She was lying on the bed in just a t-shirt and she was watching tv. "Don't be such an asshole. Just because I don't want a relationship doesn't mean that I don't want you in my bed."

"It's hard to tell anymore. It doesn't seem like there's a whole lot that I can do anymore to please you."

"There's one thing you can do." She spread her legs, showing me her bare pussy. I stalked toward her, ripping off my shirt and tossing it somewhere behind me. I barely undid my pants before she was on her knees and ripping the zipper down. Then her hands were in my jeans and she was pulling me out. I groaned and let my head drop back. I just sat there, enjoying her mouth on me, that warmth coating my dick and sending pleasure sizzling throughout my body.

"Is that better?" she asked, looking up at me like a seductress.

"It'd be better if I had another set of hands to love you with."

What? Did I just say that? What did that even mean?

"I have an idea. Something that might be pleasurable for both of us."

"Anything you want."

Where was the guy that demanded we fuck my way? I always had my way in bed.

She looked past me and motioned for someone to come over. Excitement filled my gut. She was bringing in another chick to make this more fun. I could do this. It had been a while for me, but I was all for having a little fun for one night. Hands ran over my shoulders, caressing me and then wrapping around my torso. Something was different though. I looked down and noticed that they weren't hands on me, but very large, very male hands.

What the fuck? Why are there man hands on me? Maybe it's like that Seinfeld episode and this woman just has giant hands. It could be a good thing. She'd have a better grip on my cock.

Lips touched my neck and then hot, wet breath fanned out over my skin. "I've been dreaming of this," Craig said from behind me. I jerked to the side and saw him grinning at me.

"What the fuck are you doing?"

"I thought about what the therapist said and I think she's onto something. We could be so good together. Besides, it might be easier for all of us this way. We'd always be watching out for each other like friends." He kissed my shoulder, running his tongue along my neck. "Like lovers. You just have to let yourself enjoy this."

I wasn't sure I could do that, but I was willing to try for Florrie and she looked excited for this. Hell, if she could do this, so could I.

No, you can't, because you're not fucking gay or bisexual or any of the other sexual things that people call themselves nowadays!

Florrie continued to suck my cock and Craig continued to run his hands over my body. Then he was pushing my pants down, and this was really fucking happening. I took a deep breath as his hands ran over my ass, but when his thumb rubbed against my asshole, i jerked away, not sure I was ready for that.

"Don't worry," Craig whispered in my ear. "I'll use lube."

. . .

Florrie

I laid down on the bed and took Alec's hand, bringing him closer to me. He kissed and licked at my breasts, his tongue hot and wet against my chilled skin. Craig walked around and sat behind my head on the bed, his hands going immediately to my shoulders. He rubbed the tension from them as Alec continued to kiss me.

"Roll over," Craig murmured against my neck. Alec sat up and I rolled over as asked.

"Look at those legs," Alec groaned. "Fucking perfect."

"Massage her feet," Craig said, bending over to lick the side of my neck. I moved my head to the side to allow him better access.

"That feels nice," I groaned. Craig moved to straddle my ass and then he was squirting warm oil on my back and massaging it into my sore muscles. His thick fingers rubbed and pressed against the hard knots that had formed from working too much and the warmth of his legs wrapped around me lulled me into a sleepy state.

"You like that?" Alec asked. "You like Craig rubbing your back while I dig in and fuck the hell out of these knots in your feet?"

"Yes," I moaned. "I want more."

"Oh, I'll give you more." His hand slid up one of my legs, all the way to my ass, and then he was rubbing my pussy, just getting me turned on enough to keep me from falling asleep.

Craig started moving against me, pushing his erection against my ass. "I'm gonna rub these sore spots right out of your back. You're gonna be so loose by the time I'm through with you."

"Yes, make me loose. Rub me hard."

I had two sets of hands rubbing, caressing, and loving me. It felt fantastic. At some point, I dropped off to sleep and when I woke, I still had the pressure of Craig sitting on me, but no one was massaging. "What's going on? Why'd you stop?" I asked. I started to flip over and stopped when I saw Alec and Craig kissing, tonguing each other and gripping each other's cocks and jerking each other off.

. . .

Craig

"So," Craig cleared his throat. "Are we really going to do this?"

Alec narrowed his eyes at me, like I really wanted to do this too.

"I'm ready when you are."Florrie tore off her shirt and shucked her pants, standing only in her panties. This was so fucking awesome. But then I saw Alec glaring at me and he marched over, snatching a blanket off the bed and wrapped it around her hastily.

"Umm, I'm not sure that covering her up is the way to go here," I said in confusion. "If I recall, Ms. Sunshine," I said sarcastically, "said that we should explore this...thing...openly and honestly."

Florrie threw off the blanket and stepped back from Alec. "I agree."

Alec cleared his throat several times and jerked his head at me. "I think before we do this, we need to set some boundaries."

"Good. That sounds...good. Boundaries will keep things..." I waved my hand in a circle and flicked it between all of us, trying to sign what I couldn't explain.

"Right," Alec continued. "First, Florrie can say no at any time and we have to stop."

"Of course. You don't even have to say that."

"Second, we don't touch. Ever. This is for Florrie, and Florrie alone."

"Agreed. Swords do not cross under any circumstances."

"Wait," Florrie interjected. "What if there's something I want to try? Are the two of you open to it?"

Alec grimaced. "Like what?"

"I don't know. I guess I'd have to see in the moment."

"I'm not agreeing to anything until I know for sure what you might want us to do," I argued.

Florrie glanced between the two of us. "How do you feel about doing things together?"

"No, no fucking way," Alec growled.

"I mean to me. Not to each other."

"Well, there would have to be boundaries to that. I would have to calculate the distance from his dick to mine. There can never, under any circumstances, be an instance in which Alec's dick is closer than, say, three feet from mine."

"Three feet? Did you bring a tape measure?"

"Let's just say that if he could reach out and grab my junk, he's too close," Alec said matter of factly. "I would also add that at no time should either of our dicks be facing the other's ass. Even ninety degrees is just a little too close to a direct line to Puckerland."

"So, at no time are you allowed in arm's length of each other or at a ninety degree angle," Florrie clarified.

"Correct," Alec said.

"Is this hard or soft?"

"Like, are these hard rules?" I asked.

"No, are the distances when you're hard or soft?" Florrie asked. I looked at Alec in confusion. "Well, men are always saying how big they are when they're hard. I'm assuming that it would be a significant difference. And does this measurement go from one dick to another or one dick to the other's hand?"

I wiggled uncomfortably, glancing down at my groin for just a second. "I guess it would be dick to the other. I mean, our hands won't necessarily be in the same spot all the time."

"Yeah, I agree, but we also need to think about girth."

"Why would you need to think about girth?" Florrie asked. "Are you measuring the distance from side to side also?"

I cleared my throat and then motioned front to back and then side to side. Before I could make an intelligible response, Alec explained. "Sometimes men are fatter or skinnier. Length is adjustable. I mean, depending on blood flow."

"What are we talking here? Half an inch? Five inches?"

"It varies," I croaked.

"So, how do you want to do this?" Alec asked me. "We could do some practice measurements when we switch positions."

"Like, hold out an arm to make sure we're far enough apart?"

Alec shrugged. "Not the most...romantic, but we're not really worried about that between the two of us."

"I suppose. Or we could set up a sort of coms system, you know, key words to let each other know when one is getting too close."

"I think I still have some ear pieces in my bag." Alec started back for his bag, Florrie stopped him.

"Oh, for fuck's sake. You'll be three feet from each other. If you're too fucking close, take a fucking step back. You don't need to fucking measure!" She stared at both of us and finally, Alec shrugged and started pulling his shirt over his head. "Now, can we get started on this extremely weird team exercise? Or maybe you need to check your equipment first and make sure that works too."

"There's nothing wrong with our equipment," I grumbled before pulling my own shirt over my head.

"Just who exactly are you going to be fucking?" Alec bit out as he noticed Florrie checking me out.

"Afraid of a little competition?" Florrie snapped.

"Uh, just a thought, but maybe we should put on some music. I'm not sure that I want to hear the noises Alec makes when he's fucking you."

"Seriously, this is ridiculous. You two are so worked up over where your dicks go and what noises you'll hear that you're ruining the whole experience."

"Fine," I snapped. "Just tell me what the fuck you want me to do and I'll do it."

Florrie got on all fours on the bed and Alec lined up behind her. I waited on instructions.

"This is how we'll do this," Alec said, panting slightly as he held his cock just outside of Florrie's pussy. "I'll take her from behind. You get under her and lick that pussy. Make her come all over my cock."

"You want me to put my face down there where your cock will be."

He glared at me, but I just stared him down. There was no way that was happening.

"Are you a man or a pussy? Because my woman needs you."

Never backing away from a challenge, I got down on my back and scooted under Florrie, who was on her hands and knees.

"Alright, I'm moving in. Now, you lick that pussy when I pull out and you make it good."

I took a deep breath and watched as he slid inside her.

Don't do this. This is wrong!

He pulled out and I fucking ate that pussy like she was sweet potatoes and turkey at Thanksgiving. God, she fucking tasted good. I pulled back as he pushed back inside her and moved my lips up to her clit, licking and sucking. It was a little weird because I could feel his dick inside her, but I ignored it. She wanted this and I would make it good for her.

Every time he pulled out, I feasted on her. Her moans pushed me on, making me need that cream like I would die without it. Alec started moving faster, so fast that I couldn't always pull back in time. My lips touched his dick and I tried to pull back, but then he pulled out and she moved, and the next thing I knew, Alec's dick was in my mouth.

I jumped back, yanking my mouth away from him, and squirmed out from under Florrie. "What the fuck was that?"

"You sucked my dick," Alec shouted.

"You moved too fast and shoved your dick in my mouth! That's fucking disgusting!"

"Boys, it's not that big of a deal. I kind of liked it. In fact, why can't we do a little more of that. The therapist said that we needed to get acquainted with each other."

"Not like that. I had his dick in my mouth. I'll be scarred for life. I'll never be able to look at him the same way again."

"You?" Alec shouted back at me. "I felt a warm mouth around my dick and it wasn't a woman's. And I fucking liked it! Now, you tell me who's more fucked up!"

"Yeah? Well, I liked it too!"

"Well, then maybe we should just fuck."

"Maybe we should," I shouted back. And then he was kissing me, all the while Florrie was watching.

I'm not seeing this. It's not real. This is not happening.

Chapter Thirty-Two

ALEC

I cleared my throat as I approached Craig and Florrie the next morning in the gym. It was awkward as hell to see them. Not that they knew what happened last night. It was my fucking dream, but still, just seeing them made me feel like we had all been a part of the same sordid business.

"Hey," I said uncomfortably.

"Hey," Craig said, holding out his hand for a fist bump, but then retracting it and rubbing his hand against his shirt. "Uh, what's new? I mean, anything weird...happen...last night?"

"Nope," I said quickly.

"Nope, not a thing," Florrie added. "Completely normal night. Just bed and sleeping. No dreams. None whatsoever."

"Yeah," I cleared my throat. "Me neither. Just your normal night of sleep where nothing happens. Absolutely nothing."

Craig nodded. "Same here. Nothing new to report."

We all stood there nodding and refusing to look at each other. "So, that doctor," I said after a moment. "She's kind of weird, right? I mean, the things she suggested, they could put thoughts in a person's head, right?"

"You mean, like, make people think things they wouldn't normally think?" Craig asked.

"Yes," Florrie said. "I agree. Totally weird."

"Like, maybe she might have made some suggestions that might make me dream about something that I would normally never think. Not that I did," I added quickly.

"Right," Florrie nodded. "Like maybe add elements to a dream that would never have been there in the first place without her suggestions."

"Yeah. I mean, I'm not gay," Craig said. "Not that I had dreams about being gay. I'm just saying, the power of suggestion can be very strong."

"Exactly," I said, holding up my hand like he had just hit the jackpot on ideas. "We're not gay."

"No," Craig shook his head. "And dreams don't mean a thing."

"Right," Florrie agreed. "Not that any of us had any dreams."

"No," I said, shaking my head and still not quite able to look either of them in the eye.

"So, I'm kind of thinking that we should all take the day apart from each other. You know, do the opposite of what she said and get some space," Craig advised.

"Sounds good." Florrie stepped back like she was ready to bolt.

"So, we're agreed. No more talk of anything suggestive in therapy," I said to be clear.

"Or seeing each other the rest of the day," Florrie added.

"Or talking about our dreams."

"No," I shook my head. "Definitely no talking about dreams."

We all took another step back and stood there awkwardly. "Well, I'm gonna split. I've got shit to do."

"Yeah," Craig nodded. "I've got...other things that don't involve sleep. Or beds," he added quickly. "And definitely require clothes."

"Right," Florrie added. "And mouthwash."

Craig had started to look away, but looked back quickly, eyeing me strangely. It couldn't be. We didn't all have the same dream, right?

Florrie snapped her fingers and pointed in the other direction. "Look. Bundt cake."

She took off leaving me alone with Craig. "Let's never speak of this again," Craig said quietly.

"Agreed."

Chapter Thirty-Three

ALEC

Present Day...

"Jamie Hanson?" I stepped forward and shook the man's hand. "I'm Alec Wesley. I'm your primary contact while we're protecting you. This is Florrie, she'll be your personal security while-"

"Excuse me," Jamie grinned. "A woman is going to be protecting me? I'm not trying to be sexist, but she doesn't look like she could hurt a fly."

I quirked an eyebrow in Florrie's direction. She strut up to him in her summer dress and slingback heels, her blonde hair blowing in the breeze, and laid her hand on his chest. "I promise not to let anyone hurt you."

He looked down at her and returned her smile. "I'm sure you would try." She gripped his hand, twisted his arm up behind his back, and shoved him up against the wall in the entryway of the house. "Okay, okay," he laughed nervously. "You don't have to prove it to me. I believe you," he said desperately.

Florrie stepped back, brushing the hair out of her face. God, she was sexy. I shook that thought from my head.

"Trust me, I won't let anything happen to you. This is part of the reason I'm your close protection. People will assume I'm your date and not the woman that will kill anyone that tries to come close to you."

"I won't ever make that mistake again, Florrie." He smiled at her and she fucking beamed back at him. This was all wrong. That was the smile she used to give me, only now, she was free to give it to anyone.

"Why don't I show you inside and you can go over everything with me and tell me what's expected of me?"

He stepped aside, waving an arm forward for Florrie, leaving Craig and I behind.

"Did you see that?" Craig whispered to me. "I didn't even get an introduction. I'm feeling a little put out right now." I slowly turned my head and glared at him. He took a step back and shrugged. "Okay, *maybe* you have the bigger issue right now. I can see how you would think that. She's hot and she just fell all over the floor in a puddle for JFK Jr. Who wouldn't? Did you see that guy's hair? If I had hair like that, I would definitely grow mine out."

"Are you trying to say he's better looking than me?"

"No," Craig said, but then looked back at Jamie and bounced his head from side to side in thought. "It could be close. I mean, on the one hand, you have the body and the dastardly good looks, but he does have the hair. Sometimes hair trumps everything else."

"Where do you come up with this shit?"

"Elle. Yeah, I was reading it one time when I was getting a pedicure. The article was about-"

"Hold on." I stopped him outside the living room with a hand to his chest. "Did you just say that you were reading a chick magazine?"

"Well, it's not like they have a copy of *Guns and Ammo* at a nail salon."

"So, why don't you bring your own shit to read?"

He shrugged. "I kind of like reading that stuff. It gets me inside a woman's head."

"I still can't believe you talked me into getting a fucking pedicure," I grumbled.

"Hey, that shit was good and you know it. Besides, it's not like I go just to treat myself to a day out. I get ingrown toenails. Have you ever tried running on uneven terrain when you have an ingrown toenail? Plus, seriously, a woman bowing down to you, literally massaging your fucking feet? Life doesn't get too much better than that."

He clapped me on the shoulder and headed into the room. I just stood there, staring at my teammate as he sat down, very properly I might add, and picked up a fucking tea cup and a scone. Who was this guy?

I sat down on the opposite couch that Florrie and Jamie were sitting on, glaring at him the whole fucking time. He didn't even notice. He was too busy laughing with Florrie. Occasionally, he would touch her leg. It was all innocent, of course, but I saw fucking red. Craig had to kick me twice to get me to stop glaring at him like I was going to kill him.

"Mr. Hanson," I interrupted. "We have your itinerary here with us. We've gone over the charity event and some of the other stops you added in. We believe that it would be wise to put a second team on you once we're in New York City. You'll meet them when we get there. They'll mostly be secondary security and we'll only bump that up if we feel there's a threat."

"But Florrie will be with me the whole time?" he smiled.

"Yes," I said, clearing my throat. "She will act as your girlfriend throughout the entire time we're in New York. If someone is after you, it'll make it more difficult for an attack to occur."

"I wouldn't mind having you on my arm the whole time." His smile was sickeningly sweet and worse, Florrie returned it. I could tell she was enamored with him. So, what did this guy have that I didn't?

Craig and I left Florrie to plan out some details with Jamie, mostly because I couldn't stand to be in the same room with both of them. It wasn't a necessity that all of us be in the room, but more than that, we had to hit the road and needed to get the vehicle loaded.

"They looked cozy," Craig said as we carried Mr. Hanson's bags out to the vehicle.

"Shut it."

"No, seriously. I can see why she's fawning over him. He's rich, handsome, higher life expectancy, and most importantly, probably doesn't have bullet holes all over his body. Oh, and they'd make gorgeous kids."

I tossed one of his bags in the trunk.

"Gorgeous?"

"Sorry, stunning. Is that better?"

"No, I want you to say something more manly."

"Such as?"

I slammed the trunk and turned to glare at him. "I don't know, but I don't want you to sound like you belong in a fucking dress shop while we're talking. I don't understand what's going on with you. Pedicures and saying words like 'stunning'..."

"Yeah," he snorted. "There's something wrong with *me*. You're the one that's worrying about JFK Jr."

"Because you keep pointing out that he's the better choice," I said exasperatedly.

"Because to most women he would be. I'm not trying to be a bastard. I'm just pointing out where you fall short. You know, so if you decide to get back together *again*, you can make room for improvements."

"Yeah, because I can see easily changing my looks to be more like JFK Jr."

"Well, fine, but you could...put less bullets in your body," he said slowly, then thought that one over for a moment and then sighed. "Well, you could make more money."

"Thanks for the advice, Einstein."

"I know you mean that as an insult, but I'm going to choose to hear it as flattery."

"Can we just go get His Royal Highness and hit the road?"

"Jr. wasn't royalty," Craig shouted from behind me. I flipped him the bird.

"Why didn't we just fly into New York City?" Jamie asked from the backseat where he was practically cuddled up with Florrie.

"Because going through an airport gives a greater opportunity for exposure. We can fly under the radar better when we drive," I explained. That wasn't the only reason. We wanted to be prepared as best we could, and having our vehicles that were fully equipped was best.

I had made Craig drive this time around. I didn't think that I could keep my eyes off the rearview mirror if I was in the driver's seat. Florrie had been back there for the last few hours, giggling like a fucking schoolgirl with Jamie. God, even his fucking name grated on me. Who named their son a girl's name? Fucking prick. The problem was, from what I could tell, the guy was really nice, which made my little predicament even worse. It was really fucking hard to be pissed at a guy that hadn't done anything wrong other than be really fucking handsome.

"So, tell me why you prefer Florrie over Florence," Jamie asked her with a smile. I glowered at them, but then realized that I had never thought to ask Florrie that question.

"I would love to say that it's because my mom loves Florence, but unfortunately, she named me after Florence Nightingale. She was known as the Lady with the Lamp, the nurse that made the rounds of wounded soldiers at night. She was always pushing me to go into nursing school. She thought I could heal people."

I watched as she cringed. I would too. Who wanted to be a nurse that healed the soldiers when you could be a fucking soldier?

"I didn't want to be a nurse or a doctor. I wanted to go kick ass."

I grinned. I knew her so fucking well.

"So, your mom wasn't too happy, I'm guessing, when you became a soldier instead of a nurse."

Florrie snorted. "Well, let's just say that it caused a lot of fights between us and we really haven't spoken since I was eighteen."

"What about your dad? Where does he fit in with all that?"

"He passed away a few years ago."

"Did you make it home for the funeral?"

I watched in the mirror as she chewed her lip and stared out the window. "We were in a bit of a crisis when it happened. I didn't find out he died until after the funeral. After that, my mom told me not to bother coming home."

I glanced over at Craig. When the fuck had that happened? Judging by the confused expression on his face, he didn't know either.

"I'm sorry, Florrie."

I watched as he intertwined their fingers and had to remember that he was a good guy and no matter how much I wanted to smash my fist into his face, we were here to protect him.

"You know, you should still try and get in touch with her. You only have one mother, and life is precious."

She smiled at him and quickly changed the subject. "So, do you mind me asking why things didn't work out with your wife?"

He chuckled and gave a nod. "Well played. Let's just say that I didn't realize what a money grubbing gold digger she was until we had been married for about nine months. I should have seen it coming. She was always pushing business deals on me, but I just assumed that she really wanted me to succeed. It wasn't until I was talking about opening a new charity that she really let her true colors show. She didn't like that I was giving all *her* money away."

"Talk about a wake up call."

"The real wake up call was when I sent her the divorce papers and she countered with her own set. For some reason, she felt she was entitled to half of everything even though we hadn't even been married for a year."

"And she's still coming after you? Why does she think she'll win?"

He cringed and ran his hand along his jaw. This was bad. "After I found out that she was only after me for my money, I might have gotten a little drunk and took another woman home. Not my finest moment, but I was angry. Have you ever done anything like that?"

"No, I can't say I have, but I'm not the monogamous type either."

I saw her eyes flick to mine in the mirror of the visor and then back to Jamie. He noticed too. He chuckled and removed his hand from hers. "It makes sense now."

"What makes sense," Craig asked.

"Why I'm still single," Florrie cut in, glaring at Jamie.

"Yeah," Jamie nodded knowingly. "That's what I meant."

"So, no kids then? Just living the single life and working?"

Hurt crossed Florrie's face, but she quickly masked it with a smile.

I knew that kids were still a sore subject for her, but I had told her we could make it work if she wanted. Unless I was the problem. Maybe she wanted kids, just not with me. Craig was right. She wanted a better choice, someone better looking or richer. No, that wasn't it. It was the higher life expectancy. She wanted someone that could promise her the future that I couldn't.

I slammed the visor closed and stared out the window. Now it all made sense. I was the reason that she avoided a relationship with me. Because the life that she really wanted was never a sure thing with me. There was always the chance that I would end up dead on a job and she would be left alone. I was the risk she just didn't want to take.

Chapter Thirty-Four

FLORRIE

After getting Jamie settled in the hotel, I left him alone. He had phone calls to make, and I needed to talk with Alec. After rekindling our fucking, I got the feeling that Alec thought I was somehow his again. I needed to clear the air. It wasn't that I was planning on screwing Jamie, but Alec needed to lay off the angry faces. I closed the door to his bedroom in the suite and made my way over to the room that Alec was staying in. I knocked lightly, but got no answer. Turning the knob, I steeled myself for his anger.

He was facing the window, arms crossed over his chest. I knocked on the door again in case he hadn't heard me, but he didn't turn around. Sighing, I closed the door and walked over to him.

"Alec, I think we need to talk."

"How come you've never told me any of that shit before?"

Surprised, it took me a second to figure out what he was talking about. "What? You mean about my name?"

"That and about your dad."

"Well, that's pretty simple. You've never asked."

He turned to me, his eyes cold and distant, his body rigid and full of tension. "I wasn't aware that I had to ask. I thought when you were with someone, you just volunteered that information."

"Alec, we've never talked about anything like that before. It's not exactly like you've taken me out on dates and we've gotten to know each other."

"Knowing that shit doesn't mean I know you. See, I know what makes you tick because I've worked by your side for years."

"Yeah, you're right about that, but you don't know anything about me other than what I've let you see."

He stepped forward to get in my space, but I backed away. I wasn't going to let him push me around.

"Stop trying to push your way in. We're not together anymore."

"Tell me, why is it so easy for you to open up to him, but not me?"

"Because he asked," I said incredulously. "Tell me one time that you've bothered to find out one fucking thing about me that didn't have something to do with giving me orgasms."

I was right and he knew it. We never had that kind of relationship, and maybe if he had tried, things might have been different. Though, I really doubted it. My mind was firmly made up.

"Don't bullshit me, Florrie. There were plenty of times that we stayed up talking. You could have opened up to me at any time. You chose not to, and now I know why."

"Yeah? And why is that?"

He clenched his jaw in frustration, the prickly hairs of his scruff standing rigid against his jaw. God, I wanted to rub my hands over it. "You've never given me a chance. From the moment I told you that I wanted to talk with Cap about being a couple, you've told me that it had to stay quiet. So, tell me. What's the real reason that you never wanted anyone to know about us?"

I was confused. What was he getting at? We'd already been through this.

"Is it because of my job?"

"That's ridiculous. I have the same job."

"I saw your face when he asked about kids." It felt like a knife stabbed me in the chest. "It's because of me. You want the good guy that can promise you no more bullet holes, no more hospital stays, no more risks that would put you in the position to be raising a child alone. Am I right?" he barked at me.

I blinked back tears at his accusation. He knew it would never happen for me, so how could he be so heartless? "You know I can't-"

"I talked with the doctors, Florrie. There were options for us. So don't you dare fucking tell me that it's not about kids. He's so much fucking better, right?"

"This isn't about him, and it's not about kids. How many times do I have to tell you that?"

"Maybe if you actually told me something! Anything! Do you know how frustrating it is to know that you're not wanted, but the woman you love can't actually tell you why? Your excuses are pathetic, Florrie. You can't even tell me for sure whether or not you love me. You say you don't know what love is, well, let me tell you what it is to me. Love is needing someone so much that you'd die without her. Love is needing to be sure that the person you're with is alright. Love is taking a bullet for the other person just so she doesn't have to feel a second of pain. Love is staying and trying to work things out over and over again because you know you'll be miserable without her. Love is knowing deep down that you'll never be good enough for her, but then trying even harder to be worthy of her. Love is a pain so deep inside that if you don't have it, life isn't worth fighting for. Love is..."

His eyes sparkled with unshed tears. His hand brushed against my cheek lightly and then he dropped it. "Love is...knowing you have to walk away from the woman you love because you know you're hurting her by staying."

He took a step back and ducked his head. Tears dripped down my face and I brushed them away quickly. I was hurting him. I could see it so clearly now. I had been selfish before, always pushing him away and only thinking of myself, but right now, the only person I could think about was Alec. If he was ever going to be happy, it was going to be without me messing with his head.

"We still have a job to do, but I suspect that playing Mr. Hanson's arm candy won't be too difficult for you. Maybe you'll even find that he's the man you really want."

"Alec, he's not-"

"I don't give a fuck who he is to you. All that matters is that it doesn't mean shit to me anymore."

We headed out the next day bright and early. Jamie had some business to conduct, meetings that he had to sit in on, and after that, we were going to show him off to the city. Jamie had no idea if his wife would actually try something, but now he wanted to find out.

"Okay, so we just go out and pretend we're a couple," Jamie said, blowing out a breath quickly, shaking out his hands. "I can do that. We just hold hands, right?"

"Well, and try not to look at me like you're scared of me."

"That's going to be difficult, because frankly, I'm fucking terrified of you now. Especially with your guard dog watching your every move."

"He's not watching me. He's watching you, and trust me, he's going to keep you safe."

I knew this for a fact because he had walked away from me for good last night. Now, we were working a job, and Alec would make sure that we didn't fuck it all up.

"Are you ready?" I asked as we prepared to step out of the vehicle.

He laughed slightly and shook his head. "I was never ready for this. I just wanted to do some good. I never thought that I would accumulate this much wealth from my investments. Now, every charity project I do is in the spotlight. I just...it was never supposed to be like that."

I gripped his hand, waiting for him to look at me. "It'll be fine. You just go do what you need to do and we'll handle watching your back."

He nodded and squeezed my hand, but he didn't let go as he opened the door and stepped out. He held my hand even as he shut the door. He was taking this girlfriend thing as far as he could, except, he was squeezing a little tight.

"You need to relax," I said with a smile.

"Sorry, it helps to know that I have a lethal woman standing right next to me. You have guns, right?"

"Many of them," I grinned. We headed for the building.

"How many is that exactly? And where did you hide them?"

He held the door open for me and we stepped inside past security. I showed them my badge and was taken through to a back room while Craig and Alec waited with Jamie. There were two men waiting for me and I took it all in stride. This was pretty typical, clearing your weapons with security first. Weapons in general weren't allowed in most buildings, but we had called ahead to be cleared and explained the situation.

"So," the first guy smirked. "*You're* the personal protection for a man worth a half a billion dollars?"

The man wore a nice suit, perfectly pressed and ready to shine. "Yes, I'll be by Mr. Hanson's side the entire time. I currently have six weapons on me."

The second man closed the distance behind me and brushed up against my backside. I quirked my head to the side, pissed off that these guys thought they could intimidate me. When his hand brushed against my hip, I may have lost control.

I snatched his hand and bent back his wrist. He crumpled to his knees and I flung my elbow back, hitting him in the nose and breaking it. I heard his cry of pain and adjusted my gaze on the second man who was already reaching for me. He had the nerve to try and get his hands around my neck. I slammed my head forward, cracking my forehead against his face. He stumbled back and I kicked him in the chest, sending him flying into the wall. He crumbled to the ground, whimpering in pain.

Picking up my purse that had fallen to the ground, I opened the door and walked out, my heels clicking on the tile floors as I made my way back to my team. Jamie's eyes were wide as he looked me up and down.

"You may want to go check on your men," I said to the security agent in front. "They seem to have had an accident."

The man rushed to the back and I slid my hand into Jamie's, giving him a reassuring squeeze. But when I went to move toward the elevators, he stood stock still.

"What?"

"You have...blood on your face."

Alec handed me a handkerchief and I took it, pulling out my compact from my purse to check the damage. I had blood splatter from breaking the guy's nose all over my face. I dabbed and cleaned myself up and tucked it all back in my purse.

"Ready?"

He just stared at me. "What? We had a disagreement about where he could put his hands."

Jamie released my hand immediately and I rolled my eyes, strutting away toward the elevators.

The longer I sat in the boardroom, the more I wanted to just drop my head to the table and go to sleep. My head was pounding from head butting that guy earlier, and I knew that would happen, but sometimes these things couldn't be avoided.

"We've got two suspects by the vehicle," Cazzo said over coms. "We'll see what he does and follow him."

A few minutes later, he came back on. "They placed something under your vehicle. We're in pursuit. Cops are on the way. You're gonna have to find another way out. Don't stick around."

"Sir," Alec said, stepping forward. "We need to leave."

Jamie turned to me, worry on his face. I stood and held out my hand to ease the tension. His business associates didn't look too happy that we were interrupting their time. "It was so nice to meet you. I hope we'll see you at the charity event tomorrow evening."

They seemed appeased by that and I grabbed Jamie's hand and headed for the door. He seemed stunned at first, but was now following without question.

"Cazzo, what do you have?" I asked.

"Still following. Cops are just arriving on the scene."

"We'll take him to a secure location and check in when we arrive," Alec responded.

"There are several of these buildings connected underground," Craig said, pulling a map from his jacket pocket.

"Why are we leaving?" Jamie asked.

"Someone planted something on the vehicle. We need to get you to a secure location while the police check out the SUV. Our other team is following the suspects. Hopefully, they'll be able to find out something," I said.

"Alright, let's take the elevator down to the garage. It looks like there's an access tunnel that we can head through. I'll call security and let them know to meet us there."

We got on the elevator, but had to make several stops for people that were also headed down. We stopped one last time at the lobby and when the doors opened, a man was standing near the entrance of the building. He was staring right at us, and then lifted his wrist and spoke.

"Alec," I said, grabbing my gun from my thigh holster.

"I see it." He drew his weapon, as did Craig. The doors started to close and the man ran for the front doors. "Cazzo, we've got a secondary team in the lobby. We're headed to the basement for the access tunnels that connect the buildings underground."

"I have a car on the way to you. I'll have them meet you outside the Bank of America Tower."

"Got it."

The doors opened and Alec and Craig stepped out, clearing the area. "Stay right next to me. I need my gun out, but do exactly what I say."

"No problem," Jamie chuckled nervously.

Craig nodded and I stepped out of the elevator with Jamie on my heels. We hurried across the parking garage to the access tunnel where security was waiting. He opened the door and we slipped through, running through the underground tunnels that connected the buildings.

"Cazzo, we're about to enter the Bank of America Tower."

But there was no response. "Shit," Craig said, pulling the door open. He started to move forward, but stopped and raised his gun. I immediately went on defense, stepping in front of Jamie.

"Corner," I said, turning and pushing Jamie toward a darkened corner. I heard gunshots and I heard footsteps. I spun around and raised my gun, unloading my gun into the man chasing us. Suddenly, there were more men in the tunnel, filtering in all around us. I grabbed a second clip and snapped it in place, holding my stance firm. I backed up, putting Jamie directly behind me. I felt Jamie reach for my weapon at my hip, but there were too many of them coming to stop him.

I fired repeatedly, taking down each person that dared to come close to us. Gunfire sounded in my ear and I flinched, not prepared for the sharp bark of the gun. I glanced at Jamie, who was holding the gun in his hand like it was a snake. Alec and Craig had taken down most of the men and now I just had to stay put and keep Jamie safe until we got the all clear.

"Clear," Alec shouted after a moment. "Cazzo, come in." Radio silence again. "Shit. Okay, here's the plan."

I motioned for Jamie to follow and headed closer to Alec.

"I'm going to call this in to the police department and we'll book it out of here. They already knew we were here, so we're not sticking around."

I saw the gun at the last minute, the man barely moving his arm, but it was enough. I leapt over to Jamie, shoving him to the ground just as the gun fired.

Chapter Thirty-Five

ALEC

I heard her call his name and I saw her leap in front of him. I knew it was her job, but when I saw her body jerk, it didn't matter that it was her job. All I saw was the woman I loved laying on the ground and not moving.

The man who fired was on the ground and Craig was cuffing him. He was thinking logically, while I was only thinking with my heart. We needed him alive so we could find out who was behind the attack, but rage unlike anything I'd ever felt gripped me and held on. I stormed over to the man, throwing myself on top of him, and threw punch after punch. His face was red and bloodied, but all I saw was Florrie. I could feel the blood coating my hands and my face, but I didn't relent. I was tired of people trying to take her from me. He wasn't going to get away with this. He was going to be dealt justice the way I saw fit.

"Alec, stop!"

Craig jerked at my arm, but I shoved him off and grabbed my gun, pointing it in his face. "Back. The fuck. Off," I bit out. He slowly stepped back, holding his hands up in acquiescence. I turned back to the man on the floor. He was barely conscious, but he opened his eyes and grinned at me.

"Was she your girl?" he gurgled. "It's a fucking shame. With that body-"

My hand flew to his throat and I squeezed, sucking all the life from his body. He didn't have any right to talk about Florrie that way. No man did. His eyes bulged and the veins in his forehead popped to the surface. He grasped onto my hand, but he was too weak to do anything.

"Alec, you have to stop, man. You're gonna kill him. We need him alive."

"Fuck that," I growled.

"Alec, she's fine. Florrie's not hurt."

But it didn't penetrate. In my mind, she was still laying over there, probably bleeding out on the ground.

"Florrie needs you. Just stop and go help her."

The need to see her took over and I glanced in her direction. She was standing and holding her chest, but she seemed fine. She started to undo her dress and that's when I saw that she was wearing one of Knight's skin vests. It was a bulletproof vest that he had field tested years ago. The results weren't great, so we hadn't used them. But for Florrie it made sense. Some protection was better than none.

Looking back at the man on the ground, I leaned down and whispered in his ear. "You think you've won, but we're all still standing, and you're going to hell."

Gripping his head, I leaned on his chest and snapped his fucking neck. I heard Craig sigh beside me, but I didn't give a fuck. I did what I had to do.

"Guess I'll be the one to let Cazzo know our lead is dead," Craig said.

I walked over to Florrie and pulled her to the side.

"Why did you do that?" she asked. "We needed him alive."

"He tried to take you from me."

"Alec," she sighed in exasperation. "It's my job. You would have done the same thing."

"Remember what I told you about love?" She nodded. "He tried to take that from me, and then I'd be dead inside. Yeah, I killed him. He pushed and I pushed back. And I won."

I walked away, knowing Florrie didn't want to be around me right now. Hell, I didn't want to be around me right now. And when we got back to Reed Security, I was in for one hell of an ass-reaming by Cap.

"What the fuck were you thinking?" Cap shouted at me over the phone.

I didn't say anything. There was nothing I could say to defend myself. I was on the job and I had taken matters into my own hands. There was no pretending that what I did was okay.

"Are you gonna answer me?"

"You're not gonna like the answer," I responded.

"You killed a man that could have led us to finding out who wants to kill our client." Still, I said nothing. "Craig and Florrie are staying behind with Jamie. I'm sending out another team to add support. As soon as they arrive, you get your ass back here."

"I understand."

I hung up and sat down on the couch in the suite. Loosening my tie, I yanked it off and threw it in the corner. I very well may have screwed my career over today, but I'd do it again in a heartbeat. Leaning back against the couch, I let my eyes slip closed and tried to wash the day away.

Warm hands ran across my shoulders, but I must have been dreaming because Florrie had to be pissed at me right now. But then I felt her straddle my lap, I slid my hand around her waist. Touching her instantly soothed something inside me that was hurting uncontrollably.

"I'm sorry I scared you," she whispered against my lips. I kissed her, not because I wanted to maul her and fuck her, but because I needed it to ground me.

"I'm not sorry for what I did."

"I know."

"I'm heading back to Pennsylvania." I opened my eyes and stared into hers. "Cap might fire me for this." She didn't say anything, just continued to stare at me. "I'd do it again, you know."

"I know."

"I'm not sorry. When I saw that bullet hit you..." I pressed my lips together, unable to say anything else. She already knew how I felt. "I know Cap's going to take me off the team at the very least."

I watched her for a moment, wondering why she came over to me. Why was she sitting on my lap like she was meant to be there when just a day ago, things had ended yet again between us? She didn't want me, but here she was, acting like she was mine. But I could also see her hesitation. She was afraid she was sending me the wrong signals. I wouldn't make that mistake again.

"I can see it now, why you thought it wasn't going to work. I put the mission aside because of my feelings for you. I was out of control."

I ran my hands up the side of her body and back down. I was going to miss this. I had never had a connection with anyone the way I did with Florrie. She was the one person who had the ability to light up my life when I thought everything was fine. I hadn't known I needed someone until I had her. And now it was all gone.

I didn't know if there was anything that could have changed what happened with us. Florrie was who she was and I never really stood a chance of catching her and making her mine. She was always meant to fly on her own. I left in the early morning and headed back to Reed Security, and she went back to work. I was alone again, but this time, I knew there was no chance of getting her back.

"So, now that you're back, you want to tell me what the hell was running through you head?"

I was sitting across from Cap in his office. This conversation had been a long time coming. It was one thing when we were on the run and weren't working together, but what I had just done proved that it wasn't a good idea for us to work together.

"I was thinking that the woman I loved was just shot right in front of me. I was thinking that I wanted to kill the person responsible."

"And after you found out she was okay, you killed him anyway."

I nodded, staring at a spot on his desk. His face flashed in my mind, the man smirking at me as he taunted me. I knew right then that no matter what, that man was going to die and I was going to kill him. There was no justice for someone like that. He would be taken into custody and sent to prison. If he had the right lawyer, he would get off. As it was, if he ended up in jail, it wouldn't be a hard enough sentence. Prison was nothing like it used to be. He would get the chance to be "rehabilitated". But I had seen the evil in his eyes. There was no way for a man like that to be redeemed.

"Alec, you have to give me something. You went crazy. You killed a guy in cold blood."

"Have you ever seen Maggie hurt? I mean, where you thought she was dead and it was all over? The life you wanted with her was gone. Even if things didn't work out, there wasn't even a chance now, because the woman you loved was gone." I glanced up at him and knew that he knew exactly what I was talking about. "See, even if Florrie doesn't love me, never wants to see me again, she's still out there living her life. And I know that even though it's killing me to never touch her or hold her again, never see her smile or throat punch someone, she's still alive. And I'm good with that. Because I know, deep down in my gut that I would rather have her alive and married to some schmuck than to be dead and know that someone out there isn't getting all those things that I once had with her.

"I know now that the time I had with her is over. I know that I'm never gonna get to wake up next to her again or see her smile at me like she loves me, even though she won't fucking admit it. Things went too sideways for us." I nodded to myself, knowing that what I was saying was the truth. "But that asshole that tried to take her from me is dead. And I don't fucking regret it for a minute."

I wiped a stray tear that slid down my face. I wasn't too fucking proud to admit that I was heartbroken. I also knew that real men could cry. And I was a real fucking man, so I let the tears slide down my face unabashedly, and I let myself grieve the relationship that was lost.

Cap sighed and tossed me a box of kleenex. "I want so much to be pissed at you right now, but I know exactly what you're talking about. I know that I would have killed the guy, because that's exactly what I did in that basement when that gang took Maggie. There was so much fucking blood and all I could see was her lying on the floor. And I thought she was dead." He ran a hand over his face and shook the memories off. "Give me some time to think this over. Take a few days off. I don't want to see you around here."

I nodded and walked out the door. I wasn't out, yet. But I was still fucking lost without her, and that was something I was going to have to learn to deal with.

Chapter Thirty-Six

FLORRIE

We were sitting back at the hotel in the living room of the suite. Craig had gone out for breakfast, which left me with Jamie. I had been distant since everything went down yesterday. I didn't know how to feel about what happened with Alec. He had gone crazy and killed a man because he had shot me. It was insane. I was just doing my job.

But then I remembered the look on his face when he killed that man. He had a darkness to him and it all revolved around me. Someone had threatened me, and no matter how much I tried to deny it, he loved me. I had just been pretending that he didn't really love me that much, because it made me feel better about not returning his love. But it was clear last night that Alec loved me with an all-consuming intensity that I had seen so many times with my co-workers. Now I couldn't figure out what to do.

"Your team leader is pretty intense," Jamie said as he sat down beside me.

I nodded with a smile. "Yes, he is."

"He must love you a lot. I would imagine that a man would only lose it like that if he lost the love of his life." He took a sip of coffee and studied me over the top of his mug. "So, why aren't you with him?"

"I...We work together..." I said dumbly, not quite sure if that reasoning was true anymore.

He laughed slightly. "Sounds like you're not too sure about that."

I groaned and flopped my head back against the couch. "It's complicated."

"So, uncomplicate it for me."

I sat up and faced him. "You really want to hear about this?"

He took my hand in his and stroked the back of my hand. "I was married to a woman that I thought I loved. But after seeing Alec with you, I know I didn't even have a tenth of the love that Alec has for you. I want to know what that's like someday."

I swallowed the lump building in my throat, "Well, it just happened one day. We've worked together for years, but one day, I just saw him differently. I don't know, maybe I always had a thing for him. And then I thought we would get together. Things were about to happen and then his girlfriend was there."

"Wait, he tried to start things up with you and then went back to his girlfriend?"

"It's not as bad as it sounds. He didn't want to be a cheater and his girlfriend showed up at the bar. He stopped before anything happened between us. He didn't even kiss me."

"And what did you do?"

I shrugged. "I went on and pretended that nothing had happened. I didn't want it to affect our work relationship."

"But he broke up with her?"

"After he was shot. He ended it with her and then...are you sure you want to hear all this?"

"Oh, I think I need to now."

"Well," I picked at the loose threads of the bottom of my pants. "He waited, after he broke up with her. He wanted to give me time and...and then we were together and he wanted to go talk to our boss. But I didn't want anyone to know. I didn't want all the pressure."

"So, you had a hidden relationship?"

"Not really. It was just fucking."

He looked at me skeptically. "Are you sure about that?"

"Well, it was on my part. He kept trying to talk me into more."

"Okay, so when did it all implode?"

"About a year after we got together, I found out that I have a medical condition that would make it hard to have kids. I've seen all the guys at work, the way they act when they become parents. I didn't want to take that away from him."

"So, you took matters into your own hands."

"Well, not exactly. I mean, I didn't tell him about it and I tried to end it with him, but he has a way of pulling me back in. And then I found out I was pregnant a year later. But it was an ectopic pregnancy and...it was not a good way for him to find out about everything."

"So, if I may point out something to you..."

"Go for it."

"You didn't trust him because he mislead you by wanting you when he had a girlfriend, but you lied to him for a whole year. And you think you're the injured party?"

I cringed, but I knew he was right.

"Florrie, I hate to say it, but it sounds like you're the one making the mistakes here. No matter if you wanted a relationship or not, you were the one that was doing the lying."

"I know," I finally admitted. "Believe it or not, we broke up for a good six months, but then..."

"You started fucking again. Let me ask you something. After seeing the lengths he would go to for you, and seeing it for what it really is, how can you still deny that he's the guy for you?"

"I wish I knew."

"You need to figure that out. Because neither of you is ever going to be happy without the other."

"Are you ready for tonight?"

"I don't know," Jamie grinned. "Do I tempt fate and show my face?"

"Well, you can't let them win."

He sighed and adjusted his tie. "I suppose you're right. It doesn't mean I have to like it."

He turned to fully face me and his jaw dropped. "Holy hell. Please tell me you didn't fit any guns under that dress."

"Two."

"Two? How did they fit?"

I looked down at my dress, low cut in the front and a high slit up the side. It was fire engine red and sparkled slightly. "Well, I had to store them in special places."

He groaned and rubbed his hands over his face. "Remind me that I need to find a woman like you when I get divorced. I think I like the idea of a woman that can hide weapons beneath a skin tight dress and still look sexy as hell."

"Let's go get this over with. Is there anyone you think that will be a problem tonight?"

"It should all be people that have been invited for the charity. I don't foresee a problem."

"Good. Then let's just go have fun."

"Ha," he barked out a laugh. "You've never been to one of these things, have you?"

"Happily, I can say that I haven't."

We drove across Manhattan, fighting horrendous traffic the whole way. It was a relief when we got to the event just so we could get out of the car. The door was opened and then there were flashing lights that made it difficult to spot any threats. Luckily, I knew that Craig, Cazzo, and Sinner were nearby. We made our way up the steps where a security agent stepped forward to speak with Jamie.

"Mr. Hanson, we're sorry to bother you, but your wife is here and insisted that she be allowed to attend. We didn't want to cause a scene, so we allowed her to enter."

"It's fine," Jamie sighed. "I'll deal with her."

"Be on the lookout," I said in my mic. "Jamie's wife is here."

"Oh, that should be fun," Craig commented. "Who brought the popcorn?"

We walked into the ballroom where the function was being held and I almost tripped over my own feet. I was expecting some lavish affair, but the whole room was decorated modestly and the food being served was minimal at best.

"I'm surprised. I was expecting this to look a lot different."

"Well, the whole point is to raise money, not to spend the money that is donated on a party."

I glanced around the room and spotted the soon-to-be ex-wife glaring at Jamie from across the room. "The wicked witch of the west has been spotted by the french doors," I informed Cazzo, Sinner, and Craig.

"Incoming. Looks like she's not going to stay away," Cazzo said.

I leaned into Jamie, making sure not to be overheard. "Your ex-wife is walking this way. Do not go anywhere without me tonight, understood?"

He nodded and then turned just as his wife approached.

"Jamie, I see you've brought trash along with you this evening." Her smile was tight and unwelcoming.

"I see you've pulled your hair back too tight. You might want to loosen it. It pulls your face and makes you look like you've had a face lift."

She turned red and I held my hand to my chest, trying my best to look apologetic. "Oh, I'm sorry. Did you have a face lift, but you didn't want people to know? Better find a better surgeon."

"Jamie, who is this woman?"

"I'm his girlfriend," I said, holding out my hand. "Florrie."

She rolled her eyes and snatched two glasses of champagne off the tray as a waiter passed. She handed one to Jamie and kept the other for herself.

"You're so hospitable," I grinned as I took my own glass. She just kept getting riled up, thinking she was going to make me angry, but I knew her game and I wasn't playing it.

"Jamie, we need to discuss the divorce."

"Now isn't exactly a good time for that. This is a charity event," he said testily.

"I'm aware. You did give them quite a good portion of our money."

She glanced around the room and I quickly switched glasses with Jamie, shooting him a look that said to play along.

"No, dear. Just my money. You've never worked a day in your life."

She looked back at him with a sneer. "You always were such a jerk."

"Funny," he said, taking a drink of his champagne. "You always seemed so endeared to me. Of course, that was when you had access to my money. It's funny how a lack of income can make someone so hostile."

He downed the rest of his drink and handed it off to a waiter, but I put a hand on the waiter's arm just as he was about to walk away. Snatching the glass, I grabbed onto Jamie's hand and started for the entry, keeping Jamie's original glass in my hand.

"We need an ambulance now," I yelled into my mic. "Jamie has ingested an unknown substance. I'm heading for the rear of the building. Have paramedics meet us there." Jamie looked at me in confusion, but then pretended to sway on his feet. "Somebody grab the ex-wife. She's the one behind this."

"I'm coming to you," Craig answered.

"I've called paramedics," Cazzo responded. "Head for the back door and I'll clear the path.

"Jackson, Chris, and Jules are at the backdoor," Sinner informed me. "

I pulled Jamie behind me, but eventually, he would have to start acting like he couldn't walk.

"Stumble," I muttered, and he did.

Craig caught up to me moments later and we both propped him up and started dragging him toward the backdoor.

"This is not how I saw tonight going," Jamie said as he hung his head and pretended to be out of it.

"Trust me, I didn't think I'd be dragging you around the building either."

"I've got the ex-wife," Sinner responded. "Cops are here now and cuffing her as we speak. How close are you to the back door?"

"Almost there."

"Change of plans," Cazzo said. "We've got some unfriendlies outside. Chris, Jules, and Jackson are moving out. Move to the door as planned and let it play out."

"You want us to get taken?" I asked.

"We won't let it get that far. We just want them to think they've won."

"Copy," I said, feeling slightly out of breath as we continued to drag Jamie. We were just approaching the door when Cazzo joined us.

"You ready for this?"

"Of course."

"Good, be prepared to fire if necessary, but we need answers."

I nodded, but continued to hold Jamie and the glass of champagne. It was our only evidence at the moment. Cazzo flung the door open and no less than ten men stepped out and surrounded us.

"Hand him over," one of them said.

"Damn, you caught us. Whatever will we do?" I said, faking any real fear that I would be taken. It obviously didn't come across that well because another man stepped toward me and snatched me by the hair.

"You've got nowhere to go," the man said. "You're outnumbered and your man needs to be dragged along. You've got no car waiting and no one to help."

"I'm your huckleberry," Sinner said, stepping out of the shadows. The man swung his gun in Sinner's direction, but Sinner didn't even flinch. "Did I do that right? I always wanted to play Doc Holliday. Val Kilmer does such a great job. Did I pull it off?"

"Sinner, you don't even look like a cowboy," Cazzo said in exasperation.

"But the lines. Did I pull it off okay?"

"Sure. It was fantastic. You should join Broadway."

"Shut the fuck up," the man yelled. "Stay right the fuck where you are."

"That's just my game," Sinner said to the man as he walked forward with his gun behind his back.

"What?" the man said in confusion.

"Now you say, 'Alright, longer," Sinner said, getting irritated that the man wasn't playing along.

"It's lunger, you idiot," the man replied.

"Are you sure?"

"Yes, lunger was a derogatory term for a person with tuberculosis. Doc Holliday died of tuberculosis."

"Shit," Sinner said, his face twisted in awe. "That makes so much sense." Then he appeared to get back into character and continued.

"Alright, lunger. You go to hell," Sinner said, motioning for the man to continue. "I'll put you out of your misery."

The man looked at Sinner, then over to us, and then back to Sinner.

"Say when," Sinner continued.

"Say when what?"

He looked at us and then back to the man. "I thought you saw Tombstone? This is one of the most famous scenes of the whole fucking movie. How do you not know this part? Say when you want to have a gunfight. Seriously, if I have to explain how all this works, it's just not any fun."

"What the fuck is wrong with you?" the man asked Sinner.

Jamie, irritated with this whole charade, pulled himself from our grasp and stepped forward. "He's just fucking with you. You've lost. You're surrounded and he's fucking with you."

The man shook his head. "No, you've got nowhere to go."

"Chris, hit the lights," I said into my mic.

Police lights at both ends of the alley lit up the darkness and cops started rushing forward with their weapons drawn. I handed the glass of champagne off to one of the investigators, who immediately preserved the contents of the drink and the glass itself.

The man Sinner had been fucking with was being handcuffed and Sinner walked up to him with a grin on his face. "You're no daisy. You're no daisy at all."

I rolled my eyes and walked over to where Jamie was standing by the wall. He looked pleased to say the least. "So, does this mean that I'm officially safe?"

"I wouldn't go that far. You'll need to hire a security team at least until your wife is behind bars. It wouldn't be unwise to keep them on staff now that you're rich and all."

"Damn, so the simple life is over."

"It would appear so."

He sighed, running a hand through his hair. "So, what happens now?"

"We escort you back to wherever you want to go."

"And you? Will you be staying on my staff?"

I smiled and loosened his tie. He looked so much better in jeans and a t-shirt. "I'll be moving on to the next job."

He slid his arm around my waist and pulled me in closer to him, but not in a sexual way. "You know, I wouldn't mind having a girl like you by my side, and not just as security."

"I'm afraid that I'm just a little too complicated for all that you have ahead of you. I'm not really the ballgown and charity events type of girl."

"And your watchdog? Where does he fit into this?"

If only I knew the answer to that question. I had no idea where Alec and I went from here. We had said goodbye when he left and it sounded awfully final. I didn't like it, but I didn't know how to make everything right between us either.

Chapter Thirty-Seven

ALEC

I tried to put up a fight when Cap decided to mix up the teams, but it was no use. He had me the moment he accused me of being unprofessional. The truth was, I knew he was going to do it. There was no way he couldn't. It just so happened that it fit in with his plans for everyone else.

And maybe it would do me some good. I needed space from Florrie if I was going to get over her. I wouldn't see her as often and that could only make things easier on me. We'd be going out on different jobs and there wouldn't be time to dwell on why she just didn't seem to want me.

"Hey," Cazzo said, clapping me on the back. "Cap needs us in his office."

I nodded and pulled a clean t-shirt over my head. Cazzo, Jules, and I had been training together for the last two weeks and now it was time to get to work. I headed upstairs and joined the others in Cap's office.

"Please tell me you've got a good job for us," Jules begged. "I have to get out of here."

"Ivy driving you crazy?" Cap grinned.

"I didn't say that."

"You didn't deny it either," I added. "I get it. I could use a change of scenery myself."

"Well, you're out of luck. For today, at least." Cap tossed us each a folder of paperwork. "You will be protecting Hannah Marshall. She's currently waiting to testify for the prosecution in a case against Nathan Sharpe."

"The business guy from Philly?" Jules asked.

"The very one. She says that he's guilty of insider trading and has the documentation to prove it."

"What does he say?"

"Not much, other than he's innocent. They're playing it close to the vest until the trial. Since our safe houses are a little under the weather at the moment, Hannah will stay here in the panic room until the trial begins. Then, you'll take her to Philadelphia for her to testify."

"Why are we protecting her? Has she had threats against her?" I asked.

"The prosecution suggested she take police protection until the trial. It scared her enough that she contacted us. I don't think she really thought through all it would entail to testify against one of the wealthiest men in the state."

"How long until the trial?" Cazzo asked.

"Two weeks. Since we're protecting her here and there are always other personnel here at all times, I'll only need one of you to stay with her at all times."

Cazzo and Jules turned to me with pleading looks. "Oh come on." I threw my pen down on the table. "That's just not fucking fair."

"You're the only single guy," Cap admitted. "It makes the most sense that you work as her personal security."

"This fucking sucks."

"It's not as bad as it looks. She'll be able to move about the panic room, and as long as you don't give her the fucking codes, she can't get out on her own. You need to be in here with her, but not on her ass twenty-four seven."

"Fucking great," I grumbled. "So, when is this princess showing up?"

"In about an hour."

"Fine, I'll head home and get my shit."

"By the way," Cap said as I stood. "Have you guys decided what you're going to do about housing?"

"Well, if someone buys up that property at the edge of mine, we'll all technically be on the same land and I don't have to move," Cazzo said. "Which you know I don't want to. I like the arsenal I've built up at my house."

"Well, there are still some guys looking into moving. Maybe talk to Ice. He lives in that small, shitty cabin."

"It's not that bad," Jules muttered. "He added on after they had kids."

"What about you?" Cap asked me. "Any ideas?"

"Fuck, I hate moving. Do I really have to decide right away?" I whined.

"What the fuck are you talking about?" Jules asked. "You know one of the ladies is going to do all the work for you."

"Still, there's the day of the move and I have to wake up in time for the people to get there and then there's all the organizing-"

"That you could hire a moving company to do," Cazzo added.

"And someone's gotta watch the kids-"

"You don't have any kids," Jules interjected.

"And all those heavy boxes-"

"Which the movers will be carrying," Cap said.

"And the driving-"

"You live in the same fucking town," Cazzo said exasperatedly.

"And don't get me started on the unpacking," I groaned.

"Alec," Cap interrupted. "All I'm hearing is that you're a lazy fucker and you don't want to be around for the day of the move."

"Or for the unpacking," I added.

"I think we can handle that," Cap grinned.

"What does that mean?" I asked in a panic.

"It means that I'll take care of everything."

"No, Cap, that's not what I-"

"Don't worry. I'll make sure it's everything you want," Cap smiled deviously.

"You don't really think that Cap's going to decide where I live, do you?"

"I think you'd have been better off keeping your fucking mouth shut," Cazzo said as we watched the police escort pull into the Reed Security parking lot.

"But he won't..."

"Dude, you're fucked. Just face it and move on," Jules said. "You whined to the big man and you know he's going to fucking take care of it."

The car pulled to a stop in front of us and the officer in front stepped out and opened the back door. A woman stepped out, around five foot six, average build and brown hair. There was nothing particularly special about her, but she instantly had my attention at the same time. There was an innocence to her in the way she moved. She looked nervous, but friendly at the same time and damn, I did want to step forward and protect her. Which was exactly what I did.

"Ma'am, I'm Alec Wesley. I'll be your close protection agent while you're staying here."

I held out my hand and she put her delicate one in mine. "It's nice to meet you. I'm Hannah Marshall."

"It's very nice to meet you."

Cazzo stepped forward and talked through everything with the officers while I led Hannah inside.

"This place is huge."

"This is only half the building. The other half burned down a year ago."

"Oh my gosh. Was everyone okay?"

"For the most part. We're still alive and kicking."

"That's good. I had a friend that died in a fire when I was in high school. She got trapped in an upstairs bedroom and because of the way the fire spread, there was no way for firefighters to get to her."

"That's terrible. I'm sorry."

"Thank you. So," she cleared her throat uncomfortably and glanced around.

"I know this is a lot to take in, but we will keep you safe."

She nodded curtly and gave a hesitant smile. "I didn't really realize what I was getting myself into. I was a little shocked when they said witness protection."

"How exactly did you get the information you needed to take your boss down?"

"Um..." she laughed lightly, brushing some hair behind her hair. She blushed slightly, making me think she wasn't proud of what she did. "I seduced him and then tied him to a chair in the boardroom. I told him I had whipped cream and strawberries and that I was going to get them. I really went to his office and found the proof I needed. I left him tied to the chair and he wasn't too happy about that."

"Wow," I chuckled. "I can see why he has it out for you. I can only imagine what his employees walked in on."

I led her down the hall to her room and opened the door, stepping inside to show her around. Not that there was a lot to show her. "You have a suite here. Bathroom is over there and you should find everything you need. There's a couple living with us that take care of the cooking and cleaning. Breakfast is at six every morning and lunch is a free for all. Dinner is at six. You can pretty much go anywhere you want around here, but don't go in other people's rooms. There's a workout room, but the training center is off limits. I would also recommend that you shower in your own room unless you want to see a bunch of naked men walking around."

She blushed furiously and I couldn't help but chuckle. "I'll leave you to it here. I'll be around if you need me. You won't be able to leave without one of the guys. No one is allowed to leave without the codes, so I'm afraid you're pretty well locked in here."

She nodded and slumped down on the bed. I didn't know if I should say anything else, but I figured if she needed something, she would ask.

"So, Hannah," Rocco grinned while scooping out mashed potatoes onto his plate. "I hear you took drastic measures to take down Mr. Bigshot."

Her cheeks flamed red and she glanced at me for help, but I just shrugged and gave her an encouraging nod.

"Um...I just did what I thought I needed to. It wasn't right what he was doing."

"Our own little justice warrior," I said with a laugh. "We should introduce you to Maggie."

"Oh, hell no," Chance said. "No more. One Maggie running around is enough. Cap has a hard enough time keeping Maggie in line."

"I don't know," Morgan said, swirling around her glass of wine. "It could be interesting. From what I know of my time with Maggie as a crusader, it was kind of fun. She has good connections and she always keeps things lively."

"Yeah, that's just what Cap wants after this past year, for things to be more lively."

"Speaking of lively," Susan, Raegan's mother, spoke up. "Do you know what the ladies are planning? Raegan said something about starting a new venture with some of the other wives."

"That's not good," Rocco said. "They have enough to do around here."

"What?" Chance asked. "Like taking care of your kid?"

"That shit still blows my mind," he said, shaking his head. "She's a cute little shit, but fuck, I never thought I'd be taking care of a baby alone."

"I'm sorry," Hannah interrupted. "I don't mean to be nosy, but what happened with her mother?"

"Bolted," Rocco said. "Came by and dropped off the kid and left. I didn't even know she existed."

"That's terrible. Is there any chance she'll come back?"

Rocco's face turned stormy and he clenched his knife hard. "She's not getting anywhere near Evie. It doesn't take a genius to know she was a terrible mother."

Hannah nodded and gave a small smile. "I'd like to meet her, if you don't mind. I love babies."

"Sure," Rocco said after a moment. "She's still adjusting to living here. Not to mention, she gets freaked out every time she gets stuck in that damn panic room because Knight set such a small time frame for the sensors. That thing is fucked up. She's already in a fucking panic room."

"Why don't you just tell Knight to take it out, or override the system."

"I tried. He just fucking glared at me and told me that I must not love my kid that much if I was willing to put her life at risk like that."

"Like what?" Hannah asked. "I'm sorry. I'm so new around here. I guess I don't understand. What kind of protection are we talking about?"

"Lasers, killer robots, diaper bombs, escape hatches...just to name a few," Rocco said.

"Wow...that's..."

"Excessive," Rocco finished.

"I was going to say awesome, but I could see how you think that."

I looked at her strangely, but she just shrugged. "Hey, you have this awesome world that the rest of us don't know about. I think it's cool."

The conversation continued around us, but I couldn't stop looking at Hannah. She was an anomaly in our little group. It took most of the women a few days to acclimate to our way of life, but she seemed to really get into the whole idea of what life was like here.

With having to stay around here and look out for Hannah, I didn't feel like I could just go off and do whatever I wanted. Sure, I didn't need to watch her every move, but people were always coming and going, and I needed to keep an eye on the door and make sure she didn't slip out. But I was getting fucking bored.

"Is there anything fun to do around here?" Hannah asked after breakfast.

"Uh, there are movies." She grimaced. "Well, I'm sure I could find Derek and see if he could teach you how to crochet."

Her grimace grew and I chuckled. "I don't mean to be presumptuous, but we're in this really awesome training center. Don't you have something that would be fun? Like, could you teach me to shoot? Or maybe I could do your training course?"

"Are you sure about that? It's pretty hard. We're all former military and it's built to be difficult for us."

"Well, I never said that I would be good at it, but it might be fun to see what you guys do."

"Alright," I nodded. "What if I show you how to shoot? We can get to the hardcore training later."

She beamed at me and clapped her hands together in excitement. "This is so awesome. When this is all over, my friends are going to be so jealous."

"Well, let's make sure we do this right, then."

I took her to the gun range and found a weapon that suited her. I helped her with her stance and explained how the gun worked. She soaked up all the knowledge like it was something she was dying to learn about. I kind of liked that I could show her all this shit. Michelle had never been interested in anything I could teach her. And Florrie already knew all this. If anything, she was always trying to show me up. I couldn't just be a man's man around her. I had no way to be the protector in our relationship because it just pissed her off. In reality, she was just as good as any one of us. She could take care of herself and maybe that made me feel a little unwanted.

We spent the better part of an hour shooting, just laughing and joking about anything and everything. She seemed to genuinely enjoy learning all this shit and the woman was funny as hell. It felt carefree and refreshing to have such an easy relationship with someone. Even if we were only friends.

"Looks like you don't need protection anymore," I smiled. "Nobody would dare mess with you after seeing you shoot."

"Yeah," she laughed. "I'm sure that when they saw the shot to the foot, that was meant for the head, they would run screaming."

"Hey, you still hit the target and that's what counts."

She smiled and unloaded the magazine like a pro, handing the gun and empty clip back to me. "Thank you. I really appreciate you taking the time out to keep me company."

"No problem. I had fun."

"Maybe we could sneak into the kitchen and see if Susan has any cookies left."

"I just took the last one."

I spun around and saw Florrie, standing there looking really fucking uncomfortable.

"Uh, Florrie, this is Hannah. She's staying with us until her trial. Hannah, this is Florrie."

"It's nice to meet you," Hannah said, reaching her hand out to shake Florrie's. But Florrie just stood there with a resting bitch face. Hannah withdrew her hand uncomfortably and cleared her throat. "Well, I should get back and..."

Hannah glanced between Florrie and I, but I was too pissed at the way Florrie was acting to notice. She turned and hustled away while Florrie continued to glare at me.

"She's under our protection. You don't have to be such a bitch to her."

"I didn't realize that you were so willing to entertain our clients," she snapped. "If I had come in any later, I might have walked in on you fucking."

"What's your problem? You don't want me, but you don't want me to be happy with anyone else either?"

"Isn't that the way you feel?"

I took a step back and sighed. I was tired of these pointless arguments. And I realized in that moment that most of our arguments were pointless. Florrie would never change and I should have seen that from the beginning. At the very least, when I found out that she had been lying to me for a year.

"No. I want you to be happy, Florrie. I know that's not with me, and that really fucking sucks. I thought I could never watch you walk away from me again. But when I thought you were shot and bleeding out on the floor, I realized that it didn't really matter if you were with me or not. I just wanted you to be alive and happy. So, no. I don't wish you to be unhappy. I want you to find someone that gives you something that I obviously couldn't. And I hope this time around, you see what's in front of you before it's too late."

I didn't wait for a response. There was no point. I'd heard it all before from her. She didn't want to be with me, but that didn't mean I had to stick around and continue to be beat over the head with that information. I walked away in search of the one person that actually made me feel good about myself right now.

Chapter Thirty-Eight

FLORRIE

I watched him walk away and my heart sank. My breath caught in my chest and I felt weak. He was really walking away this time. But why was I so upset? I kept telling him it would never work out, but then I was upset when he seemed to finally give up. It just didn't make sense. I was getting what I wanted, but it seemed so wrong.

I headed back inside and walked through the panic rooms, trying to figure out exactly what to do. I seemed to be wandering around, completely lost. Thinking I would see if someone wanted to watch a movie, I went in search of anyone that wasn't busy at the moment. But no one was around. I heard laughter in the distance and followed the sound. Pushing open the door to the theater, my breath caught in my throat. Sitting down and watching My Cousin Vinny was Alec and Hannah, along with some of the other guys that were still here for the day. Even Raegan's parents were there, hanging out and having a good time.

"She fits in pretty well around here," Craig said as he stepped up beside me.

"Who?"

"Don't pretend you don't know who I'm talking about. That girl is funny and kind, and Alec is all over her."

"He's not all over her," I snapped. "They're just hanging out."

"Yeah, you're right. But how long will it be before that becomes something more?"

"There's something off about her. I don't trust her."

"You don't know her. And the only reason you think there's something off about her is because you're jealous."

"I'm not jealous. I'm telling you, it's weird. She's too calm, too relaxed."

"Yeah, because she's being protected and is in a fucking bunker. She doesn't have anything to be nervous about. Besides, when you have a man like Alec sitting right beside you, what do you have to be concerned about?"

I couldn't take my eyes off the two of them as they sat in the theater. Alec had his arm draped over the back of her chair, and while it was innocent, it felt way too familiar for me.

"He's just doing his job."

"She pays attention to him, you know? She finds what he says interesting. You know, earlier today I overheard her talking about all her friends and family with him. They were talking about places they'd like to go on vacation and even talked about what they'd like to do once they hit retirement."

"So? That's all just talk."

"Yeah, that's the point. They talked. When was the last time you tried just sitting and talking with Alec?"

I didn't say anything because I had never made an effort to really try to get to know Alec. I had just assumed that he would always be around.

"I don't know how to be anything else with him. We're so similar. I just assumed that there was really nothing to say."

"Even after all the times that Alec tried to get you to open up to him? You know, when he was asking for more from you, he wasn't just talking about having a label on your relationship. He wanted all of you, but you never could open up to him."

My heart started beating a little faster with every minute that passed that I watched them. They seemed so comfortable together, so relaxed in each other's company. How could I compete with that? I didn't know how to just sit and relax with someone; how to enjoy their company.

"I've walked away too many times," I said, tears filling my eyes. "He'd never want me back now."

"You might be right."

I turned to him, hurt that he wasn't going to try and encourage me to try.

"What do you want me to say, Florrie? You've jerked the guy around for three years. He's not going back to you. He's made peace with the fact that it won't work between the two of you. What could you possibly say to change things now?"

"I could tell him that I want to try," I said desperately.

He shook his head and pulled me away from the door, shutting it behind him. "Don't you dare fuck with him anymore. He's been through enough with you. You've lied to him, you've made decisions for him, but not once have you given him a real chance."

"Then what do I do?"

He sighed, running a hand through his hair. "I think the question you need to ask is do you really want him or do you just not want to see him with someone else? And when you figure that out, you need to decide if you could see a relationship with him, because he's already told you what he wants."

"I don't even know how to figure any of that out."

"Maybe that therapist could help you. She was very insightful, but you have to give her a chance to help. There's something fucked up going on in your head, Florrie. I love you for who you are, but you can't drag Alec back into something that isn't going to last."

"You sound like you don't approve of me." I ducked my head to hide the tears slipping down my cheeks. He grabbed me by the arms and made me face him.

"Florrie, you know I love you and I would do anything for you. I don't approve of how you've treated Alec in the past, but you can change that. I would give anything to have the two of you back together again. You two were made for each other. But if you want him at all, you have to figure out what's preventing you from committing and you need to figure out how to fix it. And you'd better have all those answers before you even think about talking to Alec."

I nodded and cleared my throat. "I will, I promise."

"Good. And if you have trouble figuring it out, check out Elle magazine. They have some good tips."

I had been seeing Delilah Sunshine for a few weeks now, but I wasn't really feeling like I was making any progress. Up until now, everything seemed like random questions or things that I just didn't know.

"I have to say," Delilah raised a brow at me, "I'm surprised to see you here. The past few sessions haven't been very productive. I sort of thought that you would have given up by now."

"I'm not a quitter."

"Aren't you?" I stared at her in confusion. What the hell kind of comment was that? "Why don't you tell me why you're really here?"

Her eyes bored into me and I could feel the sweat beading all over my body. It was now or never. I could feel it. She wasn't going to put up with me dodging questions too much longer.

"I need to figure out why I can't accept Alec. I don't know why I'm pushing him away. I don't know why I don't love him back."

"Are you sure you don't?"

"I don't know. I thought I knew, but then I saw him with someone else and...it was the worst feeling in the world."

"Do you want to love him?"

I thought about it a minute, but I had to be honest with her. "I don't know what love is. I don't know what it feels like or how to give it."

"Well, what did it feel like when you were a little girl?"

"I'm confused by the question."

"How did your family show you love?"

"Um, well, my dad...he was busy a lot. He worked a lot to support our family, so he wasn't really there all that much."

"And your mom?"

I tried to think back to a time that my mother could have been seen as anything other than a stern person that you listened to or got the fuck out of the way. I didn't really know what normal was like. We were just the way we were.

"I'm getting the sense that your family was not full of hugs and kisses."

"We were all...busy."

"Busy?"

"Well, Dad was at work and Mom kept up the house and had a part time job on the side. We were expected to do our chores every day and then we had our homework. When Dad needed help around the house, we did as we were told. I'm not sure what you're getting at here. Things were pretty normal."

"Let's move on to something else. When you're with Alec, do you feel happy?"

"Most of the time. I mean, he irritates the fuck out of me when he gets overly possessive."

"And why do you think that is?"

"Well, I can take care of myself."

"Have you always taken care of yourself?"

"Yeah. I was raised to be self-reliant. I've never waited on anyone to do anything for me."

"Do you have any siblings?"

"A brother."

"And you were around him a lot?"

"I wouldn't say that. I would go with him sometimes if I wanted to get away, but I was usually off doing my own thing."

"Playing with barbies and doing your hair?" she smiled.

"No." I knew my face said she was an idiot. "Who does that shit? No, my dad taught me to shoot. I would go hunting or you know, practice throwing knives."

"And did you ever catch anything?"

"Of course."

"And your dad was proud?"

"Well, I guess. He usually just told me to go skin it and get it ready for dinner."

She nodded and wrote down some notes.

"What does all this have to do with me loving Alec?"

She smiled at me, but didn't answer. "You said once that Alec had been shot. How did you feel?"

"Well, obviously I was upset. He means a lot to me. He's my teammate."

"And you would have been upset if he died?"

"What kind of question is that? Of course I would have been."

"But you don't care that your baby died?"

My jaw clenched hard and it took everything I had not to get up out of that chair and beat the shit out of her. "Yes, I fucking cared."

"Sorry, but you don't really seem to care about a whole lot when it comes to other people. You actually seem very selfish, from what I gathered from our last few times we've met."

"I do care about people–"

"Then why do you push them away? Why didn't you accept Alec's love with open arms?"

"Because it wasn't what I was offering."

"And what would it take for you to accept him? Does he have to lay down his life for you? Or maybe he should spell it out in blood."

"What the fuck are you talking about? I knew he loved me–"

"You just didn't care. Because if you did care, you would have taken his feelings into consideration at any point in time that you were together. But it was always about you, wasn't it?"

"Look, I don't need to explain myself–"

"No, you don't need to," Delilah said testily. "Because I'm not the one that you've hurt over and over again. We've been meeting several times a week for the last few weeks, and frankly, I don't think you're ever going to get it. So, let me explain to you what's really going on and then you can let that sink in. You have mommy and daddy issues. They obviously never showed you a day of love in your life, so you've basically been conditioned to do the same to others in your life. You have the ability to feel love, but you don't recognize it. And frankly, the way your parents raised you, so cold and detached, has left you to lead the same kind of life. You care only about yourself and everyone else doesn't really matter, because everyone should be able to take care of themselves, right?"

I stared at her, not knowing what to say. It was a lot to take in all at once. I half wanted to punch her and half hear out what she had to say. No one had ever been so blunt with me before or laid out what was happening in such a clear and concise way.

"Did you feel happy when you were with Alec? Was that a feeling you wanted to keep? When you found out that you couldn't have kids, were you sad or happy? Did you feel bad for Alec that a child had been taken away? At any point in your relationship with Alec, did you think that what you had was really good and it felt right?"

I just sat there, trying to digest it all. I hadn't really figured that I was the problem. I guess some part of me knew because I had come here in the first place, but to have it laid out so clearly for me just blew my mind.

And for the first time in my life, I felt something deep inside. Hurt so unimaginable that I just couldn't bottle it up. It was like she had opened my mind up to a side of myself that I had never really explored in all my life. Because I had never thought I had a need for it. But right now, I needed to ask some very important questions to myself and figure out what I really wanted.

"I can see that what I'm saying is impacting you in some way. Now, I don't want you to take this as a chance to blame your parents for not giving you enough love or blame them for everything that's ever gone wrong in your life. This is a chance to recognize something you've been missing out on and snatch it up before it goes away and leaves you feeling empty inside."

"So, what do I do? Do I talk with Alec?"

"I would say that you need to figure this out for yourself first. Don't drag Alec into this until you truly understand what you feel."

"How do I figure this out?"

"Do some self-reflecting. Ask yourself what you really want out of life. Think about what it was like with Alec and what you could have had and if you can still have that. You have to figure out if you're happy with the way things are or if you want what he was offering all along. And are you ready to open yourself up to all the love he has to give and accept that, and can you return it?"

I didn't know how to answer any of that stuff. But luckily, I was surrounded by people that had been in the same situation as me at one time or another.

———————

"Florrie, what's this all about?" Hunter asked. I looked at the other guys- Ice, Derek, Burg, Jules, and Jackson. All of them had one thing in common. They had the fear at one point.

"I need advice."

"Nope. I've been here with you before," Hunter said as he stood. "I'm not doing this again."

"Just hang on a minute. I just need some advice on how you know."

"Know what?" Ice asked. "Know when to pull out? When to shoot? What are we talking about here?"

I took a deep breath and dove right in the deep end. "I need to know how you know when you're in love."

The guys all stared at me for a moment and then burst into laughter.

"She doesn't know," Ice laughed.

"I bet she even thinks she has a choice," Jules said, choking on his own laughter.

"Now, guys, think about what it was like for you," Burg said, trying to calm them down. "Ice, you passed out."

"True story."

"And Hunter, well, it took stalking your woman to get it through your thick skull."

"Hey, I was trying to woo her. And I wasn't as bad as Jackson," Hunter pointed out. "It took him a whole fucking year to figure out that he was in love with Raegan."

"At least I didn't forget the woman I loved," Jackson snapped.

"Hey, low blow. I was hit in the fucking head with concrete."

"What does any of this have to do with me?" I said, shouting over their bickering.

"Do you feel that burning in your gut?" Burg asked.

"You mean heartburn?"

Derek rolled his eyes at me. "Like, if he's away from you, do you worry about him or wonder what he's doing?"

"Hey, guys," Ice interrupted. "This is Florrie. Let's talk on her terms." I glared at him, but he just shrugged. "It's true. Okay, when you go to bed at night, do you reach for your gun or Alec?"

"Well, when Alec was there, I reached for him. But I didn't need my gun."

"And when Alec is on a job, do you worry about someone getting the drop on him?" Hunter asked.

"No, I worry that his gun will jam."

"Ah," Hunter said with a nod. "Very telling."

"What's very telling?"

"Condom or no condom?" Jules asked.

"No condom. Why?"

But I didn't get an answer because Derek interrupted. "And when you see a new weapon on the market, who do you want to tell first about it?"

"Alec."

"When you see the Napoleon cannon in his house, what feeling do you equate that to?"

"Um, joy?"

Hunter stepped forward, rubbing his hand across his jaw. "Final question. When you stay over at his place, how long do you stay in the shower?"

"I don't know. Fifteen, twenty minutes."

"See? I knew you weren't a fling girl," Hunter grinned.

"How do any of those questions relate at all to whether or not I'm in love?"

Jackson grinned, folding his arms over his chest. "The cannon? That's how you see your life with Alec. It represents the joy that you feel when you're with him."

I looked at him in confusion, but then Jules piped up. "And the no condom represents the trust you have in him."

"And the worry you have over his gun jamming says that you worry about him, not that he can't handle himself, but that something uncontrollable will happen and you'll lose him," Derek said.

"And the fact that you reach for Alec instead of your gun says that you trust him to keep you safe," Ice said.

"And that twenty minutes in the shower?" I asked.

"That means you love him," Hunter grinned.

I looked at him in confusion. "I'm sorry. Because I spend twenty minutes in the shower means I love him?"

"Well, yeah. I mean, if you didn't want to stick around, you wouldn't spend twenty minutes in the shower."

"Or it means that we got really fucking dirty while fucking and I needed a long shower."

"Well, yeah, it could mean that," Hunter acquiesced.

"If I may take over," Burg said, pushing the others out of the way so he could stand right in front of me. "Florrie, forget what these guys said and answer one question. Do you want Alec more than anyone else in your life? Can you see your life without him?"

"That's two questions."

"Florrie," he growled.

"It's complicated. There's so much-"

"Bullshit!" he shouted at me and I jumped, not expecting the harsh tone in his voice. "Stop making fucking excuses!"

"What do you want me to say?"

He looked at me sadly, shaking his head in disappointment. "Stop lying to yourself. Maybe these guys don't see it, but I do. You're so fucking scared because you don't know what love feels like. You're afraid to admit that it might be true. But Florrie, if you can't fucking admit it, then you're the one that loses. The rest of us, we already have what we want. When I met Emma, I just knew there was something different about her. No, I didn't know that she was the one, but I knew I wanted to be with her more than anyone else. So, I jumped. I took a huge fucking leap and I went all in. If you can't live that way and take that jump that gives you the man you want, then you don't deserve him."

I nodded, understanding what he was saying. And I felt like shit for it. Because I had played it safe. I had hung back and made myself unavailable for all possibilities because I didn't know what love was. No, that was a lie. I didn't want to believe that someone loved me, because then I couldn't be the hard ass that I always had been. I would have to soften myself up and open up to how love might change me.

"So, do you want Alec?"

"More than anything."

"Would it kill you to see him with someone else?"

"Yes," I said, knowing that I had already felt it deep down inside.

"Then what the fuck are you still doing standing here?"

I smiled and almost leapt forward to hug Burg, but then I remembered that I was Florrie fucking Younge, and I didn't need to change everything about me just because I figured out that I was in love. I turned and headed for the door, hearing Derek call after me.

"Good talk! It was the Napoleon cannon question that got you thinking, right?"

Chapter Thirty-Nine

ALEC

"Are you all packed?" I asked Hannah.

We were taking off this morning for her trial in Philadelphia. She appeared pretty calm, but appearances could be deceiving. She'd been in a bubble for all this time and when we got to the court house, shit was gonna get real for her.

"Yeah. I'm ready to get this over with and move on with my life."

"Good."

I held the door for her and was just pulling it shut behind me when I caught her scent. I took a deep breath as I secured the door and turned to face the woman I would never have. Over the past few weeks, I had made peace with the fact that Florrie and I were just too different and it would never work between us. It would be okay though. I still got to see her, just not as much as I used to. That was for the best though. Having space from her had both hurt like hell and given me the chance to really look at our relationship, or lack thereof, and see that she was just too independent for me. In the six months that we had previously been broken up, I was more angry and letting that anger fuel my thoughts. I hadn't really let her go. I hadn't really accepted things for what they were.

"Alec, do you have a minute?" she asked. She looked a little nervous and was usually never anything but put together.

"You know, I have to get to Philadelphia for the trial. We can catch up another time."

She glanced at Hannah and then back to me, lowering her voice. "Please, it'll just take a minute."

I shouldn't do it. Florrie didn't deserve my time. No, that wasn't true. That was the anger talking. I reminded myself that some couples just didn't work out. That was life. Love wasn't always returned, no matter how much I wanted it. I couldn't make her love me or want me in the same way. It didn't mean there was something wrong with me or that I needed to change. It just meant that we weren't supposed to be together.

"Hannah, why don't you go down and I'll be there in a minute."

Hannah turned, looking at me with concern, and left. She knew a little about Florrie and I. Just that we had been together for three years, but it was over now. When she was gone, I turned back to Florrie, waiting for her to talk.

"I wanted to say that I'm sorry. I know now that you were right about everything."

I stood there, not sure what to say. What was she getting at? We had said goodbye. There was no need to go through this and rehash who was right and who was wrong.

"I've been seeing Dr. Sunshine and I figured a few things out."

"I'm glad, Florrie, but I have a job to do. Can this wait until I get back?"

"No," she said quickly, wringing her hands together. "I need to get this out and I need to do it now."

I crossed my arms over my chest and waited for her to continue.

"I love you," she blurted out, tears filling her eyes. "I know that I'm too late and I know that I screwed with your head so much that you could never want me back, but I'm asking that you take one more chance. For me. Say that you still want me. Because I only want you for the rest of my life, and it would kill me to see you with someone else. I just couldn't take it."

She swiped the tears from her face, licking the salt from her lips as she waited for me. But I didn't know what the fuck to say. I sure as hell wasn't expecting that. I didn't think that I would ever hear those words from her, and I thought if I did that I would feel this earth shattering feeling deep inside, but instead, it just made my chest ache in pain. Time had done too much to us. It had ruined what we used to have and turned it into something ugly.

"Florrie," I sighed and ran my hand over my beard. I never thought I would be the one giving Florrie the shove off.

"Don't say that," she pleaded. "I know you want to walk away right now. I know you want to give up and tell me that I'm not worth the trouble, but the thing is, I think I am. I'm just a screwed up girl that is asking you to return the love that I tossed away."

"It's not that easy," I said, taking her hand. "You know that I'll always love you." She hiccuped a sob, something that I never thought I would hear from Florrie and it broke my fucking heart, but my heart had already been tattered to shreds, and I just couldn't put it back together with one declaration. "We're not meant to be together. There was a time when I thought we were perfect for each other, but too much has happened. It's never worked between us before. What makes you think now will be any different?"

"Because I know now that I love you."

I stepped forward, cupping her face in my hands. I brushed her tears that were still flowing, and rested my forehead against hers. "I'll always love you, Florrie. There's not another fucking woman in this world that could ever make me fall to my knees the way you do. And I'll never regret a single minute with you. I just can't do this again. My heart's already shredded. Believe me, I wanted you more than life itself, but I just...please don't ask me to do this again."

I pressed my lips to her forehead, trying to give myself the courage to walk away from the woman I still loved. She would always be the one. But someday we would both move on and she wouldn't find it so fucking hard to tell that guy that she loved him, and then she would know for sure that it was right. And me? Someday I'd find a way to love again. It wouldn't be as good and it wouldn't be with such an amazing woman, but it would be enough. I was just so fucking glad that I got these three years with Florrie, no matter how fucking hard they were. We almost had everything. We almost had forever.

I stepped back and stared at the woman I loved. Her beautiful face was streaked with tears and her eyes were shining bright. She'd never looked more fucking beautiful. I wanted to stay, but I forced myself to take another step back and then another. I turned and walked downstairs and onto my job. It was time to move on.

Chapter Forty

FLORRIE

He stepped away from me and I knew I had lost. I had poured my heart out to him, but it wasn't enough. I had pushed him away for too long and he'd had enough. I couldn't blame him. I didn't even want to be with me. I watched his tall frame walk away from me. Those rough hands would never touch me again. I would never feel his lips on mine or feel the warmth of his body next to me.

I couldn't let this be the way it ended though. I raced down the hallway, my heart pounding as I ran after him. I got to the living room and was just about to call out for him when I saw Hannah wrap her arm around his waist. She turned back to me and shot me a look that had unease shivering down my spine. Something was wrong here, and I had felt it from the moment she came. But I had pushed it aside, thinking that I was just jealous of her connection with Alec. I knew that something was off, but if I went after Alec and told him that I didn't trust Hannah, he would accuse me of looking for danger where there wasn't any because he had rejected me.

I turned and ran for the IT room. Becky was sitting at the computer, doing shit that I had no idea about. "Becky, I need your help."

"Can it wait? I'm trying to get Reed Security back up and running so that I can move on with my life."

"Whatever," I said, shoving her stuff aside so that I could get her attention. "You know you don't actually want to leave us. Besides, I have something important, something that could get our guys hurt if I'm right."

"Alright, you have my attention. But I'm still leaving. What's going on?"

"This girl, Hannah, what do you know about her?"

"Um, just what the prosecutors sent over about the case. Why?"

"Something's up with her. I just get a bad feeling when I'm around her."

"Okay," she said slowly. "Do you have something for me to go on other than your gut instincts?"

"Isn't that enough?"

"I don't know. I mean, you let Alec get away. I'm not sure your instincts are working properly."

"We can worry about that later. If I'm right, he could end up dead because of this woman."

"Alright, I'll get to work, but I'm not sure what I'll find."

"Good." I stood there and waited. After a moment of her typing, she looked up at me expectantly.

"Are you just going to stand there?"

"Well, yeah. I need to find out what's going on."

She sighed, but started working again. Our first lead came an hour later. "Okay, after looking over the case, the only thing that strikes me as odd is that Nathan Sharpe, the guy she's accusing of insider trading, just inherited a crap ton of money."

"What's odd about that?"

"Well, he's extremely wealthy. He claimed his inheritance about a year ago. Most people that are that wealthy don't need to pull off illegal activities to get ahead. I mean, from what I see, he's a pretty ruthless businessman, but everything I'm reading about him shows that he's also pretty fair to his employees and business associates. Why would a man that's good to his employees do something that could hurt his employees?"

"But that's still just a theory. And if she has documents that prove he's guilty, then that doesn't help us at all."

She scrolled through some more information on the man and paused. I was dying to know what she was reading.

"What is it?"

She held up her finger, her lips moving as she read something.

"Come on, tell me what it is."

Her finger stayed up and she continued to read.

I tapped my foot in irritation, waiting a good five minutes for her to finish. She spun around with a smile on her face. "Well, I think I have a lead for us to go on."

"Okay, what is it?"

"His inheritance."

"What about it?" I asked impatiently.

"He inherited, but there was a second person that would inherit in the event that he performed any illegal acts."

"Like, even a parking ticket?"

"I would have to see the amendment to the document, but I doubt that would disqualify him."

"And he knew about this?"

"Most likely. I'm sure that any good lawyer would have informed him to be on his best behavior."

"How long is that valid? You said that he inherited a year ago."

"It stands as long as he's living. He can only change it when he writes his own will."

"Okay, so who does the inheritance go to?"

"A man named Jason Moran. He was the caretaker's son. But he's been living in Montana for the past two years."

"So, it's unlikely that he knew about the will."

"Well, the only way he would know is if he had somehow seen the will beforehand, which is highly unlikely."

I was getting frustrated. This was going nowhere. "I don't see what this has to do with Hannah."

"Maybe nothing, but she's the one that's accusing him. Why don't you get ahold of Sharpe's lawyer. See if you can find out what they know."

"They're not going to tell me anything. Besides, with the trial starting soon, they'll be focused on their gameplan."

"Then you'd better be really convincing."

"Knight," I yelled, running up to him in the training center. He turned and scowled at me.

"What the fuck do you want?"

"I need your help."

"Not interested."

"Please! I think Cazzo's team may be in trouble and we need to warn them."

"You mean, the same team that Alec's on?"

I rolled my eyes, growling angrily at him. "This does have to do with Alec, but I think something's seriously wrong and I need your help."

"And why would I help you?"

"Because it's secretive, dangerous, and highly illegal."

He quirked an eyebrow at me, turning to give his full attention and crossing his arms over his chest. "Okay, I'm listening."

"Okay, long story short, I think Hannah is conspiring with someone to steal Nathan Sharpe's inheritance."

"Who the fuck is Nathan Sharpe?"

"The man that she's accusing of insider trading."

"And what makes you so sure she's conspiring against him?"

"It's thin."

"Explain how thin."

"Well, Sharpe's investigators had been following her after she accused him. They didn't get much because she came to us soon after, but from what they could tell, she goes to a public library to use their computers."

"She doesn't have one?"

"No."

"Okay, that's a little odd, but not proof that she's guilty."

"Exactly. They couldn't find anything to show that she had contact with the guy who would inherit if Sharpe was guilty of committing a crime."

Knight sighed and ran a hand over his face. "Florrie, they have police that handle this. Why are you so adamant that we go after this?"

"Because I think she's going to do something to strengthen her argument against Sharpe."

"Based on all this conjecture?"

I winced and nodded. "I know it's not a lot to go on."

"You've got nothing to go on," he said. "I don't know what you even want to do that's highly illegal that would do anything to prove your case."

"Well, she has a UPS box that she rents."

"Does she have a mailbox?"

"Yes."

His eyes narrowed and I knew that I had him. He smelled something fishy too. "So, she rents a UPS box even though she has a regular mailbox."

"It looks completely innocent."

"She's checking the mail," he surmised. "It looks completely fucking innocent."

"Exactly, but if she's communicating with this guy in Montana, the other person that would inherit, nobody can track that."

"Unless we break into her mailbox and go through her mail," he smirked.

"Right. So, will you help me?"

"You should have just said that you wanted me to break into a UPS box. This would have moved along a lot faster."

―――――――

"Are you sure this is going to work?" I asked Knight from my position outside the UPS store.

"You came to me. You really need to ask that?"

I rolled my eyes and watched through my binoculars as Knight walked around the back of a UPS truck, dressed in the signature brown shorts and shirt with the shoes.

"You know, a man should not look that good in that uniform."

"I'll pretend I didn't hear you say that," Knight muttered. "I'm fucking uncomfortable as hell right now."

"Okay, the shift change starts in two minutes."

"Do you have confirmation that our new employee friend is still broken down on the side of the road?"

I looked at the screen where I had hacked into the feed from the street camera. He was still on the side of the road, trying to change his fucking tire.

"Still broken down."

"Good. I'll be out in five."

Knight walked into the UPS store and nodded at the employee behind the counter. "Hey, Smith broke down on the side of the road. Central sent me over to do his route."

"Right, well all the mail is in the back. Let me show you the crates and you can start loading."

"No problem," Knight said as he followed the man back.

"How the hell do you pull off being so congenial to other people, but to us, you're a complete asshole?" I asked him over coms.

"Magic," he muttered.

"What's that?" the other man asked.

"Nothing."

The man started showing Knight the crates to load and that was my cue to enter. I crossed the street, package in hand, and walked through the front door.

"I'll be right with you," the man yelled.

I rang the bell up front repeatedly and heard the man curse his annoyance.

"I've got this, man. Don't worry about it," Knight told the man.

"Can I help you?" the man asked as walked behind the counter.

"Yeah, I need to mail this package to Yemen."

"To Yemen," the man deadpanned.

"Yes, Yemen."

"Okay, fill out this form. I'll be right back."

"Wait, I've never filled this out before. I need help."

The man glanced to the back and then sighed, coming back to the counter. "Okay."

I watched as Knight slipped over to the mailboxes and grabbed the mail out of the back and started shuffling through it. The man slid a piece of paper over to me, showing me what wasn't allowed to be shipped.

"What does it mean by anything flammable?" I asked.

"It means that if you're sending anything flammable, you can't send it."

"Oh." The man started to turn. "What exactly is considered flammable?"

"Fireworks, ammunition," he waved his arm as if to tell me that was the kind of stuff that was prohibited.

"Huh? So, I guess I can't ship a nuclear bomb over there," I laughed, but he just stared at me. "Okay, no sense of humor." He tried to turn back again. "Oh, nuts! I can't send human remains?"

"No. Were you planning to?"

"Well, that's what I have in this package. See, my grandfather fought in the Yemen Civil War and he wants to be buried over there with his friends."

"Wasn't that in the early 1900's?" the man asked.

"Yes, he was very young and didn't have my mother until he was almost fifty!"

The man stared at me with a deadened expression. "Thrilling."

"I know," I grinned.

"Well, you still can't send remains through the mail."

"But he's cremated," I said dumbly.

"I guessed that based on the size of the package. Unless you somehow figured out a way to smash remains into a nine by eleven package."

"That would be pretty funny," I laughed, but the man just stood there staring at me. I saw Knight slip out the back door and decided to make my exit. "Well, I guess I'll just have to find some other way to get Grandpa over there."

"Looks like it," he said in a bored tone before turning around and heading to the back. I walked out the front door and hurried over to the truck where Knight was already waiting.

"So, what did you find?" I asked as I hopped in the passenger side. He handed me a postcard.

"Check it out for yourself."

I looked at it, but all I saw was a picture of the Grand Canyon and a postmark.

"There's nothing here."

"Look closer."

I checked the side with the picture and looked at the back again. I still didn't see anything. Knight rolled his eyes and peeled the corner of the postcard. Underneath was a message.

"It's all set for when you walk out of court." I looked up at him and he raised an eyebrow at me. "You think there's going to be an attempted assassination?"

"Wouldn't that make her case look stronger?"

"Like someone's trying to shut her up," I surmised.

"Except, she has a security detail and it's not going to be her that's taken out," Knight added.

"How are we going to prove this? We found it illegally. Even if we take this to the prosecutor, they won't be able to do anything about it."

"We have to show opposing council and let them do the digging. All we can do is get our team out of the way."

He started the truck and headed over to the courthouse. "Court gets out in fifteen minutes. What are we going to do?"

"We have to get inside the courthouse and get to Cazzo."

"What if Alec walks out of the courthouse with her? You know he's going to be the one that takes the bullet."

"We'll just have to make sure that doesn't happen."

I called Alec's number, but it went straight to voicemail. He wouldn't have his phone on in the courtroom. I called Cap next.

"Sebastian."

"Cap, it's Florrie. I need you to listen. I'm with Knight and we have a lead that says that Hannah is not who she says she is. We have good intel that says she's part of an attempted hit to prove her case to the court. She's really working to help secure an inheritance for someone else."

"What? Florrie, this doesn't-"

"Just get ahold of Cazzo and let him know not to let the team leave the building. Talk with Becky. She knows what's going on!"

"And why the fuck wasn't I told-"

"Cap, I don't have time to explain. Just get the message to Cazzo."

I hung up and prayed that he was able to get the message through before they left the building. We drove in silence the rest of the way, Knight driving much faster than he should. We arrived just five minutes before court let out, but with all the security measures we had to go through, court was already out by the time we made it in.

"I'll go this way," Knight said. "You go the opposite way and let me know the minute you see someone. I'll do the same."

I nodded and scanned the crowds as I moved to the right. There were so many people that were filtering out of the courtroom that I couldn't make out our team at all.

"I'm not seeing anything, Knight."

"Neither am I. I need a fucking map of the place."

I spun around and caught sight of an exit off to the side. I ran in that direction, my gut telling me they would exit that way. And then I saw him. Alec was escorting Hannah out the door with Jules on the other side of her.

"Alec!"

But he had already walked out the door. I tried to push through the people, but the crowd was too thick. Turning, I followed the flow of people, shoving my way to the front doors.

"Knight, they went out the east doors. I can't reach them that way. I'm heading for the front and going around."

"Copy that. I'm making my way to you."

I finally pushed through the door and ran along the side of the building. Alec and Jules were walking with Hannah down the stairs to the SUV that Cazzo had waiting for them.

"Alec!"

He heard me and turned in my direction, but then pressed his hand to his ear and looked to Jules in concern. I raced toward them and then something caught my eye. Something caught the sun on the top of the roof in the distance. I went into a full on sprint, running down the stairs.

"Shooter!" I shouted.

Alec rushed forward with Hannah while Jules pulled his gun and looked for the threat.

"Northeast rooftop," I shouted.

"Down," Knight shouted, running around from the back side of the courthouse. But I wasn't taking cover. Not when Alec was still in the open. I heard the first shot ping off the SUV. I heard Hannah scream. Rushing filled my ears as I was just steps away. I jumped behind Alec, providing as much cover as I could. My body jerked as a bullet hit me in the back. I slammed into Alec from behind, shoving his body into Hannah, who was now in the vehicle. My body crumpled to the ground.

The sky swirled above me, the blue swirling with the clouds. Alec knelt down beside me, his face contorted in pain.

"Are you hit?" I asked.

"No, I'm not hit. You are."

"I know, but you look like you're in pain," I gasped.

"You stupid fucking woman," he swore and rolled me to the side. I cried out in pain when he pressed against the hole in my shoulder. "Why the fuck did you do that?"

He was holding something against my wound, but rolled me back into a more comfortable position. Staring into his eyes, I finally got it. All those things he said to me about love, it finally made sense. I grinned at him slightly, feeling a little dazed, probably from blood loss.

"Love is taking a bullet so the person you love doesn't have to feel even an ounce of pain," I said softly.

He shook his head in disbelief. "You didn't have to take a fucking bullet for me."

"How else was I going to prove to you that I was serious?"

He bent down and kissed me hard, taking what little breath I had away. "I fucking love you, you crazy bitch."

I smiled as big as I could. "It's about time you said it."

He helped me to my feet, staring at me in that domineering way that I always used to hate. Now, I was so fucking glad to see him staring at me that way, and I would never tell him to back off again.

"Can we go?" Hannah shrieked. "They're shooting at us!"

"Because you sent them," I said before stepping forward and slamming my fist into her face. It pulled like hell at my shoulder, but it was totally worth it.

Alec grinned at me right before he kissed me hard. "That's my girl."

Chapter Forty-One

ALEC

"Stop, Alec. I don't need you to baby me."

I growled at my woman and pushed her back in the bed. I had a tray of food here and I was going to spoon feed her every single fucking mouthful until I was satisfied that she was taken care of. After all, she had been shot protecting me. Reed Security had officially dropped Hannah as a client as soon as Knight showed us the postcard from her UPS box. Nathan Sharpe's lawyers were trying to find a way to prove conspiracy, but that wasn't our problem.

"Would you just let me take care of you?"

"I don't-"

I pressed my finger to her lips. If we were going to be together there were a few things we needed to get straight.

"Just shut the fuck up. You've done enough of the talking in this relationship. Now, I've let you set the rules all along, but if you want to be with me, there are a few rules I've got for you to follow. Are we clear?"

"Yes," she said, rolling her eyes at me.

"Good. Number one. When you are injured, I will take care of you and you can't complain."

"Fine."

"Number two. You will fucking tell me every single medical issue you ever have, including when you have your fucking period so that I know what the fuck is going on with you. No more secrets. Got it?"

"I think telling you when I have my period-"

"Ah- Did I say this was up for discussion?"

She rolled her eyes again and nodded. "Fine. I'll tell you."

"Rule number three. You will fucking tell me exactly what you want out of life. If you want kids, we'll discuss it like adults. No hiding from me because you think you can't give me what I want. There will be no more of you deciding what I need or want. Are we clear?"

"Fine."

"Rule number four."

"How many fucking rules do you have?"

"As many as I want. Now, rule four. No more fucking hiding from me. We're in this together and you will fucking tell me what you need at any given time. And in return, I'll do my best to listen and not fuck it up."

"I suppose I can live with that."

"Rule number five. We will work together on a team and Cap will probably make us go to counseling. I will do my best not to piss you off and you'll do your best to handle my protective side."

"If we're going to be on the same team, you have to let me do my job. No more treating me like I can't take care of myself. You always trusted me before. You have to trust me again."

"I swear it. Are we agreed on all that?"

"Yes."

"Good. Now, I have one final rule and this is probably the most important rule above all of them."

"Okay." She looked at me warily, but I knew she'd agree.

"Craig is never allowed in our bedroom alone with us for any reason."

ALSO BY GIULIA LAGOMARSINO

Thank you for reading Alec and Florrie's story. There's still more to come further down the line, so keep reading. The Reed Security gang will be back in Storm's story!

Join my newsletter to get the most up-to-date information, along with new content in the Reed Security series.

https://giulialagomarsinoauthor.com/connect/

Join my Facebook reader group to find out more about my obsession with Dwayne Johnson!

https://www.facebook.com/groups/GiuliaLagomarsinobooks

Reading Order:

https://giulialagomarsinoauthor.com/reading-order/

To find the individual series, follow the links below:

For The Love Of A Good Woman series

Reed Security series

The Cortell Brothers

A Good Run Of Bad Luck

Made in the USA
Monee, IL
09 September 2023

42436461R00163